MYTHICAL DOORWAYS

A Fellowship of Fantasy anthology

To Julia^
Enjoy the adventures!
♡ Lawrie Lundmy

Dear Readers,

Welcome to Mythical Doorways, the third anthology from the Fellowship of Fantasy. We present to you our tales of gateways to marvelous places. These doorways open into adventure, wonder, and even danger.

Within, you will accompany heroes on their way to fairy worlds. Brave the dangers of the past through a portal in time. Eavesdrop at the door of a forbidden workshop. Follow a girl on a search for a better life in her choice between three tempting magical doors. Help a sorcerer close a gateway before an unspeakable horror escapes, and slip through a portal on a quest for delicious chocolate!

There are many perilous journeys ahead of you, but no graphic content. All the stories here fall below a PG-13 rating.

The Fellowship of Fantasy is an online group of writers dedicated to presenting the best in clean fantasy stories of any stripe. Some tackle epic quests to save the world, while others prefer more urban settings. Whether you enjoy contemporary tales, romantic re-tellings, or something else entirely, you're sure to find stories that speak to you.

Thank you for joining us on our trip through these doorways, and may you find adventure and entertainment on the other side!

Sincerely,
The Fellowship of Fantasy Authors
www.fellowshipoffantasy.com

CONTENTS

Jenelle Leanne Schmidt

Gwyna was hunting to bring home food for her family. She never expected to encounter a dragon. She certainly never expected to become the prey...

Lauren Lynch

On a quest to explore the past he should have had, an escaped slave makes a leap of faith and a strange discovery.

Everwild

J. M. Hackman

Flint North dropped into the chair next to Ms. Matthews's desk. The study's fluorescent lighting deepened the lines on the stern lady's face. She offered him a plastic smile. "This is an exciting day for you."

He grunted and slumped deeper into the chair. Aging out of the foster system was exciting? Try terrifying. He swallowed hard against the lump in his throat.

"Your paperwork's completed, and I've written down a few contact numbers and addresses. The Job Center, the admissions office of North Community College, the apartment building on Main." She handed him a thin beige folder. "Remember, your apartment's furnished, and the first week's rent is paid. Send a thank-you note to Foster Aid; they stocked your refrigerator with food for the week. And don't forget your interview at the temp agency tomorrow."

His life and opportunities condensed into a simple manila folder. He blinked and rubbed the nape of his neck. "What about the apprenticeship?"

She gave him a condescending smile. "Oh, Flint. You're talented, but Mr. Anton doesn't often take apprentices."

"But he said I was good. We're meeting tonight to discuss it."

"Very well. Meet with him, then. Good luck." The skepticism in her voice cut like a razor blade.

He nodded, refusing to look into her dead, gray eyes.

She tapped a slim box on the edge of her desk. "Oh, this box came for you in the mail. I didn't feel it was my place to open your mail, now that you're of age. But you're welcome to open it now, if you like." She leaned forward, her eyes shifting between his face and the box.

"Nah, I'm good." Stifling his curiosity, he slipped the thin package into his jacket pocket and sat back in his chair. She'd have to handle her nosiness. Privacy was a rare commodity, especially in a group home.

"Well, if you're sure." She offered up another smile, the action unnatural.

She was probably thrilled to be rid of him.

Grabbing the folder, he pushed a "thanks" through his dry throat and left. He had a backpack of clothes, thanks to the shopping trip at the superstore last week. The nonprofit group, Foster Aid, had also purchased sheets, dishes, and some hygiene items that were waiting at the apartment. A few personal belongings. No family. Limited prospects, save the highly improbable apprenticeship with famed local artist, Mr. Anton. Community college was out of the question. He wasn't smart enough, skating through school with Cs and sometimes Ds. Higher education would be torture, and the resulting loans would eat him alive.

Strolling through the entryway of the group home, fear was a gray shadow behind him. He refused to look back. The kids here weren't his friends, so he hadn't bothered with goodbyes. This place had been a prison for most of his life, and the only thing he missed was the security of having somewhere to sleep. Now, that was all on him. If only he'd been able to see Lila this past Saturday. His best friend attended a private prep school across town, but they usually met in the library on Saturday mornings. She hadn't shown up this weekend.

He walked the few blocks to the apartment complex on Main, checked in, and listened to the landlord give her spiel—no drugs, no parties, rent due on Sunday, doors locked at midnight. After he signed the contract, she left him alone in the stark apartment.

The small room held a single bed, a worn wooden dresser, and a miniature kitchenette in the corner. A minuscule bathroom was tucked into another corner, and his lone window displayed a lovely view of the cinder-block building next door. School paste-toned walls closed in on him. No commonplace photos or nondescript watercolors brightened his surroundings, nothing to indicate anyone lived here. His fingers tingled with the urge to sketch a landscape, or a self-portrait, anything to cheer up his living space. At least he had a place to sleep. Home, sweet home.

Pulling the thin box from his pocket, he wondered what lay inside. No return address, just his name and the foster home's address typed on a plain, white mailing label. He wrestled with the tape and the uncooperative box before it finally opened, a golden key falling into his hand.

He blinked and tossed the box onto the bed. What did the key open? He turned it in his hands, searching for an identifying mark. It shimmered in the light slipping through the curtain. Having missed its target, the box lay on its side near the edge of the bed. He picked it up, and a piece of folded paper fell out. His fingers glided over its expensive linen texture. The message was two lines. *Meet me at the library today at 11:00. This key can answer all your questions. ~Lila*

Flint snorted. Hardly. The key's metal warmed in his hand. Maybe it was real gold. She attended that fancy school, so she could probably afford it. Normally, he'd pawn it—secure a few bucks to take him farther into the unknown journey stretching before him. He clenched the key tighter in his fist. Not this time—Lila's gift would be squirreled away as a souvenir of their friendship. Dread coated his stomach, a painful reminder his future was one big question mark. Pocketing the key, he left the house. His first stop—Burger Den on the corner, to see if they were hiring. He'd avoid the temp agency if he could.

Outside, the brisk wind ruffled his hair. Christmas decorations hung from the city streetlights—beat-up, tinsel-trimmed Christmas stockings. The shop windows also boasted Christmas displays to encourage shoppers to open their wallets. Winter fairy figurines poised above pond-like mirrors, skating delicate snowflakes into the glass. He tucked his chin into his collar. The major holiday was a month away, but a cold snap rode the breeze.

The fast-food joint held only a few people eating a late breakfast, mostly retirees, judging by their white hair. He approached a female cashier. "Are you hiring?"

She fished an application out from under the counter and handed it to him with a full-wattage smile. "If you come back in an hour, the manager will be here." Another flirty smile capped her sentence.

He thanked her and tucked the paper into his jacket pocket. She was cute, but he wasn't going to fill out the application here and wait like a loser. The library was a block away. He'd go there and kill some time before returning.

As he walked down the street to the library, he felt like a tourist. It was a nice city with plenty to do if you had the money, but nothing inside felt a connection to this place where he grew up. People on the street scurried to do their business. He was a random puzzle piece. He didn't belong here, never had. Maybe now that he was on his own, he could travel to another city that would feel like home.

The warmth of the red-brick library hit him as he cleared the door. A group of kids sat in the children's section, listening to the librarian read a story. He found a quiet table in the nonfiction section and shed his jacket. Opening the application, he began to fill the blank lines. Name, address, et cetera.

"Well, you're early. I thought you'd be busy setting up your apartment this morning."

He looked up and smiled, his heart lifting. "Lila! You cut out on me last weekend."

"Sorry." The petite blond gave a shrug. "When I called, they said you were out."

He nodded. The housemates never bothered with taking a message. "I was probably already here. You skipping school today?"

With a *thunk*, she dropped her bag onto the wooden table and pulled out the matching chair before slipping into it. "We have today off. What's that?"

"A job application for Burger Den."

"I thought you were going to apprentice with that artist."

He hitched a shoulder. "It's a long shot, so this is if things don't pan out. But I've got a question for you." He pulled the key from his pocket. "What's this?"

Her gaze skimmed the room, the table, the books, the patrons, before it settled on the key. "A present. Happy Aging-out Day."

"Thanks. And how does this answer all my questions?"

She sighed. "You know you're one of my best friends, right? And I'd never lie to you—about anything."

He looked into her eyes, and his heart thumped once in his chest before resuming its normal rhythm. He'd developed a crush on her when they'd attended elementary school together, before she'd moved across town. Lila Grayfeather, the coolest girl in first grade. The crush had never really vanished. "Sure. Why?"

"That key is the answer to your heritage, Flint. It's a fairy key."

"Fairy? As in a little person with wings?"

Frowning, she pointed a finger at him. "That's not what a fairy is. They're magical beings and can be any size. Your mom is a fairy."

His mind latched onto the statement, even though it sounded like nonsense. "Sure, she is. And you know this how?"

"I was briefed. Your dad was human. That makes you half-fae."

"I'm half-fairy?"

Several patrons turned and gave him uncertain looks before moving deeper into the nonfiction section.

"Yes. Now that you have the key, you have to make a decision by noon tomorrow."

"Back up. What else do you know about my parents?"

Leaning back in her seat, she gave him a half-smile. "Your mom had to give you up. And your dad didn't know she was pregnant. He died before you were born. She couldn't raise you alone, and she thought the hospital would find a family for you."

The total absurdity hit him. His disbelieving laugh carried a hint of hysteria. "Okay. That's a good one. But you can stop now. How long did it take you to think up this story?"

She remained silent until his laughter tapered off. "I didn't make it up, Flint. As your Guardian, I'm responsible for notifying you about your heritage and your upcoming decision." She stopped, her deep, blue eyes studying his face, probably gauging whether a freak-out was imminent.

"You? You're my fairy guardian?" It was so strange how a totally normal kid could grow up to have mental problems.

"I do *not* have mental problems." Glaring, she crossed her arms.

"What? Did you—"

"Yeah, I can read minds. So what? And, dude, that was totally uncalled for. Just because you can't understand, explain, or believe my ability doesn't give you the right to assume I'm delusional."

"You're right. I'm sorry. So, what's the big decision I have to make?"

"Whether to stay here or move to the fairy realm."

He shut his gaping mouth. What dimension had he fallen into?

"This isn't another dimension, Flint, just your life."

"You've really got to stop that. It's rude. And invasive."

She blushed. "Sorry."

The rise of children's voices stalled his reply. A swarm of little kids hurried past their table on the way to the checkout desk, picture books clutched in their arms. It also gave him a chance to think. His mom was a fairy; he was half-fairy. He still couldn't wrap his mind around it all.

Lila sat quietly and continued to scrutinize him, her eyes narrowed.

"I don't even know what questions to ask. Why would I want to live with fairies? I can't even believe I'm saying that." Shaking his head, he shoved a hand through his hair.

Pulling her bag from the table, she stood. "Why don't I just show you? You'll never believe me otherwise. Come on."

He pocketed the application, threw on his jacket, and followed her back out into the cold. As he fell into step next to her, she cupped her hands near her mouth and blew into them. "I hate winter. Anyway, have you seen the rundown bridge near the North Forest?"

"That huge stone thing? Who can miss it?"

"That's where we're headed." She grabbed his hand and pulled him into a deserted alley.

The scents of rotting food and a nearby Italian restaurant mingled, turning his stomach. "Lila? Is this a shortcut?"

"We can't walk there. It'll take too long. Hold on." She gripped his hand tighter.

He blinked, and the alley disappeared. Another blink and they were standing next to the gray stone bridge.

"What just happened?" His breath frosted out in little clouds.

She grinned. "Did I mention I can teleport, too?"

"You read minds, and you teleport. Sure. Why not?" Nothing would surprise him today. The very foundation of everything he believed had been called into question.

Including whether this bridge was safe. Two crumbling columns stood at the entryway to the bridge. Missing stones left gaping holes in the arched pathway leading across the small river. He'd heard the city had chosen not to replace the bridge due to the cost. Instead, they'd built a concrete bridge a mile downstream.

Lila stepped closer and touched the stone supports. The bridge shimmered before disappearing, the forest vanishing. A beautiful bridge with a filigreed silver gate arched into view, leading to a green meadow. Beyond the gate, grasses waved in the breeze, flowers bloomed, and the briny scent of the ocean teased his nose. A worn path furrowed through the meadow.

Flint took a step, but Lila laid a restraining hand on his arm and shook her head. "This is the doorway to the fairy realm. Your key unlocks the gate, but you can't go in until you make your decision. I wanted you to see its beauty for yourself."

The ache in his chest built with the urge to explore, to follow where the path led. His fingers itched for a drawing pencil. This was going down in his sketchpad as soon as he got back to the apartment. He shoved his hands into his pockets. "Why can't I just visit whenever I want to?"

"Once you've made a decision to live in the realm, you can come and go for short periods. Usually five hours at a time with a twelve-hour rest in-between. But you must use the key by noon tomorrow with the intention of staying or the opportunity's gone."

"You're saying I have to give up everything to move somewhere I've never been? Is there anything special about this realm? Other than the fairies, of course."

"It's called Everwild."

He grinned and waggled his eyebrows. "Wild, huh? Sounds promising."

She rolled her eyes. "Don't be a dork. Everwild's beautiful. It's a seaside realm, full of farms and flower gardens with warm weather year-round. The residents help the environment flourish, so these next few months are the slow season. It gets busier in the spring and summer."

The apprenticeship with Mr. Anton was the chance of a lifetime. He couldn't miss it, just because he was half-fairy. *If* he was half-fairy. "I have until twelve o'clock tomorrow to decide?"

She nodded. "Your fae blood allows you to touch the bridge support and perceive what's really beyond. Insert your key to unlock the gate. That's it."

"Hold on, Lila. This apprenticeship could change my life."

"But you don't even know what could happen beyond the gate."

"Exactly. It could be a disaster. Why didn't you tell me about this sooner?"

"We had to wait. What if you had been adopted? Your new family would've been devastated if you disappeared into the fairy realm. So we held off until you became an adult."

"We? Who's we?"

She crossed her arms and scrunched her neck into her coat collar as a cold wind whipped her hair. "The counsel and your mom."

His eyes went wide before he looked away. "Of course. My birth mom's alive."

Lila touched his arm. "She had to give you up, Flint. She was just a kid herself, and she was afraid of what her father would do to your real dad. That's why I was assigned as your Guardian, to let her know how you were doing. She loves you and tried to do the right thing."

After a moment, he shook his head. "I don't know. I need time."

Her shoulders stiff, she turned away and kicked at the cold dirt path.

"Hey, this is a big deal. I can't make a split-second decision right now. But that doesn't change our friendship, does it?" He swallowed, afraid he'd revealed too much. "Are we still friends?"

Disappointment shadowed her eyes. "Of course. I hope you get what you want, Flint."

"Thanks. If the meeting goes well, I'll take you out for ice cream to celebrate."

When they parted ways an hour later, Flint hurried back to his room. His fingers flew as he sketched the realm revealed to him for only a few minutes. He spent the rest of the afternoon shading and adding color. He sank onto his bed when he was done. It was better than most of his work. After a few minutes admiring the piece, he picked up his pencils to store them. What the—?

From the end of one pencil, a green tendril curled out, a tiny, delicate leaf extended like a flag. Dropping it on the desk, he backed away and wiped his eyes. When he looked again, the green tendril retreated, disappearing into the top with only the leaf sticking out. He stored the other pencils, but left the weird one on the desk and refused to touch it. Checking his watch, he muffled a curse. He had to meet Mr. Anton in an hour.

They met in a little coffee shop tucked in among older shops. Flint walked the ten blocks in the cold to save money. When he entered, the scent of coffee and yeast mingled in the warm shop. Books filled one wall, while black and white photos hung on the others. Back-to-back booths filled the floor space. Mr. Anton waited for him in a far booth, a plaid scarf still wrapped around his neck.

After they ordered coffee and muffins, the famous artist asked Flint about his life, his work, what he wanted for the future. Mr. Anton's little mustache wiggled, and his thick gray eyebrows moved up and down as he talked. They finished their coffee and pastries, and Mr. Anton wiped his mouth with a napkin. "Your work shows promise, but you have much to learn. If you apply yourself, I will teach you. Are you still interested?"

Flint opened his mouth to say yes. The words stuck, and he cleared his throat. "Um. Sir, can I think about it and let you know tomorrow?"

Pursing his lips, Mr. Anton raised an expressive eyebrow. "I was under the impression this was exactly what you wanted."

"Yes, but it's a big decision."

"Very well. If you choose to pass on this opportunity, it won't come around again. There are plenty of other eager artists who are waiting, so contact me as soon as you've decided." He laid a business card on the table next to Flint's coffee cup.

"Yes, sir. I understand."

Mr. Anton left shortly afterward, and Flint kicked himself on the walk home. Why hadn't he jumped on the offer? He'd dreamed of it for weeks, spinning visions of days spent under the artist's teaching. But Lila's words twirled through his head, the key's presence in his pocket a burning reminder of Everwild.

He hurried home, his fingers and nose numb from the cold, still pondering the events of the evening. It was ludicrous to wait. A wise, reasonable person would accept Mr. Anton's apprenticeship and learn as much as he could. Surely, Lila would understand—many Saturdays ago, they'd talked about his ideas for the future and where he wanted to be ten years from now.

That night, his dreams filled with grassy meadows and a blue sea that lay beyond. The scent of fresh blooms filled the air. Upon waking, he stretched, the sweet perfume lingering. He pushed himself up, colorful shapes shifting on his comforter. His eyes went wide, and he scrambled toward the headboard. A profusion of daffodils covered his bed. Blooms of fragrant yellow, pinkish salmon, and creamy white lay strewn like a blanket. Where had all of these daffodils come from? He gathered them from the bed and laid them on the couch. His temples throbbed with the start of a headache. Several minutes of head-scratching later, he gave up on an explanation and left to take a shower.

After a quick bowl of cereal, Flint called Mr. Anton and accepted the apprenticeship. They made arrangements for him to start the following day. He hung up and breathed out a sigh of relief. He frowned. Where was the excitement, the thrill, the anticipation of starting his dream? Only a vague quiver of apprehension strummed down his neck. It must be nerves.

He dialed Lila, hoping she'd be happy for him.

When she answered, he swallowed the golf ball in his throat. "Hey, it's Flint. Guess what? Mr. Anton offered me the apprenticeship last night. I just called him. You are talking to his new apprentice."

A beat of silence passed. "Congratulations, Flint. I know you've worked hard for it."

"Thanks! We should go celebrate."

"Maybe later. I'm not feeling so well." For the first time ever, awkwardness filled the spaces in their conversation.

"Oh, okay. I'll talk to you later. Feel better soon."

For the rest of the morning, nothing held his interest. He nodded off while reading, every attempted sketch resembled a three-year-old's art project, and his television reran sitcoms from the 80s. He threw away the wilting daffodils and pulled the key from his pocket. The gold gleamed, taunting him of a world he'd never know.

Sitting on the edge of his bed, he eyed the key. Giving up everything here, especially the apprenticeship with Mr. Anton, was a bad choice. His head knew it, but his heart refused to listen. Getting paid to learn under a famous artist? How could anything be better than that? Still on edge, he left the apartment, hoping a long walk in the cold would clear his head.

For a long time, he threaded through the streets without a particular destination. His thoughts swirled. Although he'd accepted the position with Mr. Anton, it didn't feel right. For reasons he couldn't explain, Everwild called to a place deep inside. As he left the concrete path, rustling sounded behind him. He turned to see flowers shoot up where he'd stepped—daisies, tulips, lilies in all shades. What was going on? Was he going crazy? He shook his head and hurried away from the strange flower path blooming in November. Moments later, he stood in a showdown with the stone bridge. His feet had carried him to the very place he needed to be.

Slipping his hand deep into his pocket, he touched the key. Despite his circumstances, an apprenticeship with Mr. Anton wouldn't fill his need for a connection. He checked his watch, and his heart jumped. The blue numbers read 11:55 a.m. Walking over to the collapsing column, he placed his palm on it. The derelict bridge disappeared, and the gorgeous stone one replaced it. He pulled the key from his pocket, already feeling a warm breeze from the other realm caress his cheeks. With a glorious fullness filling his chest, he slid the key into the silver lock and turned it. With a soft click, the gate swung open.

"Flint?"

He turned. Lila stood behind him, her mouth hanging open.

"Hey."

"But I thought—you said—did you change your mind?" Her eyes brimmed with hope.

He tapped his chest. "In here, I know Everwild is where I need to be. I can't explain it."

She smiled. "I saw your flower trail."

"Is that normal?"

"For a fairy? Absolutely."

"I also had ivy sprout from my pencil yesterday, and this morning I woke to find daffodils on my bed. Those things have never happened before."

She laughed. "They're normal for an adult fairy. You'll get used to it. Mind if I walk in with you?"

He smiled in return. "No, not at all. One question, though, just to clear things up. You live here, right?"

She nodded. "Yeah, I'm a full-blood fae."

"Can I visit you some time?"

She slipped her hand into his, and they crossed into the fairy realm. "I'd like that a lot. But you'll be pretty busy for a while."

"Why?"

"Well, there's one more thing you should know." She continued to hold his hand as they followed the path across the meadow.

"What's that?"

She grinned, her eyes sparkling. "Your mom? She's the fairy queen. So, you're the Prince of Everwild. Welcome home."

J. M. Hackman loves bookstores and libraries. She spent her childhood visiting these magical places and writing. After graduating from Penn State, she held many positions: assistant librarian, office assistant, office manager, substitute teacher, author, wife, and mother. She still holds the last three jobs. Her YA fantasy Spark (Book One of The Firebrand Chronicles) was released in 2017. She spends her days writing stories, consuming massive quantities of dark chocolate, and looking for portals to other worlds.

www.jmhackman.com

Well of Fate

Savannah Jezowski

Nine worlds hang from Yggdrasil,
Watered by the Well of Fate.
The sisters carve young destinies
On dew-draped branches of the tree.

Beneath the tree, evergreen,
The Gatekeeper guards the door—
Beyond the bleak Shore of Corpses
Where only Death may enter there.

What was before cannot be changed,
And what is to come must be.
The sisters draw it from the well
And children live the tale.

Ratatosk wanted to change his fate.

The life of a squirrel was hardly epic. Nut-gathers and tale-spinners, squirrels kept to the trees while others built great halls and mighty longboats and forged paths through the mountains and across the seas. It simply wasn't fair. If given the opportunity, Tosk was sure he could be a mighty hero.

So he'd gone searching for the one thing in the Niflheim that might give him that opportunity, the fabled Well of Fate. Tosk twitched his fluffy red tail and leapt onto the branch above his head. Distracted by his musings, his claws only just caught the rough bark of the ash tree. He yelped and scrabbled frantically with his back feet until he had wormed his way onto the branch. He sat up, tail twitching in agitation, and glanced over his shoulder to make sure no one had seen his misadventure. It was bad enough he was not destined to be a hero, but he would rather the rest of the world not know it.

The words of the owl who lived above Tosk's borrow in the Ironwood Forest came back to haunt him. "Who? You? A hero? Only good for gossip," he had hooted, probably annoyed with Tosk's chatter. The ridicule had stuck to him, like burrs in his tail.

Good for nothing, was just as easily what the cranky old bird meant.

Perhaps he wasn't good for much, but he had to be good for *something*. Tosk's lower lip quivered as he stared into the endless tangle of branches of Yggdrasil—the legendary tree that connected the nine worlds and guarded the entrance to the Well. Although, Tosk was beginning to wonder how many of those legends had been exaggerated because he had been up and down the tree twice already, and he had found nothing besides bird nests and a squirrel stash. He had sampled some of the nuts, just to make sure they were still good. He didn't want the poor squirrel who had hidden them to come back to a stash of rotten nuts.

And he wouldn't, because they were still quite good. Tosk licked his lips and gave his pronounced stomach a pat. Still good, although perhaps a mite fewer in number.

"That was a close call, little rodent." The voice, piercing and sharp like the northern winds that ripped across the Niflheim, sent Tosk tumbling to the branch below. He clawed at the bark with all four paws and barely managed to save himself from a nasty fall.

He righted himself and peered up through the leaves of the tree, brightened by the sunlight streaming down from the sky. A great round eye blinked at him. Then, the foliage shifted, the leaves shivered, and a great brown queen of the sky eased into view. It was an eagle, and a mighty one at that, with a head as white as the winter snows and a beak as sharp as a dragon slayer's blade. Tosk hunched his shoulders and sidled backward.

Even a squirrel of his heroic tendencies would be an easy snack for such a creature.

"Have no fear from me, little rodent. I have had my fill of feasting this day," the eagle said with a chuckle. It was a nasty sort of chuckle that did nothing to calm Tosk's nerves.

"I wouldn't mess with me, if I were you," he said. His voice, although said with as much heroic bravado as he could muster, squeaked like the pathetic mewling of a forest mouse. He cleared his throat and pulled himself up straighter. "And I am *not* a rodent. I am Ratatosk, he who single-handedly battled the dragon Fafnir to rescue Odin's son from eternal—"

"It was my understanding," the eagle interrupted, "that it was a dragon slayer who battled Fafnir—and a raven. Clever bird." The bird preened the feathers under her wing, sliding them through her beak with a clucking noise.

"Dragon slayer's daughter," Tosk corrected. He had told the tale often enough that he should know.

"Ah. So you did *not* battle Fafnir, then."

Tosk squirmed. "Poetic license. Besides, I *would* have defeated him if I'd been given the chance. But that rotten bird and dragon girl were determined to hog all the glory."

The bird clucked at him and paused her preening. "Is that why you are here, rodent, to regale me with tales? Tell me, what is that wingless serpent up to down below? *That* is a tale worth your life."

Tosk gulped and took a step backward. "What serpent?" he squeaked.

"Nidhogg. Naturally, he has sent you here to spy on me." The eagle left her branch and swooped down to sit next to Tosk. He shrieked and scampered backward until he pressed up against the bark of the tree. He clutched his ear tufts and hugged them against his cheeks.

"No, he hasn't! He really hasn't!" Tosk yelped. "I'm here to find the Well of Fate."

The eagle froze, her snowy head turning to the side so that she could stare down at Tosk with her glittering eye. "What does a little rodent like you want with the Well of Fate?"

"To change it, of course! To change mine, I mean." He needed to prove the owl wrong. Somehow, he had to prove he was worth something, worth more than gossip.

The eagle threw back her head and screeched, so loudly Tosk stuffed his fists into his ears to drown her out. She looked back at him, her beak opening and closing as she spoke. Tosk removed his fists and shook his head to clear away the ringing in his ears.

"What was that? I can't hear you over that infernal ringing."

"I said, why would a tale-spinner wish to change his fate?"

Tosk frowned at her, feeling rather like a mouse batted around by a cat. "I am not resigned to being a tale-spinner for the rest of my life. I want to be a hero." More than anything, he wanted to prove the owl wrong. His lower lip began to tremble again as the words not quite spoken seemed to echo in his ears.

Good for nothing, good for nothing, good for nothing…

"Ah, but you are so good at your gossip. Tell me, Nidhogg really did send you, didn't he? What does that worm wish to know this time?"

Tosk's frown deepened. "Where is this Nidhogg exactly?"

"Beneath the roots of the tree. Speak quickly, because I think I have discovered a hollow place in my gullet that you should fill nicely."

Tosk gulped and pressed harder against the tree. "If you tell me where I can find the Well of Fate," he squeaked, "I will find out what Nidhogg is saying about you."

The eagle leaned closer and stared at him, unblinking. "You drive a hard bargain, rodent, but I grow bored up here and could use a diversion. Very well. Bring me news of my nemesis and I will go hungry."

"And the Well?" Tosk prodded.

"That," the eagle said with another piercing shriek, "is a question only the

Gatekeeper can answer."

Tosk planted his fists on his hips. "That wasn't our agreement! You were supposed to tell me where—"

The eagle shrieked again. "I think that hollow place in my gullet is talking to me," she said, her claws raking the branches of the tree as she moved closer. "Yes, I can hear it now. 'Fill me,' it's saying. 'Fill me with crunchy, delicious rodent—'"

Tosk gripped his ear tufts, his heart slamming against his chest. "I accept your terms!" he yelped. Then, he frowned and straightened himself to his full height as he strove to regain the dignity of a hero. "And I am *not* a rodent."

The eagle dipped her head. "Very wise of you. Now go. You will find Nidhogg beneath the roots of the tree, along the shore."

Tosk frowned. If there was a shore, then it must stand to reason there was also a lake. But he had been all around the tree and up into its highest branches and had seen no signs of a lake anywhere. "What lake? I never saw one."

"Go!"

Tosk threw himself off the branch. "I am going!" he yelled as he landed with bruising force farther down the tree. He scrambled along the length of a swinging limb to the trunk and hurried downward as fast as he could possibly go. Above him, the eagle began to laugh, each peal sharper—and nastier—than the last.

"Be careful what you search for, little rodent, because you may just find it," she called down to him and then dissolved into more unpleasant laughter. Tosk's poor ears rang with her laughter as he ran for his life, down the length of Yggdrasil.

Laughter, gossip, good for nothing.

It took him several hours, but Tosk finally found what he was looking for. The roots of the ash tree were a snarled mess, diving in and out of the soil like a tangle of worms. He scratched around them, testing them for weakness until he finally found a great hulking root with a hollow space beneath it. He wiggled down inside and dropped a rather disturbing distance. When he landed and recovered his wits, he discovered what seemed to be a tunnel. His hopes, rather dashed by his unfortunate encounter with the eagle, began to rise as he scampered down the length of the tunnel, down, down into the earth beneath Yggdrasil.

He did not have to go far before the tunnel widened. Ahead, pale blue light flickered against the tunnel walls. Soon, he could hear water lapping against stones. Tosk ran even faster, until he burst free of the tunnel and skidded to a halt in a massive cavern filled with flickering blue light. The light emanated from the water lapping against the shore of the cavern floor, the rippling waves iridescent and bright. He gaped, unsure what he was seeing.

"So, there really is a lake beneath the tree!" He gasped. His voice echoed out and back to him.

Something clattered to his right. Tosk yelped and dove for cover behind a large rock.

"Of course. What were you expecting? Soil and worms?" This voice was as different from the piercing cry of the eagle as day was different from night—deep, and guttural, like the rush of great rivers through mountain caverns.

"Yes, actually," Tosk squeaked, head buried beneath his arms, tail bushed above him.

A laugh rolled through the cavern, shaking the very ground beneath him. Tosk huddled tighter into himself, quite sure he was going to die before he ever did anything heroic.

"I like you. You're honest. Come out, my friend, that I may meet you."

Tosk gulped and tried to steady the frantic beating of his heart. "No, thank you. I'm quite fine where I am," he stammered. He was beginning to fear the owl was right about him.

"Come *out!*" the terrible voice demanded. "Please."

Tosk was not inclined to obey, but the nicety the creature tacked onto the end of his demand changed his mind. Perhaps Nidhogg was more reasonable than the eagle had been. He eased out from behind his rock and found himself staring into a massive face twice the size of the eagle. Covered in black scales that reflected the light of the water, the creature grinned down at him.

"You're—you're a dragon," Tosk stammered, wishing he had stayed behind his rock. He was beginning to wish he had stayed home, period. Perhaps, being a hero was overrated. The fate of a tale-spinner was not so bad after all. At least, in the safety of his hollow, he had never been in any danger of filling empty spaces in cranky gullets.

"Yes, of course. Is that a problem?"

"Oh, no!" Tosk squeaked. "I, er, love dragons. Truly. I'm old friends with Fafnir. You know him."

The dragon snorted, sending a wave of putrid hot breath over Tosk. "A pathetic worm of dragon." He reared backward, his head rising toward the ceiling of the cavern where the tangled roots of the tree spread out in place of rock. The dragon resembled a giant snake, with only some fins along his belly to differentiate him from the serpent kind.

Tosk shivered and wrinkled his nose. He had never liked snakes, for they could swallow a squirrel whole, no crunching required. "Perhaps I overstated my affiliation with Fafnir. Hardly more than acquaintances, really—"

The dragon laughed, shaking the cavern again. "I like you."

Tosk wondered exactly what the dragon meant. Liked him as in, they might be friends? Or liked him the way the eagle liked crunchy, delicious squirrel? "Er, thank you. I think."

"Tell me, why have you come to the Shore of Corpses?"

"Ahem. Well, I am here, oh great Nidhogg, to seek entrance to the Well of Fate—wait! What did you say? The Shore of What?"

"Corpses."

Tosk gulped and looked around him, paying more attention to the rocks that littered the cavern floor. Upon closer inspection, he realized they weren't rocks at all, but bones. The rock he had been hiding behind was actually the skull of some large creature, perhaps a bear or a giant wolf. He wondered how he had missed it before. The skull gleamed white in the light from the water, as unlike a rock as a squirrel was unlike a dragon.

"Yes, I see what you mean. Ahem. Yes. Well, I should be going—"

Nidhogg surged forward with alarming swiftness, coiling his scaled body across the entrance to the tunnel. "Don't go. You've only just arrived. It's been so long since anyone brought me news of the outside. Besides, if you've come seeking the Well of Fate, you've come to the right place. The Doorway lies just across the lake. I could take you there."

Tosk lifted his face, eagerly, but the expression on the dragon's face caused him to reconsider. Nidhogg seemed far too eager to help him. What was the catch? There was always a catch. Doorways to powerful and dangerous places were never accessed easily. Tosk had told enough stories to know that. "You can just take me there? I don't have to answer a riddle, or battle a demon, or anything of that nature?"

Nidhogg bellowed a laugh. "You only find that sort of thing in fairy tales, my little friend. It's quite simple. All you need to do is climb onto my back and I will swim you across the lake."

"That's all? No deathly trials or whatnot?"

"No." Nidhogg chuckled with a toothy grin. "No deathly trials. Just a short ride across the lake."

"Is that allowed? Doesn't seem right that there isn't some sort of dangerous quest," Tosk objected. He tugged on his ear tufts as he tried to remember a tale where the hero did not have to accomplish some dangerous task. He couldn't think of any, but that didn't mean there was no precedent for it.

"I'm the Gatekeeper," Nidhogg said as he curled around Tosk, his scales scraping across the bones littering the cavern floor. He leaned down so that he was nearly nose to nose with Tosk. "I would know if it were not allowed."

"Er, very well then," Tosk squeaked. He was beginning to think it may not be healthy to argue with the dragon further. "I'll climb up."

He scampered along the winding back of the dragon until he perched directly behind his head. Nidhogg slithered forward and eased into the gleaming waters of the lake. Tosk breathed a sigh of relief as the Shore of Corpses faded away behind them. He wasn't at all disappointed to leave it—or the bleached bones—behind. This being a hero thing was a lot harder than it looked. There were so many hazards to worry about, eagles with hollow gullets and bone-cluttered beaches. At least Nidhogg wasn't like any Gatekeeper Tosk had ever talked about in his stories. They were normally devious, dangerous folks who exacted terrible prices for their services, but Nidhogg seemed very amiable. It

24

was a refreshing change of pace.

He chatted to the dragon as they swam across the lake, regaling him with the details of Fafnir's final battle, the water flickering as Nidhogg's fins churned through the water. A thin mist developed and hovered above the water, dimming the lights below. By the time they reached the shore on the other side, Tosk was quite certain they were friends. He hopped off the dragon's back and onto the shore, pleased to note this side was blissfully lacking in bones.

"Thank you so much for the ride," he said to his new friend.

Nidhogg inclined his head. "It was my pleasure." He eased back into the water with a hiss and a grin. "The sisters will guide you from here."

"Sisters?" Tosk echoed, but Nidhogg had already disappeared into the mist. With a shrug, he turned back to the shore and hopped through the mist, searching for the doorway to the Well of Fate. It was not hard to find. He just followed the mist. It curled and eased forward as if tugged by an invisible breeze that Tosk could not feel, leading him down a wide, rounded tunnel. When Tosk reached the end of the tunnel, the mist parted to reveal a giant archway carved into the tunnel wall. The arch had been inscribed with runes, but Tosk had never paid much attention to human lettering. The best tales were told by word of mouth, not written into stone. He paused to squint into the mist swirling beyond the doorway and wondered what lay inside.

Tosk's hopes began to rise as he realized how close he was to his goal. Surely, if he had come this far, he would be successful. But as he hopped through the doorway, a shiver tingled from the tips of his ears, across his spine, and all down the length of his glorious tail. He froze and looked frantically from side to side, but when nothing else happened, he allowed himself a small laugh.

"You're just being paranoid," he scolded himself. "There are no monsters here—and no deathly trials either."

He looked around the cavern he had entered. There was so much fog he could not really see much, so he hopped deeper into the room. The mist seemed to part for him, thinning as if the morning sun were beating down and chasing it away. Emboldened, he scampered onward until the rocks beneath his paws gave way to sand and the mist parted completely to reveal a low stone wall. He hopped onto the top of it and realized it was actually a round wall filled with water.

The Well of Fate.

Tosk stared down into the dark, still water. His heart began to pound as he wondered what he was to do now. Was he supposed to drink from it? Was he supposed to call out and ask for help? Perhaps there were instructions on the doorway—why had he not thought to bring a human along to translate?

The water stirred, rippling at the center as if someone had tossed a stone into it. Then, the unthinkable happened, as the water began to rise from the well, taking shape as it swayed side to side, pulsing and rippling. Tosk's heart beat so hard he feared it would beat right out of his chest, but the water creature did not approach him as it finished taking its form. It was a woman, a water woman, translucent as the waves with seaweed for hair and a string of milky white pearls around her throat. She smiled at him.

"You have come a long way," the water woman said. Her lips moved, water spilling over them as she spoke. She had eyes, like a human woman, except they were completely white. It was quite unsettling. "My name is Verdandi—I tell the present."

"Erm." Tosk cleared his throat, trying not to look into her unusual eyes. "Um, hello?"

"Hello." She swayed side to side as she studied him. She had a pleasing way of talking, soft and kind. "My sisters are coming, as well. Do not be alarmed." She motioned with a translucent hand as the surface of the well began to stir again. Two more humps of water rose from the surface and slowly took form. The one on the left was composed of black water, and a rank smell filled the cavern as she rose from the well and took form. She too had seaweed for hair, but it was black and slimy, and she wore dark pearls around her throat. Her eyes were completely black as they looked, unblinking, down on the squirrel. Tosk shrank away from her.

"This is Wyrd—she tells the past," Verdandi explained. Tosk wondered if that was why she looked and smelled so bad. Perhaps she was very old. Her skin was not translucent like Verdandi's, as if she were made of rank water left to foul in a basin instead of the clear, cool waters of a mountain stream.

The final hump of water seemed to be taking longer to form and kept changing, as if it were having trouble determining what it wanted to look like. "This is our little sister Skuld," Verdandi continued. "She tells what will be."

The third sister finally took her form, and Tosk breathed a sigh of relief, for she was just a little girl holding a long string of colorful pearls, which she seemed to be stringing. She held up a bright green pearl and winked at Tosk with a very human-looking blue eye as she slipped it onto the strand and slid it down until it clinked against the others.

"What *must* be," the little girl corrected, with a stern but fond look at her older sister. Verdandi inclined her head in agreement. The little girl had seaweed hair as well, but hers was short and spiky and stuck up around her head in a way that almost made Tosk want to laugh. It fluttered around her head as if stirred by river currents. He liked Skuld the best—she seemed the most normal—as normal as a water girl could be. She winked at him again before she reached down and fished around in the dark waters of the well. She gasped with delight and pulled out another pearl, this one purple.

"Why have you come?" Wyrd spoke for the first time.

Tosk jumped a little, for her voice was that of a cranky-sounding old woman, and she spoke very loudly. He studied the foul-smelling water woman and wondered if maybe he should retreat while he still had the chance, but Verdandi smiled at him and Skuld winked, so he lifted his nose and stared up at

Wyrd. "I've come to change my fate," he declared, trying to sound bold. "I don't want to be a tale-spinner; I want to be a hero."

Wyrd cackled and spit dark water to one side. "What makes you think we can help you, foolish creature?"

"Sister," Verdandi scolded. The old water woman hissed at her younger sister but fell silent. Verdandi turned back to Tosk with a smile. "You are a very brave creature to have come so far to change your fate."

"But no one will care about it—no one will tell stories about me. I don't want to *tell* stories. I want to have stories *told about me.*" His lower lip quivered, and he bit down on it hard with his pronounced front teeth. When he had composed himself, he sat up a little straighter. "Can you help me? Can you change my fate?"

Skuld sighed and set aside her string of pearls as she moved toward him, stirring the waters of the well as she approached. She propped her elbows on the edge of the wall and smiled down at him. Tosk's paws became soaked in the water running off her and spilling over the wall and down to the sand below. "Poor Ratatosk," she said as she leaned down and place a wet, slimy kiss on the top of his head. "Don't you know? Your destiny has already been carved into the tree—it cannot be changed."

Tears filled the squirrel's eyes. "But I've come all this way," he wailed. "If you can't help me, no one can!"

She ran a damp hand down his back, soothing him. "There, there. You do not understand. Your fate cannot be changed, but the path you take to get to it…ah, now that is a different matter."

Tosk swiped a paw beneath his eyes, chasing away tears. "What do you mean?"

She grinned at him and leaned down to kiss his head again. "There are dark days ahead for you—many dark days, and many good ones. You will have choices to make, choices that can determine what sort of life you will lead."

Wyrd spat to one side again. "You can continue to be a tale-spinner, like your father and his father before him."

"Or," Verdandi interjected, "you can choose a different path."

"A more *heroic* path. Only *you* can change your fate." Skuld smiled at him and gave him a pat on the head. "The choice is yours."

"Choose wisely," Wyrd grumbled ominously. "You'll get your chance sooner than you know."

Tosk wondered what she meant by that. He really was finding himself less and less fond of the old water woman. He scratched behind his left ear. "Surely, there is something you can do to help me," he argued, irritated and worried that he had come all this way for nothing.

Because he was nothing.

Verdandi shook her head and began to sink back into the waters of the wall. "I'm sorry, little friend," she said as she lifted a hand in farewell.

"Wait!" Tosk shouted, but she had already disappeared. "You have to help me! I can't just leave."

"Now you're getting it," Wyrd muttered with a black look toward Tosk. Her body began to lose its form as the black water spread across the well. Skuld batted the foul water away from herself with an annoyed look at her sister before she pushed away from the wall and glided toward the center of the pool.

"Please," he begged her. "I want to be good for something. I have to be a hero. *I have to be!*"

She cast him a sorrowful look and shook her head. Water droplets landed on his face. "You must forge your own path," she said. "We just carve it into the tree. You write the tale."

Tosk began to cry as she sank into the water, melding with Wyrd's rank water until only ripples remained. He sat there and cried until the ripples faded and only still, dark water remained. At last, he scrubbed his eyes and hopped down from the wall. He couldn't stay down here forever. As much as he dreaded facing the owl with his failures, he dreaded starving to death more.

He dragged his paws across the ground and followed the mist back up the tunnel toward the shore of the underground lake.

"Nidhogg!" he called out when he arrived. His voice, still rusty from crying, echoed out across the iridescent water. "Nidhogg!"

"He won't come."

Startled, Tosk leapt backward away from the quiet voice, but when he crept forward again, he saw that the speaker was actually a small boy, thin and pinch-faced. The child sat with arms around his knees, huddled near the shore of the lake. He swiped a hand under his nose and then used his shoulders to dry his cheeks.

"What's the matter?" Tosk asked, scampering up to the lad and dashing up his arm to perch on his shoulder. He wasn't the only one who had been crying.

"I've come searching for my parents," the boy said. "The dragon said I would find them, but he didn't tell me I couldn't bring them back. They're dead, you see. And now I can't get back either. He tricked me."

Tosk clicked his tongue. "There, there. Must be some sort of mistake. Nidhogg and I are old friends. I'll get this sorted for you." He dashed back down the boy's arm and to the edge of the water. He yelled the dragon's name as loud as he could, racing up and down the shore. Finally, he saw the mist curl and ripples stir the water as Nidhogg disturbed the surface of the lake. The dragon paused a few yards away from the shore.

"You called, tale-spinner?" he asked.

"There you are! This young chap seems to be confused. He says you refuse to take him back across the lake. I told him that was nonsense, of course—"

"I'm afraid the journey is one way." Nidhogg huffed loudly, steam curling from his nostrils.

"I beg pardon?" Tosk asked as the first tendrils of doubt began to churn in his full belly. He began to wish he had not sampled so many of those nuts earlier.

"The journey from the Shore of Corpses is one way. Once you pass over, you cannot return."

Tosk lifted himself upright, outraged. "You didn't tell me that! You said there wasn't a catch!"

"You didn't ask about the return trip," the dragon replied with a grin.

Tosk floundered into shocked silence. He should have known better than to trust a dragon, but he had been so focused on finding the Well that he had not considered the creature might have an ulterior motive. "You're despicable!" he cried.

"That's a mighty big word for such a tiny little morsel." The dragon laughed.

"There's more where that one came from," Tosk declared hotly. "Tale-spinners are never at a loss for *words*. The eagle was right about you—"

"What has that bird been saying about me?" Nidhogg asked as he surged forward.

"Nothing good, let me tell you," Tosk muttered, angry at the dragon but angrier at himself for having been fooled. He was no sort of hero at all.

"Tell me what she's been saying," Nidhogg demanded.

Tosk looked up at him, wondering how he had ever seen friendship in those gleaming dragon eyes. "No. I won't tell you unless you change your mind about that return trip."

Nidhogg hissed angrily and coiled toward them, his body easing onto the shore. "You drive a hard bargain, mouse."

"I am not a mouse!" Tosk cried. "Why can't anybody get it right?"

"Why the fuss?" the dragon said as he leaned closer, his lips parting to reveal sharp fangs. "You're all edible; I don't see why the distinctions are necessary."

Tosk gulped noisily, realizing he had pushed his luck rather too far for one day. "Ah, well, a bargain is a bargain. Shall you give us a ride in exchange for some gossip?"

"Us?" A deep, taunting laugh spilled out of the dragon. "Who said anything about *us*? I agreed to bring *you* back. A bit of worthless gossip isn't worth two return trips."

Tosk turned to stare at the boy, his mouth suddenly dry and stomach churning. "That's—that's not fair," he stammered. "I meant—"

"But you didn't *say*," Nidhogg interrupted smugly. "Now, are you going to come or shall I eat you both?"

Anger exploded in Tosk's chest. This had been a rotten day from the beginning, and he'd endured as much disappointment and trickery as he could possibly stand. "You're despicable!" he shouted. "He's just a boy, and you're—you're despicable!"

"You said that already. Are you coming?" Nidhogg began to slink back into the water. Tosk's heart beat frantically as he realized their escape was slipping out of his grasp. A part of him wanted to just hop on the dragon's back and try to send someone else back to help the boy—surely there were heroes plenty enough who would be willing to undertake the task, heroes more capable than a tale-spinner who couldn't even barter passage across a stupid, shimmery lake. But he stared back into the boy's angry, tear-filled eyes and realized he couldn't leave him behind. It just wasn't nice.

It wasn't right.

He turned back to the dragon, steeling himself for what would surely happen next. "I am *not* coming. You're a slimy, tricky sneak who doesn't deserve to know what birds or beasts are saying about you. I've never met a dragon as abominable as you, and I've met my fair share, let me tell you—"

"You know of other dragons besides Fafnir?" Nidhogg froze, only his head visible above the lake. Tosk stared, open-mouthed, up at the dragon, whose hairless eyebrows were lifted in interest. The dragon *had* said he wanted news of the outside…perhaps such news would be worth something to him. Worth, say, a return trip across the lake? A return trip for, say, two?

Tosk felt his spirits begin to rise as he realized their situation may not be hopeless after all. One thing he had learned about this dragon on their swim across the lake was that he did need catching up on the local gossip. He was terribly out of date down here in the caves beneath Yggdrasil. Perhaps this was a battle that could not be won by the wielding of swords but rather of words.

And there wasn't a creature in the Niflheim better equipped for wielding words.

"Well, naturally, I know other dragons," Tosk began as he planted his hands on his hips. In reality, he had only personally met three in all his life, but what Nidhogg didn't know wouldn't hurt him. "I was going to suggest I tell you another tale while you swam this little boy and I back across the lake—but, alas, if the trip is only *one way* and a tale isn't worth *two*…" He trailed off meaningfully.

Nidhogg reared out of the water, his huge head swaying side to side. "Now, that isn't fair," he complained. "You will tell me the tale or I will just eat you."

"If you just eat me, you won't hear the news *or* the story," Tosk shot back as he smugly curled his tail around his body and brushed it with his paw. "I was going to tell you about Thor and the Fenris Wolf—but, I'm afraid it wouldn't be your kind of story. I mean, who wants to hear about a giant wolf, or a dragon egg, or dragon tears—ah, but the story of the great and terrible battle for the Frostfire is one of my best—" He glanced at the dragon from the corner of his eye.

"Dragons don't cry—dragons never cry," Nidhogg interrupted with a scornful bark of laughter. "And what exactly is the Frostfire?"

"Alas, I've said too much," Tosk said with a careless wave of his paw. "I shouldn't want to bore you with the details."

"Oh, do bore me! Tell me about the dragon who cried." Nidhogg leaned down, so low his head nearly rested on the surface of the water.

"No," Tosk said, crossing his arms and turning slightly away, but only far enough that he could still see the dragon out of the corner of his eye. "I won't tell you anything unless you take us back across the lake."

Nidhogg's eyes narrowed in frustration, his tongue licking out between his teeth as he grumbled to himself. "You are surprisingly cunning for a dragon-morsel. I will strike a deal with you because I am bored. But, I warn you, if this story is not a good one, I may change my mind and eat you."

"Not a good one?" Tosk gasped as he whirled back. "My stories are *always* good ones. I am the most renowned tale-spinner in the Niflheim."

"I've never heard of you," Nidhogg said as he coiled his body around so that it rested on the shore. Tosk hopped onto his back and motioned for the little boy to join him. The boy moved forward cautiously but soon settled himself behind Tosk on the dragon's back.

Tosk bristled, outraged. "Never heard of me? That's rubbish."

Nidhogg turned and slinked back into the water. "So, the dragon who cried," he prompted.

"Ah, yes," Tosk began with a dramatic sigh. He cleared his throat, taking as long as he dared. He did not trust Nidhogg—not this time—and needed to make sure the story lasted the entire trip across the lake. He didn't want Nidhogg changing his mind halfway over.

"I'm getting hungry," Nidhogg grumbled.

Tosk cleared his throat hurriedly. "Yes, er, no reason to get snippy now. I was just remembering the details. In order to tell you about the dragon, I must first tell you about the wolf. Have you heard of the Fenris Wolf? He was a beast of great renown, equal to a dragon in size and ferocity."

Nidhogg hissed contentedly and swam a little faster, swaggering as he pulsed through the water of the lake. "Nothing is as great and terrible as a dragon," he scoffed.

"Are you going to tell this tale, or am I?"

"Very well, but tell it quickly, because this lake is not very large, and I want to hear the whole story."

Tosk was counting on precisely that. So, as Nidhogg swam across the glowing water, back toward the Shore of Corpses, Tosk began to spin his tale. He soon lost himself in the recounting of his tale, as all good storytellers do. The Well of Fate lay farther and farther behind, but Tosk had forgotten all about it, caught up in his own story.

Nidhogg slithered onto the shore just as Tosk finished the climax. The boy jumped off the dragon's back and scurried toward the exit, but he paused to wait for Tosk, who finished the story with a dramatic flip of his tail as he bounded off the dragon and onto the bone-littered shore.

"Wasn't that a good tale?" he asked proudly. "Easily worth the passage of two?"

"Come on," the boy hissed urgently.

Nidhogg curled toward Tosk, offering him a fang-filled smile. "Yes, it was. It was such a good tale, it's made me terribly hungry."

Tosk's stomach lurched as he realized he may have finished the tale a bit too early. He inched backward, fur bristling as Nidhogg rose above him like a cobra about to strike. Well, he had no intention of hanging around for post-story snacks. Tosk spun on his paws and lurched across the beach, shooting small pebbles and bits of bone behind him in his frantic burst for freedom.

Nidhogg howled, blinded by the debris Tosk accidentally hurled into his eyes. The boy turned to run just as Tosk launched onto his leg, digging into his trousers and scampering up to cling to his shoulder. He pounded back up the tunnel, one hand wrapped around Tosk's quivering body to keep him from falling off. As they neared the end of the passage, Tosk remembered how small the opening had been and wondered how the boy would fit through it.

But he kept running, past the place where Tosk had fallen into the tunnel. Behind them, Nidhogg bellowed in fury, his angry shouts growing louder as he caught up to them.

"Hurry!" Tosk shouted around the boy's fingers.

They rounded a corner and light spilled into the passage. Ahead, the roots of the tree formed a tangled sort of ladder leading out of the tunnel and toward the forest above them. Tosk leapt from the boy's shoulder and scurried easily up the roots. The boy labored behind him, slower as he searched for hand- and footholds to pull himself toward the sunlight.

Tosk shouted a warning as Nidhogg launched himself toward the boy's legs, but the dragon recoiled in pain when he moved into the patch of light streaming from above. Blinking furiously, the dragon slunk back into the shadows, cowering from the brightness of day.

The boy heaved himself out of the tunnel and scrabbled across the ground on all fours.

"We did it!" He gasped. Behind them, Nidhogg's roars of frustration echoed from the passage, frightening sparrows in the branches of Yggdrasil. They shrieked and scattered into the air. As the leaves shaken loose by their flight littered the forest floor around them, Tosk finally allowed himself time to breathe. He sat down hard, chest heaving with frantic gasps, as he took stock of himself and his companion.

"We're alive!" he stammered, hardly able to believe it.

"Thanks to you!" the boy said, grinning. "That was amazing. The way you outwitted the dragon? It was the most incredible thing I have ever seen."

Embarrassment surged through Tosk's trembling body. "It was nothing, really," he argued as he tried to calm himself.

"No, it was," the boy said, kneeling in front of him. "You could have left me and saved yourself, but you didn't. You risked everything for me. It was the bravest thing I've ever seen. May I ask your name, little warrior?"

Warrior? Tosk sat up a little straighter. No one had ever called him a warrior before. Was being a warrior nearly the same thing as a hero, perhaps? "My name is Tosk," he said, slowly, as it occurred to him that perhaps the sisters had been right. After all, saving the little boy from Nidhogg's cruel trick was rather good of him. Some might say, even *heroic*. It had never occurred to him that he could be both tale-spinner and hero—one did not have to exclude the other.

He hoped the boy was a good storyteller, because it would be up to him to help spread the news that even the smallest creature in the forest could outwit a dragon and change his fate, that a tale-spinner could be a hero and a good-for-nothing worth something.

"Thank you, Tosk. I have learned a valuable lesson this day."

Tosk smiled at his new friend, wondering if he had learned the same thing about heroes and destiny, but something in the boy's expression sobered him. Where he would have expected to see sunny gratitude, he found steely determination instead—perhaps anger as well. "What is that?" he asked cautiously.

The boy set his jaw. "I want to be like you," he said in a voice as firm as the roots of the tree beneath them. "The trickster who misleads others. I don't want to be the fool who is tricked ever again."

Tosk had never seen such determination in a child so young before. "What is your name?" He wanted to know. He suspected this boy may need watching—a lad with such determination was sure to live an exciting life, worthy of many tales.

The boy offered a half-smile that didn't quite reach his dark eyes. "Loki," he said proudly as he stood to his feet and squared his narrow shoulders. "My name is Loki."

Savannah Jezowski lives in Amish country with her Knight in Shining Armor and a wee warrior princess. Her debut novella "Wither" is featured in Five Enchanted Roses, *an anthology of Beauty and the Beast, and is a prequel to* The Neverway Chronicles, *a Christian fantasy series filled with tragic heroes and the living dead. She is also the author of* When Ravens Fall, *a Norse fairy tale retelling featuring Tosk the squirrel. When she isn't writing, Savannah likes to read books, watch BBC miniseries, and play with cover designs. All of her books are available on Amazon.*

dragonpenpress.com

Jericho and the Magician's Daughter

H. L. Burke

"We have a lot of work to do." Magician Hedward Spellsmith dabbed at his forehead with a clean handkerchief then brushed his graying brown curls away from his face. He settled on the stool beside the workbench.

"Yes, sir." Sixteen-year-old Jericho Carver waited for his instructions. Windows lined both sides of the long, second-story workshop, letting in bright summer sun and relentless heat. He tried to ignore the sweat dripping from under his short, dark hair and wondered if it would be disrespectful to roll up his shirtsleeves. When he'd helped out in his uncle's carpentry shop, going shirtless on a hot day hadn't been unheard of. However, magic was a gentleman's trade. Gentlemen did not work half-dressed…at least he didn't think they did.

He'd been Master Spellsmith's apprentice for a little over a year now and had only recently moved up from sweeping floors and stacking the wooden and paper quires on which Master Spellsmith wrote his complex spell formulas to doing some small spells of his own, under close supervision, of course. Hopefully soon he could learn to enchant his own stylus, the small, iron rods magicians used to channel fey energy from the air onto quires.

Master Spellsmith pulled a large, leather-bound book across the table and flipped it open. "We have a large order of anti-theft spells for the local sheriff."

"Anti-theft, sir?" Jericho frowned. Mountain's Foot was a small town where everyone knew everyone's business. He couldn't imagine anyone getting away with theft for long.

"Yes, apparently something has been filching poultry, and the anti-pest wards I set up didn't help, suggesting it is a person, not an animal." Master Spellsmith pointed to the other side of the table at a stack of wooden sheets cut into perfect squares: quires.

Jericho sprang into action, gathered up the quires, and brought them to Master Spellsmith's side.

"Thank you." The master drew his stylus from his vest pocket along with a slip of paper. "Here's a list of spells I want to test you on. See if you can write out the formulas for all of them. Don't guess. If you aren't sure, mark the spell to look up later. Remember, a single incorrect symbol in a complex spell formula can have disastrous results."

Jericho unfolded the paper and read the list. Frost ward spells, pest deterrent spells, tracking spells, lighting spells—all of which he'd gone over a hundred times and knew by heart. He swallowed a groan. When was it going to be his turn to work some real magic?

He took up a slate and a fresh piece of white chalk. Writing magical symbols with an instrument other than an enchanted stylus was like sewing without thread. Only a stylus could channel the energy into the symbols to create magic. Still, Master Spellsmith was a firm believer in old-fashioned rote learning. Jericho wrote out the first string: commencement symbol, sun spell for warmth, a proximity symbol for the area the frost ward would cover, then finally an activation symbol. With that done, he moved onto the next.

Master and apprentice worked in silence until the clock across the workshop chimed eleven.

Master Spellsmith set down his stylus. "Blast. Not even half done, and I have an appointment in a half hour."

Jericho's ears perked up. "Sir, if you wish, I could finish the order. I know the theft wards by heart."

"You're only a first-year student, Jericho." Master Spellsmith chuckled. "You don't even have your own stylus."

"You could let me use your spare." Jericho stood. "Please? Let me show you."

Master Spellsmith let out a long breath then passed the young man his stylus and a paper quire.

Jericho shook his head. "An anti-theft spell needs to be written on wood, sir. Otherwise the energy will expend it too fast."

Eyes twinkling, Master Spellsmith took back the paper quire and passed Jericho a wooden one. "First test passed, then."

Jericho's fingertips prickled as he grasped the stylus. Yes, he'd used one before, but always with Master Spellsmith reading out the symbols he was supposed to use or copying them from a ledger. Now, if he chose the wrong symbols, whatever happened would be his fault. He clamped his mouth shut and focused on the spell.

When the iron stylus touched the planed wood, it singed a dark line into it, as if it was burning, but with no perceptible heat. He whipped through the line of symbols before he could doubt himself. Magical energy buzzed across the quire, tracing the writing in glowing light.

"Perfect." The master took the quire and examined it. "You *are* ready for this, I see. Impressive. Perhaps you'll merit that stylus before the two-year mark.

Yes, you can handle these while I'm out." He buttoned up his embroidered vest and placed his stylus in his pocket. "You know where my spare is?"

Jericho motioned toward the door on the back wall. "In your desk, second drawer, with the inkwell and quills."

"Good man." Hedward patted his shoulder. "If you see Rill about, tell her I'll be bringing something from the baker's home for dessert. She'll like that." Rill was Master Spellsmith's thirteen-year-old daughter, a sweet girl, quiet, but with a pent-up energy that occasionally bubbled up like sparks behind her blue eyes. Just thinking about her made Jericho smile.

As Master Spellsmith left the room, Jericho sat on the edge of the worktable and let out a long breath. He'd done it. The shop was his for several hours, a stylus at his disposal...would this be what it was like when his apprenticeship ended and he was a full-fledged magician?

Jericho prided himself on keeping a cool, stoic exterior, but now he wanted badly to leap into the air and give a whoop. He was doing it. He was actually becoming a magician!

Hurriedly collecting the spare stylus from its nest in the master's messy private study, he set to work. He'd have all the anti-theft spells done in record time...and perhaps play with some light spells or illusions afterward. After all, Master Spellsmith hadn't said to *only* do the anti-theft spells.

He sat on the stool and stretched out his long legs. Over the summer, his already lanky body had shot up several more inches. He was now one of the tallest if not the tallest man in Mountain's Foot while arguably not quite a man yet...though the prestige of that lessened every time he caught sight of his ribs when shirtless before his bedroom mirror. No matter how much he ate, it didn't seem to add anything to his sparse frame.

As he wrote the first few symbols onto the wood of the quire, a rustling caught his ear, coming from the supply cabinet in the corner. He paused. That was odd. Could they have mice? No, Rill's pet, Jaspyr, would pitch a fit if there were rodents on the premise. It had to be his imagination or perhaps beams shifting in the manor house's framework. Before he could resume his task, however, something thumped. The right-side door of the cabinet shook ever so slightly.

What in the world? He tiptoed across the wooden floor and yanked the door open. Glowing yellow eyes blinked at him. Then like a taut spring, a bronze creature exploded from the shadows. Four metal paws splayed against Jericho's chest, knocking him onto his backside.

"Jaspyr, what the—" Jericho bit back an oath as the clockwork fox nosed at his face. "What were you doing in there?" Jaspyr's ears flattened. Jericho hesitated. Enchanted as a companion, Jaspyr was rarely without his mistress. That could only mean one thing. Jericho opened the cabinet's left-hand door. "Rill?"

The teen girl flushed and crawled out of her hiding spot.

"Blast you, Jaspyr." Her pale blond hair stuck up in unruly tufts and dust streaked her sky blue frock. The fox hopped into her lap and gave an apologetic whine.

Jericho forced himself to put on a stern face. "Rill, what are you doing in here? You know how your dad feels about you hanging around the shop."

"I'm not touching anything! I just wanted to listen." Her bright eyes clouded. "You and Father do so many interesting things. Me? I'm stuck in the library reading mundane history and etiquette and…I just want to be a part of the magic, Jericho. Even if he won't let me practice it, I want to know about it, so I don't feel like an outsider when you two talk shop over dinner."

Jericho's heart softened. He'd never liked the way Master Spellsmith shut the door in Rill's face whenever she tried to participate in training. In fact, it seemed downright unreasonable. If magic was so harmful, why was he teaching it to Jericho and why did he practice it himself? "You know if he finds you—"

"He won't, though. I was in here when he said he was going to town. He won't be back for hours." She clasped her hands. "Please? He'll never know. Please, Jerry? Let me stay."

His heart twisted. She was the only one who called him that. "All right, but don't touch anything. Just watch."

Mouth clamped shut in an obvious attempt to suppress a squeal, Rill nodded excitedly. He let her have the stool and sat instead on the edge of the worktable.

"How do these spells stop people from stealing things?" she asked, leaning closer.

He hesitated. Master Spellsmith was very clear about not wanting Rill to interact with magic, but answering that question really wouldn't teach her how to do magic, just demystify it a bit. "It doesn't really. Magic is simply the manipulation of Fey energy. It can't change the behavior of people. However, energy can mark objects with a traceable signature. What this does is mark a person's belongings with identifiable energy, so they can be tracked in the event of theft and lead right to the person who took them. Hopefully, just spreading the word around the village that these are in place will prevent any future thefts. I'm still half-convinced it was just a weasel or something. Those can be clever about evading traps." He picked up a quire. Rill's eyes followed his hands.

"Every spell begins with a commencement symbol, doesn't it?"

He cleared his throat. How did she even know that? "Yes."

Jaspyr curled up at her feet, his plume-like tail sweeping from side to side.

"And it ends with that other symbol? The one that looks like a commencement symbol only backward?"

"Yes, that's the activation symbol." He stopped writing. This was coming dangerously close to breaking Master Spellsmith's rules. Of course, they were kind of stupid rules. He shrugged. "Those inform the Fey energy of the—"

"Rill!"

Jericho dropped the stylus, and Rill nearly toppled off the stool. Her father stood in the doorway to the shop, his eyes wide, his hands clenched into fists. A memory of a similar expression on his own father's face shot through Jericho like a knife. Instinctively, he stepped between Master Spellsmith and Rill.

"It's not her fault, sir. I—"

"We weren't doing anything." Rill pushed her way in front of him. "I was just watching, not touching."

Master Spellsmith approached his daughter. "I have one rule for you, Rill, one rule for your own safety and well-being, and you constantly ignore it." The man's voice quavered. "And now you drag Jericho into your willfulness?"

Jericho's heart pounded. Memories of his mother's cries of pain, of his father shouting, echoed in his brain. Rill flinched at her father's scolding. Jericho tracked the master's hands. If he raised them toward Rill, employer or not, Jericho would knock him down so fast—

Rill's gaze darted toward Jericho. Her eyes widened, then she bolted from the room, past Master Spellsmith, who made no move to stop her.

Her father covered his eyes, moaned, and shook his head. The tension between Jericho's shoulders eased. This family conflict wasn't going to end in violence. Rill was safe. With that established, Jericho's mind turned to his own problems. He'd violated one of Master Spellsmith's most sacred rules. Would he be fired? Sent back to his uncle's shop?

"Sir, I'm—"

"I am not angry with you, Jericho." Lowering his hands, Master Spellsmith fixed his calm gray eyes on his apprentice. "I know how Rill can be. Saying no to her is like crushing a flower. Breaks my heart every time, and I've had thirteen years of practice. Leaving you at her mercy is foolish. Still, you must understand; my rules aren't arbitrary. Magic is dangerous for Rill."

"But not for me or you?" Jericho raised his eyebrows.

"Someday I will explain further, but I don't have time to go into it today. I'm already late." Master Spellsmith strode over to the workbench and picked up a small felt-bound notebook. "If I hadn't forgotten my notes, I wouldn't have come back at all, though thank God I did." He held out his hand.

Jericho hesitated, at first uncertain what to do, then he remembered the stylus. He picked it up off the worktable and passed it to his master.

"Your skill I do not doubt, nor your desire to do right with magic, but you have yet to fully grasp its dangers. Let's take a step back, all right?"

Jericho hung his head. "Yes, sir."

"Take a few hours off. Maybe read something or enjoy a stroll in the garden, all right?" Master Spellsmith squeezed Jericho's shoulder before departing.

Jericho kicked at the leg of the worktable. That couldn't have gone worse. Perhaps a walk outside would clear his head.

A few minutes later, he strode beneath the overgrown trees of the Spellsmith's crowded garden. The summer sun filtered through the heavy canopy of green leaves, casting dappled shadows on the gravel path. The smell of freshly cut grass and roses wafted about him. He paused and listened to the rustle of the wind and the humming of the bees—and the sobbing.

Jericho stiffened and followed his ears off the path. After a few quiet steps, he picked out words from within the sniffling.

"It's fine, Jaspyr, I know it's going to be fine, but it is…it is so stupid."

The mechanical fox gave a tinny yip.

"I know. I know. He says it's to protect me, but from what? Magic isn't going to bite me, and it certainly won't make me go mad."

Jericho pinpointed the voice as coming from behind the hedge. He could make a break for it. She'd obviously come out here to be alone, but if she wanted to talk, perhaps he could be a better listener than Jaspyr…perhaps.

"Rill?" he called, hopping over the hedge with his long legs.

She gasped, flushed, and covered her dripping eyes with her handkerchief. He grimaced. Yeah, this was stupid. What was he thinking?

"Oh, Jerry! I was just…I mean."

Jaspyr bounded off her lap and leaped at Jericho's knees. Jericho patted the fox's ears and sat cross-legged across from Rill.

"I'm sorry," he said. "I should've known he'd catch us. I didn't mean to start a fight."

She laughed. "That wasn't a fight. My dad's not capable of really fighting with me, Jericho. At most he blusters for a moment then gets that reproachful look."

He furrowed his brow. "But…you ran away?"

"Yes, because when I looked at you, I thought you were about to punch my father on my behalf." Her cheeks reddened. "Seriously, I've never seen you look like that. Are you all right?"

He swallowed. Was *he* all right? All he'd been thinking of was keeping her safe… "Yeah, of course, I…" Her eyes peered into his soul. He swallowed again. "I thought he might hurt you. I wanted to be ready in case he tried, so I could stop him."

Her pale eyebrows melted together. "Hurt me?"

"Yes, well, when my dad got angry, he—" He coughed and looked away. "It's silly. I should've known Master Spellsmith wouldn't—"

Her fingers caressed the back of his hand, and every muscle in his body seized. "Your father hit you?"

Shame welled up within him. "I don't like to talk about it."

With a slow nod, she withdrew her hand. "If you don't want to, that's fine, but if you need to, I'm here."

His stomach twisted within him. How could she make him feel like that? She was just a kid, a sheltered kid who could never understand. Still, she meant well. It wasn't her fault that she'd had a comparatively happy childhood. "What about you? Do you want to talk about what happened?"

She closed her eyes. "I know he just wants to protect me, and I understand what he *thinks* he's protecting me from."

"I don't." Jericho frowned. "Will magic hurt you?"

"It…it changed my mother." She pulled Jaspyr onto her lap and stroked the length of his shiny bronze back. The fox gave out a low, humming purr.

Jericho rubbed the back of his neck. Master Spellsmith's wife and her disappearance had been the fodder for a lot of town gossip, but none of it painted a complete picture. The long and short of it was she'd disappeared one day and no one knew why. Most just assumed she'd tired of domestic bliss and run off.

"He wasn't always like this." Rill smiled sadly. "Mother and Father used to work together in the workshop. Then she changed, grew distant, paranoid almost. He says the magic got to her, addled her, made her forget what was important, but I don't think it was the magic. I think…I think she just chose to leave. Auric, my brother, thinks so too. That's why he and Father always used to fight. That's why Auric left for the city as soon as he got old enough, and why I'm not sure he'll ever come back either."

Jericho had never met Master Spellsmith's son or wife, but the sadness in the master's eyes when either of them came up spoke for itself. "He's a good man, your father. I do believe he wants to keep you safe."

A tear trickled down her cheek. "Yes, but…oh, Jerry, I want to learn magic. It's like a beautiful toy, locked in a glass cabinet, so I can see it but never touch it. It calls to me. It sings to me, and to see Father teaching you—and I *like* you, I swear, and I'm glad you're learning magic and working with Father, but I should be there, too, with you both, and it breaks my heart that every time I try, he shuts the door right in my face."

Uncertain what to do, he drew a handkerchief from his pocket and wiped her tears away.

She giggled uncomfortably. "You must think me an awful baby, crying like this."

"Not at all. Do you want me to stay with you? Or walk you back to the house?"

"No, I'm fine, thank you. I'll see you at lunch. I'd just like a few minutes alone, out here in the quiet. I'll be all right." She bent and kissed her pet between the ears. "I have Jaspyr, after all."

Jericho stroked Jaspyr's nose before wandering back toward the house.

Rill was right. It wasn't fair.

Traditionally in Mountain's Foot, trades passed from father to son, but mother to daughter or father to daughter was not unheard of. When Master Spellsmith had offered Jericho the position, Jericho had assumed it was because both the Spellsmith children had declined it, that Rill was only interested in domestic things, like so many of the village girls, dreaming of husbands and babies, and Auric—well, Auric was simply gone. That Rill wanted to learn but wasn't allowed to had eaten at him since he'd discovered the truth. It wasn't fair, and Jericho loathed things that weren't fair.

He entered the servants' wing where he had a small room to himself with a bed, a cabinet, and a dressing mirror. Opening the cabinet, he scanned for the small, cloth-bound book, the first thing Master Spellsmith had given him during his apprenticeship: *Pierson's Handbook of Basic Magic*. Tucking the volume into his vest pocket, he darted out into the hall then up the stairs to the family wing. No one seemed to be around. He knocked on the door he knew belonged to Rill. No one answered.

Good.

She was probably still in the garden. He had to act fast. The door proved unlocked. Her four-poster bed was covered in pillows and one stuffed fox toy. The whole room had a floral scent that nearly knocked him over, but in a good way. Forcing his thoughts back to the matter at hand, he considered his options. If he left it out in the open, there was a chance the maid might find it before she did. No, best not to risk that. Instead, he slipped it under a pillow then retreated, easing the door shut behind him.

There.

If Master Spellsmith found out, Jericho would probably be fired, but hopefully that wouldn't happen. Hopefully, this would make Rill happy.

Jericho shoveled scrambled eggs into his mouth as fast as he could, trying not to wonder if Rill had found the book the night before. He'd been the first to the breakfast table, and the kindly cook, Annie, had filled his plate with eggs, bacon, and toast, saying something about getting some meat on his bones. Jericho had laughed at this.

"Lost cause," he'd mumbled, before thanking her for the food and digging in. He was starving.

Apparently, Master Spellsmith had chosen to eat in his study. Rill usually took her meals in the breakfast nook rather than the kitchen, so when the door opened and she hurried in, beaming at him, he froze mid-chew.

She glanced at Annie, who was elbow-deep in suds, cleaning pots and pans, then grinned conspiratorially at Jericho. "I found it."

His stomach dropped, worried Annie might've heard, but settled as Rill sat across from him and Annie kept working, her attention apparently elsewhere.

Rill leaned closer. "I stayed up so late last night. I think I read half the book. Oh, Jerry, thank you so much. No one has ever done anything like that for me before. If—" She glanced at Annie, flushed, and dropped her voice to a whisper. "If Dad finds out, what will happen to you?"

"He won't. This is between us, all right?" He smiled. Yes, this was why he'd taken the risk. It was wonderful to see her happy.

After he finished eating, they walked into the foyer together.

"I'm heading to town this afternoon for tea with some friends," Rill said. "Do you want me to pick anything up for you while I'm there? Say hi to your family for you, maybe?"

He shook his head. "I just visited with them a few days ago on my afternoon off. No need to go out of your way for me." He eyed the stairs to the workshop.

She dropped her gaze. "Yes, I suppose you'd better get to work."

"Jericho?" The door at the top of the stairs opened, and Master Spellsmith peeked out. "Come up here. I have something you need to see."

"Excuse me." Jericho nodded to Rill before taking the stairs to the workshop three steps at a time. When he entered the long room, Master Spellsmith stood over one of his rift detection wards.

All magical energy came from the Fey Lands, a mystical world parallel to their own filled with fairy creatures and crackling energy that magicians could harness to power spells. The energy reached the mortal world through rifts in the invisible barrier between the worlds, fissures that opened naturally to allow its passage like steam rising through cracks in a pie crust. Sometimes, larger ones let in other things, though, such as trickster Fey intent on causing mischief for mortals. It was rare, of course, like lightning strikes, but Master Spellsmith worried about it a lot and kept a close eye on the detection wards for larger rifts.

"What is it, sir?" Jericho gazed down into the ward, a crystal ball with a spiraling dark line inside. The line grew thicker whenever the Fey energy in the area increased, like when a rift opened. At a glance, Jericho noted a particularly thick section which would've correlated to the day before. "A big rift, huh?"

"Yes. I was distracted by the orders yesterday, so I didn't check it. It's probably nothing, but we should be on the lookout—"

Metal paws clinked across the floorboards. Jaspyr pushed his head between Jericho and Master Spellsmith and smiled up at them.

"What are you doing in here, you silly fox?" Master Spellsmith picked Jaspyr up and rubbed his ears.

Rill poked her head into the shop. "Sorry, Father, he got away from me." She gave an apologetic smile.

Jericho put his hand over his mouth to hide a smirk. Sure he got away from her. She hadn't used him to slip into the forbidden workshop or anything like that. Jaspyr might be a fox, but Rill was a clever vixen in her own right. If Master

Spellsmith suspected this, though, he didn't let on.

"You shouldn't be in here, Rill," he said calmly, holding Jaspyr out to her. The fox wriggled and yipped.

"Is something wrong with your ward?" She craned her neck, trying to see around him.

"No, just a particularly large rift—but while we're on the subject, I'd like you to stay near the house for a couple of days. Keep Jaspyr near you. He can sense Fey meddling and will protect you if one is in the area, but just to be safe, don't go wandering outside the manor's grounds."

Rill's shoulders slumped. "But Father, my tea party in the village is today, remember? You promised me I could go, and I've been looking forward to it all week."

Weary of being held at arm's length, Jaspyr twisted himself free. He positioned himself beneath Rill's skirts with only his head sticking out.

Jericho cleared his throat. He didn't want to insert himself into the argument, but again, it seemed Master Spellsmith was being unreasonable. Rifts opened on a weekly basis, and while this was a larger one, it was incredibly unlikely that anything malevolent had come through it.

"It's too dangerous, Rill." Her father frowned.

"But it's the village." She crossed her arms. "I am just as safe there as I am here, certainly. The whole town knows me and will look out for me."

"And on the five-mile ride between here and the village?" Master Spellsmith frowned.

"I won't stop anywhere along the path." She tilted her face up toward him, eyes pleading, bottom lip quivering ever so slightly.

He hesitated. "Well… Maybe if I could go with you, Rill, but I can't today. I have too much to do around the shop."

"I could go, sir," Jericho heard himself volunteer. Father and daughter both stared at him. He shifted from foot to foot. "If you don't need me around the shop, that is. I can drive her there in the gig, wait for her outside the tearoom, and take her home when she's done."

Rill pressed her hand over her heart—a gesture he suspected she may have read in a novel. "You'd do that for me?"

"It's not a big deal." He shrugged, suddenly warm under the collar.

Master Spellsmith gave a slow nod. "I suppose if Jericho keeps an eye on you, and you come straight home afterward. Go get ready. I wish to speak to Jericho."

Rill skipped out of the room, Jaspyr at her heels.

Jericho faced Master Spellsmith, but instead of speaking as promised, the man walked across the room and entered his study. When he returned, he held the spare stylus.

Jericho's head spun. "But…but you said—"

"I know what I said, but Rill's safety is everything to me, Jericho, and if I'm entrusting her to your care, I'm not going to leave you unarmed."

The stylus felt strangely heavy in Jericho's hand. "I won't let anything hurt her."

"You better not." Master Spellsmith put on a face he probably thought was stern and threatening, but Jericho had faced down real monsters. Rill's father wasn't one. Still, the knowledge that a good man trusted him with his daughter carried far more weight than thinking a bad man might hurt him if he failed. "To make certain, you're going to get a crash course in defensive magic right now."

A few hours later, Jericho held the reins of their open, single-horse carriage as Master Spellsmith helped Rill into the seat next to him. He passed her Jaspyr, who curled up in a tight ball on the bench between Jericho and Rill and began to purr.

"Take care, you two, and come straight home after the party." He squeezed his daughter's hand and stepped back as Jericho snapped the reins and they pulled away.

As soon as the manor gates closed behind them, Rill removed her sun bonnet and gave Jericho a sideways glance. "Your lessons this morning certainly seemed exciting."

He chuckled. "Listening through the keyhole?"

"Maybe." She smoothed her skirts, wearing a demure expression like a mask.

"Yes, well, your dad wants to be certain nothing came through the rift that's going to eat you."

"Oh, I know." She sighed. "Sounds like it worked out for you, though, getting to learn all those flashy new spells."

His chest inflated. "Yeah, it's good to finally get some useful magic in my toolkit. My favorite is the confinement spell. It's essentially constructing a box out of Fey energy that keeps your attacker in one place, an invisible, portable jail cell. I already knew a similar spell used for rounding up chickens and small livestock, but this one could hold a full-grown steer or even a bear."

"Really? How do you—?" She dropped her eyes. "Sorry. I shouldn't ask about it. It's selfish."

He raised his eyebrows. "Selfish?"

"Jericho, I love to hear about magic, but you already risked so much giving me that book. I'd hate to get you fired. You enjoy magic so much, and you're so good at it." She stroked Jaspyr.

"I guess you're right."

They rode in silence for a few minutes. Why had he been so stupid? Getting carried away talking about his studies when he knew she could never take part? Blast it, she looked so sad. He hated when she looked sad. It made him want to punch something, preferably whatever had made her sad, but in this case that was him, and punching himself would just be awkward. He gritted his teeth and made his choice. After all, he'd already broken Master Spellsmith's rules by giving her the book. Might as well go all in.

"If you don't tell your father, I won't," he whispered.

Her eyes lit up, then she smirked at him. "You're a bad influence, Jericho Carver."

"So, to make the confinement spell, you use an activation symbol, barrier symbol—which is essentially a square—then an enhancement symbol for extra strength, and a proximity symbol to either cast it around yourself—as a shield—or in front of you, in which case you need…"

She listened in rapt attention as he detailed the various spells he'd learned. From her handbag, she produced a small diary and a pencil stub and wrote out some of them, occasionally asking, "Like this?" She had a knack for it. By the time the church steeple of Mountain's Foot appeared on the horizon, she'd memorized several basic spells. He pulled up in front of the small tearoom. A half-dozen teen and preteen girls bunched together at the door in various shades of pastel, many in ridiculous feathered and flowered hats. They giggled like a flock of cooing pigeons. When he helped Rill down from the gig, several pointed and one squealed. Rill turned crimson.

"Don't mind them," she whispered. "They all treat boys like some separate species to be collected as pets. It's kind of disturbing."

"I'd like to see them try to collect me." He snorted. "Have fun?"

"Honestly, if it wasn't the only outing Father would accept me leaving the manor for, I'd rather be anywhere else." She tucked a strand of flaxen hair behind her ear. "Do you think instead we could slip away somewhere and you could teach me more magic?"

"It's too small of a town for that. Someone would tattle on us."

She sighed and snapped her fingers. Jaspyr stirred, opened one eye, and sniffed reproachfully.

"There are scones in the tearoom," she said.

The fox sprang to his feet and wagged his tail.

"Do you want to come in and get a bite to eat?" Rill focused on Jericho.

He considered the swarm of girls, several of whom still eyed him. While he didn't consider himself handsome, he'd realized in the last year or so that his height as well as his training in a "gentleman's trade" made him a prime target for matrimonial-minded girls. He did not enjoy the extra attention in the slightest. "No, I ate before we left. I brought a book, so don't hurry on my account."

She squeezed his hand before darting into the group of young ladies.

Jericho made sure their horse was set with a bag of feed before settling down on a bench outside the tearoom. He could still hear the girls twittering, as well as an occasional yip from Jaspyr. Probably begging for scones, the scamp. Jericho sank into the novel he'd brought from the Spellsmiths' library, a tale of adventure on the uncharted continent across the Great Sea. The world faded around him, until a hand on his shoulder jolted him out of his imaginary vacation.

Rill stood over him, hands clasped, face drawn. "Jericho, I can't find Jaspyr anywhere."

He sat up straighter. "Really?" For all his impishness, the metal fox rarely left his mistress's side.

"Yes. I thought he was sleeping under the table. I mean, he ate like a dozen scones. That would make anyone drowsy, but when I looked for him just now, he wasn't there or anywhere in the tearoom. Did he slip out this way?"

Jericho stood and looked around. "I don't think so." Of course, he'd been staring at his book. A fine guardian he'd turned out to be.

Rill grasped her skirt in her hands and turned away from him. "Jaspyr? Jaspyr!" She started down the wooden sidewalk, her calls gaining in pitch and volume. Jericho followed.

As they neared the first corner, a streak of light dashed to greet them, the sun reflecting off polished bronze. Jaspyr flew into Rill's arms, knocking her backward into Jericho. Grabbing Rill's shoulders to steady her, Jericho exhaled.

"Oh, you bad, bad fox." Rill nestled her face against her metal pet. "Where were—"

"Come back here, thief!" Footsteps pounded, and a red-faced man with a copper-toned beard rounded the corner. When he saw Jaspyr, he pointed an accusing finger. "There you are!" He barreled forward and ripped Jaspyr from Rill's arms. Rill whimpered. It took all of Jericho's willpower not to tackle the man, who he now recognized as Mr. Butcher, the owner of the local meat market.

"Give me my fox!" Rill's voice grew shrill.

"This fox is a thief! I caught him sniffing around my hen house, and sure enough, I'm missing another chicken."

"That's ridiculous. Jaspyr is a magical familiar. He doesn't need to steal poultry to survive." Rill reached for her pet, who whined in the burly man's grasp.

Mr. Butcher angled away from her. "So you're saying he doesn't eat?"

She bit her bottom lip. "Yes, he does, but mainly baked goods. He isn't going to devour nasty raw chicken like an…animal."

"Still, quite a coincidence that he's lurking near my hens the same day one goes missing." Mr. Butcher held Jaspyr up by the tail. The fox's legs clawed at the air. He yipped piteously.

"Stop it!" Jericho barked. He darted for the fox, but the butcher put out a beefy arm, holding him back. Jericho was taller than him by a good six inches, but bulk-wise was clearly outmatched. He drew a steadying breath. "You can't just take Miss Spellsmith's pet that way, without proof."

"I think I'm well within my rights to hold him until the sheriff can sort things out." Mr. Butcher's grasp tightened on Jaspyr's tail. "After all, I'm not the only one to lose livestock this last week. If this little beast is the culprit—" He spun to avoid Rill's grasping hands.

"You let him go, you bully!" Tears welled up in Rill's eyes. "You're hurting him!"

"Look, give Rill her fox and I'll figure out what took your chicken." Jericho crossed his arms. "I know some tracking spells. It can't be too hard to find whatever vermin took your bird."

Mr. Butcher squinted at him. "You really think you can, boy?"

Jericho squared his shoulders. "Yes." Of course, he wasn't really that certain, but he wasn't about to let this man know it. Rill needed Jericho's help.

Scowling, Mr. Butcher passed Jaspyr to Rill. The fox hid his muzzle in her hair, trembling until his metal plates vibrated together like ringing bells.

"I know your uncle and her father, so don't think you're going to slip away from me." Mr. Butcher waved a fat finger in Jericho's face. "You best find out what took my chicken, or I'm going straight to the sheriff about that fox."

Rill's hold on Jaspyr tightened. Placing a hand on her shoulder, Jericho steered her away from Mr. Butcher.

"Look, I won't be long. Just wait for me in the tearoom, all right?" he whispered.

"I don't like it. We don't owe that horrible man anything." She shot a glare at the butcher. "We should take Jaspyr home."

"It's best not to make enemies in a town this size, all right." He stroked Jaspyr's ears. "Maybe get him a couple more scones to calm him down. I promise, I'll be right back."

Her lips pursed. "Be careful."

Jericho tramped through the trees, following a line of golden light. Master Spellsmith's anti-theft wards had worked brilliantly. The moment he activated a revealing spell, sparks had raced across the ground from the butcher's chicken coop, leading through the back lot, into the nearby forest. Whatever the creature who had taken the chicken was, it had dragged its prey deep into the trees. Obviously not Jaspyr, who had returned to Rill after being missing only a short while. He stopped and dabbed the sweat off his forehead. Would that be enough proof for Mr. Butcher? Maybe, maybe not, but since he'd already lost sight of the village, he might as well keep going and maybe find the creature's lair.

Considering that it had left no tracks in the soft earth around the chicken coop and hadn't had to break any fences to slip into the yard, it was likely a small creature, probably not dangerous. Deeper in the forest, the deciduous trees gave way to a stand of pine. Instead of cool, green grass, dried pine needles now covered the forest floor. A singed scent wafted through the air. Jericho paused and examined the ground. Strange dark scuffs marked the forest floor beside the tracking line. He bent down and picked up withered needles, scorched by some extreme heat.

He looked around. What could've done that? Most of the villagers knew better than to play with fire in the woods past midsummer. Also, this didn't look like a hunter trying to start a campfire or a stupid kid playing with matches. In fact, from the regular spacing, it looked a bit like animal prints.

Another smell now joined the pleasant odor of the scorched pine: a harsh, stomach-churning whiff of burnt feathers and flesh.

Drawing his stylus from his pocket along with a paper quire, he continued onward. A spell took time to write, and he wasn't certain what he was about to face. He considered his options then wrote out a restraining spell, including all but the last stroke of an activation symbol.

A crunching, cracking, slurping sound rose from behind a thick line of fir trees. Smoke wisped into the air, tickling his nose. Jericho crept forward.

Behind the branches, a small clearing opened up. In the middle of it lay a brilliant orange creature about the size of a large dog, tearing into the remains of a chicken. White feathers circled in the air above it, perhaps being held up by hot air which seemed to rise from the beast. Jericho resisted the urge to pinch himself.

The strange animal had a long, feline body but with scales instead of fur on the majority of its body, the exception being its luxurious, twitching tail, a scruff of scarlet fur along the ridge of its back, and its feline head. Pointed ears lay back against its head and two bat-like wings folded at its side.

He mentally thumbed through the list of Fey creatures and came up with a name: dracoline. Setting stylus to quire, he made the last mark in the activation symbol. Energy dashed across the spell, consuming the quire which turned to ash in his hand. A rope of golden light shot forward and wrapped around the Fey-beast. It tangled around the creature's wings and limbs.

The dracoline gave an earsplitting yowl and thrashed back and forth. It twisted its spine in an unholy angle so it could glare at Jericho. Green eyes flashed. It opened its fanged jaws, and something shouted at Jericho to hit the ground.

He dropped to the earth and covered his head as a wave of flame shot over him.

Blast! Of course it could breathe fire. Why wouldn't it? He fumbled for another quire as the creature continued to struggle against its bonds. The magical cords flexed and stretched but held fast—for the time being. Jericho needed something stronger: a confinement spell? A sleeping spell to put it out?

He rolled to the side and behind a tree just as a second blast shot from the beast's maw. The needles curled and crackled in the heat. Heart pounding, he took out a second quire. Technically a spell could be written on any smooth surface. Paper was simply the most portable. If need be he could write on a rock or a bit of wood. Good, because he'd only brought three quires. He started scratching out the confinement spell but went too fast and switched the second and third symbol. Cursing, he tossed the wasted quire aside and tried again.

Something snapped, then quiet. Panic jolted through Jericho. He peeked from around the tree. The dracoline was gone.

Get away from here while you have the chance, common sense shouted at him. Slowly rising to his feet, he turned to run.

The dracoline crashed into his chest like a charging bull.

Knocked flat on his back, Jericho gasped for air. Wait? Where was his stylus? Before he could even look for it, the Fey-beast attacked again. It swiped at Jericho's face with glowing-red claws. He threw up his arms. The blow shredded the sleeve of his shirt. Its claws burned rather than cut, sending searing pain through Jericho's forearm.

Kicking out, Jericho scrambled away on all fours. The dracoline pounced on his back. They rolled together. The beast was hot to the touch, not unbearably so, but not pleasant either, especially with the bulk of its body pressing down on its intended victim. Its teeth snapped at Jericho's neck. Getting an arm free, he swung with all his might. His knuckles cracked against the beast's jaw. It growled and leaped back.

Jericho scooted backward and hit a tree stump. He sat, watching, as the dracoline paced before him. Testing it, he feinted to the left. The dracoline followed the movement then settled back down with its head between its front paws and its tail twitching like a snake.

"Why don't you just get it over with?" Jericho snarled.

The dracoline *purred* and playfully batted at Jericho's booted foot.

Maybe it wasn't actually going to eat him. Jericho tried to stand up. It hissed and let forth a fireball that sent the young man cowering again.

It's playing with me like a cat with a mouse, he realized in horror. He'd known enough mousers in his life to know how that ended.

Cold sweat broke out across his forehead. He needed to calm himself, to think. But this creature was faster, stronger, and...fire-breathing-ier than him. With his stylus lost and no weapon at hand, what could he do?

Not die sitting like a cornered rat, for sure.

He sneaked a hand behind his body and scratched through the thick carpet of dried pine needles to get a handful of dirt. Toss that in its eyes, then run while it was blind. Not a perfect plan, but better than waiting to have his face ripped off.

With all his might and what he hoped was a fierce, disconcerting shout, he hurled the dirt into the dracoline's face. The creature hissed and sat back on its haunches. Uncoiling like a spring, Jericho vaulted toward the tree line. A swipe of claws against his back and he hit the ground again. He rolled face up, spitting dirt. The dracoline's jaws opened wide. Hot breath still tainted by the odor of burnt feathers buffeted Jericho's face. He threw his arms over his eyes.

Clang!

Something metal crashed into the dracoline's head. Jericho's breath escaped him.

Jaspyr held onto one of the beast's pointy ears with clamped jaws. His body clanked as the dracoline thrashed back and forth, meowing and yowling like an aggressive tom cat.

"Get to cover!" a familiar voice shouted.

Rill? Oh dear Lord, what was she doing here? He couldn't protect her. He couldn't even protect himself.

"Jaspyr, get away!" Rill called out. The fox opened his mouth, and the next shake of the dracoline's head sent him flying across the clearing. Fey energy sizzled in the air. The dracoline growled, whirled, and lunged at Jericho's throat.

It hit a barrier of golden light and bounced back onto its own tail. The creature shook itself off and pawed at the air. Energy buzzed before it. It hissed and turned in a desperate circle, trying to find a way out of its invisible prison, but every step it took ended in a buzz of magic and no passage.

Jericho's whole body went limp.

Rill strode out of the trees, something small and glinting in her hand. "I think you lost this." She held up his stylus.

His face grew hot. "Yeah, I guess I did."

She glanced at the dracoline, her smile fading. "Do you think it can get out?"

He shook his head. "No, a confinement spell will hold until someone casts a dispersal spell. Thank you, Rill. I...I thought I was a goner."

"Yes, well, you were the one who told me how to write one." Her brow furrowed, and she touched his arm below the rip in his shirt. "Are you all right?"

He held up his arm. Now that his adrenaline was fading, his skin was really starting to sting every place the dracoline had struck him. Examining himself, he found a series of raised welts, like mild burns rather than cuts. Apparently, heat was the beast's primary weapon.

"It's not bad. Would've been a lot worse if you hadn't... Thank you, Rill, again. You saved my life."

She clutched her skirt in her hands, her mouth a thin, worried line. "I guess we can't just pretend this didn't happen. Between your wounds and the rips in your clothes and that...thing—" she nodded toward the dracoline. "Father's going to know what happened."

"We could leave the thing here and pretend I just had a run-in with a bramble patch, I guess." Jericho shrugged. His energy flagging, he lowered himself to the ground and sat cross-legged. Jaspyr bounded over—apparently none the worse for wear—and nudged at his face, whimpering and purring. "I'm all right, boy," Jericho soothed, petting the fox's ears.

Rill tilted her head at the dracoline who paced about in anxious circles, ears back, tail between its legs. "What happens to the...cat dragon? Is that what you call it?"

"Dracoline, I think."

"Ah...what happens to it if we just leave it here? Won't it starve to death?"

"Probably. I have a hard time regretting that, since it almost incinerated me."

"It doesn't really seem evil, though, just a wild animal, acting on instinct." She sat next to Jericho. Her hand strayed to his knee. He started but didn't move away. "I'd hate for it to suffer like that."

"Your father could probably find a way to send it back to the Fey Lands, but I don't know how." He tapped his fingers thoughtfully against his leg. "If your father finds out that you put it in the confinement spell, Rill, he's going to know we're practicing magic behind his back."

"He doesn't need to know it was me. You came out here. You found the dracoline. You put it in a confinement spell after a bit of a struggle. I waited patiently in the village and in no way got worried and came after you in spite of your warning to stay where I was safe."

He chuckled. "For what it is worth, I'm very grateful you ignored me in that."

"So am I." Her fingers tightened on his leg then returned to her lap, where she clasped her hands and sighed. "Yes, that story should do."

"It means I get credit for something you did, something you should be celebrated for." He shook his head. "I don't like that."

"It's how it needs to be." She lowered her eyes.

He stared at her. Even now, she looked like a sweet, innocent kid, but there was a talented magician beneath that facade, a sharp brain that could probably be better at the trade than Jericho if given a little nurturing. Jericho couldn't help himself. Yes, he respected Master Spellsmith, but this wasn't right, and he was going to do something about it.

"Rill, for now, that's how it will be, but someday your father is going to retire, and when he does, I'll be the practicing magician in Mountain's Foot, and I can choose my own apprentice."

Her chin jerked up, her eyes widening. "You mean you'd...you'd...you'd choose me?"

"In a heartbeat."

Tears formed in her eyes, and he had to look away.

"Oh Jerry, that is the most wonderful...thank you. Thank you so much!"

"Don't be like that. I'm only righting a wrong. You're going to be a brilliant magician, Rill, and I am not going to sit by and watch your father slam the door in your face over and over again. I know his heart is in the right place, but you deserve better."

She flung herself into his arms. Jaspyr gave an offended yip and skipped out of the way. Jericho's heart skipped painfully in his chest, but then he returned the embrace. It was oddly pleasant, and he had to remind himself again that she was just a kid.

After a moment, he withdrew and gently pinched her nose. "Come on, Rill. Let's get home."

Hand in hand, they walked back to the village, Jaspyr frisking along beside them.

H. L. Burke is the self-published author of multiple fantasy novels including the Dragon and the Scholar *saga, the* Nyssa Glass YA Steampunk *series, and* Coiled. *She is an admirer of the whimsical, a follower of the Light, and a believer in happily ever after.*

"Jericho and the Magician's Daughter" is a prequel to the Spellsmith & Carver Gaslamp Fantasy Series. *Follow Jericho's continuing adventures in* Spellsmith & Carver: Magicians' Rivalry.

www.hlburkeauthor.com

Dragon's Oath

Katy Huth Jones

"Where are you off to this time, Ethaniel?"

Peniel was gatekeeper today. Though the older youth's voice was friendly, he eyed the ewes trailing obediently behind Ethaniel. Making his face appear stern, Ethaniel hunched over and stamped the ground with his staff. His glossy black braid slipped over his shoulder like an extra appendage. Which, he supposed, it was, since the hair had never been cut and never could be, now that he'd taken the Brethren's Oath of Peace.

"Why, Gatekeeper," he said in a raspy voice. "I am taking these hungry ewes to the near pasture. Let us pass, boy."

Peniel chuckled. "You sound just like old Reuel, but don't let him hear you mock him."

Ethaniel straightened with a grin. "Don't worry. I'm always careful."

Peniel leaned closer, serious now. "Then why are you going to the near pasture? Melody is there gathering herbs."

"I know." Ethaniel glanced over his shoulder, but there was no one else nearby. "I have to speak to her."

Gravely, Peniel shook his head. "If anyone catches you, you'll be put in the stocks for sure this time. Or worse, since she's now betrothed to the Healer."

"I'll be careful." Ethaniel stared into his friend's eyes. "Please, Peni, I have to see her one more time."

Peniel scanned the compound and then sighed. "All right. But don't forget, I'll be in trouble too, if anything happens."

Ethaniel clapped his friend's shoulder. "Thank you. I promise, nothing will go wrong."

After securing the ewes' attention with his staff, Ethaniel clucked his tongue and led them out the massive gate of the wooden palisade encircling the Brethren village, home for all of his seventeen years. Now an apprentice shepherd to old Reuel, Ethaniel's life had been decided for him every step of the way. Lately, he'd begun to chafe under the restrictions of the Brethren's ways, especially in regard to the impending marriage of his beautiful cousin, Melody.

Fortunately, the palisade had no towers or windows, since the peaceful Brethren would never wage war on anyone. That would give him and Melody a bit of privacy in the pasture adjoining the back wall, at least.

There she was, to him an angel of light. Melody bent over to snip a handful of herbs, her long auburn braid slipping over her shoulder to brush the plants. He longed to loose that shining plait of hair and run his fingers through the silky softness.

"Hello, Melody." Ethaniel waited until he was nearly upon her to speak, and she jerked back, startled.

"What are you doing here?" Her large eyes with their long lashes widened in alarm. "We should not be alone together. You know what Father and Uncle Daniel said."

"I brought the ewes to graze." Ethaniel gestured back to the contented sheep. "And I know what our fathers said, but I don't care." He pressed on, despite the horror on her face. "I love you, Melody. I can't bear the thought of you being married to that dour Joel, even if he is a Healer. He can't make you happy like I can." Before he lost his nerve, Ethaniel stepped forward and cupped Melody's cheek with a trembling hand.

With a gasp, she stepped back, her face coloring. "It doesn't matter if we love one another. We're not here to be happy, Ethaniel. Our purpose is to serve others."

"That's my Uncle Uriel talking." He forced himself to stay calm, but his voice betrayed him. "You know we can serve others and still find happiness in this life."

"Sometimes, we must lay aside our own desires to serve the greater good." Melody swallowed noisily, and he knew despite her brave words, she was as distressed as he was. "Our fathers have made their decision. We must accept it."

"I can't accept it." A groan escaped his lips. "How can I live without you, Mellie?"

She took another step back and dropped her shears in her basket. "Your father will find a wife for you when the time comes."

Before he could reply, several of the ewes began to bleat, running away. A river dragon's roar filled the air. Ethaniel gripped his staff and started toward the sound.

"Get back to the village and send help," he shouted over his shoulder.

After making sure Melody was safe, Ethaniel broke into a run. The frightened sheep didn't notice he was there, but those, at least, were safe. He had to see if any of the others were in danger from the river dragon.

At the edge of the meadow, the land sloped downward toward the river. Below him, the dragon crouched half out of the water, droplets glistening on its long scaly body. Blood dripped from its powerful jaws, reddening sharp teeth while it finished eating one of the ewes. A second ewe stood dumbly on the bank, bleating in terror. Ethaniel stamped the ground with his staff and shouted at her, but she did not hear him.

He scrambled down the bank as quickly as he could, but he wasn't fast enough. The river dragon opened its bloody mouth and clamped down on the poor ewe, pulling it under the water to eat later. At least her death was mercifully quick, and all became quiet at the river.

Taking in a ragged breath, Ethaniel hurried back up to the pasture to find the lead ewe and restore some kind of order. To his horror, both Father and Uncle Uriel came toward him, while a couple of the younger boys helped gather the scattered sheep.

"What happened this time?" Father asked with a scowl. Uncle Uriel, the village leader, stopped and stared silently, balling his fists on his hips.

Ethaniel lowered his head, too ashamed to look his father in the eyes. "I brought the ewes to graze and let them wander too close to the river. Two of them were eaten by a river dragon." He swallowed against the tightness in his throat. Until this moment, he hadn't realized how much he cared about those sheep. They had complete trust in him, and his carelessness had caused their deaths.

"Come with us, Ethaniel." Uncle Uriel turned away and strode toward the village gate, expecting him and his father to follow.

Clenching his fist around the shepherd's staff, Ethaniel strode alongside his silent father. Worry mixed with grief and rose within him as anger. He stared at Uriel's dark braid bouncing against his rigid back and wondered what happened to the kind uncle he'd known as a young boy. Since becoming village leader, the man had become a stranger, severe and distant.

Once they entered the compound, Ethaniel's gut knotted. Not only Melody, but most of the other villagers stood waiting. Uncle Uriel turned and spoke in his commanding voice.

"Your inattention to duty caused the loss of two precious ewes. Your poor choices will have grave consequences."

Ethaniel looked up at his uncle. "Poor choices?"

Uriel's hard eyes narrowed. "Did I not expressly forbid you to be alone with my daughter?"

"Yes, sir." Ethaniel set his jaw and looked at Melody, who stared down at the ground. He did not regret that choice.

"Do you repent of your actions?" There was no softening of his uncle's voice.

After squaring his shoulders, Ethaniel took a deep breath. "I repent of my inattention which caused the deaths of the ewes, but I do not repent of speaking to your daughter. Sir."

Uriel's eyes glittered with barely contained rage. "Then I sentence you to three days in the pillory."

Around him, many of the villagers gasped. Melody jerked up her head and opened her mouth to protest. But Ethaniel did not want her punished, too.

"No," he shouted. "I won't accept your bloody decree."

"Ethaniel," his father began, but Uriel gestured him to silence.

With mixed bitterness and regret, Ethaniel realized his father would never stand up against his elder brother to speak for his only surviving child. He'd been a broken man since losing his wife and daughters to a fever last year.

"Then, for your unwillingness to repent and humble yourself in the sight of the God of Peace and these witnesses, you are banished from the Brethren," Uriel intoned with the finality of a decree. "You will leave with nothing but the clothes on your back. From this moment forward, you are dead to us all. Your name will nevermore be spoken in the Village of Peace."

Ethaniel met Melody's gaze. Would he never see her again? Joel, the village Healer and her betrothed, came to stand beside her. When he narrowed his eyes at Ethaniel, it strengthened his resolve. He welcomed banishment as the only way he could bear Melody's impending marriage to this man, since she was already lost to him.

Without a word, Ethaniel threw down his staff and strode to the open gate. He faltered a moment as he stared at the massive wooden door propped open beside the shocked Peniel. How could he live outside these walls? He'd never been beyond the pastures in his life. Where would he go?

Then his heart burned with the injustice of forcing a young woman to marry someone she did not love, and he clenched his fists, regained his stride, and exited the Brethren village for the last time.

He didn't stop walking until he was well away from the palisade. Then the enormity of the situation struck him, and he doubled over in pain, falling to the ground.

"Oh, my stars, what have I done?" he whispered. While publicly defying Melody's father had been satisfying in that moment, he had not fully considered the permanent consequences of his actions. Yet, even if his pride would allow him to return and beg forgiveness, he knew the Brethren leader well enough to know that *his* pride would never allow him to forgive Ethaniel's crime of loving

Melody and thereby tempting her with his daily presence.

Tears pricked his eyes while he pushed himself upright. He straightened and trudged along the path leading south beside the stream. Except for keeping a wary eye out for more river dragons, Ethaniel scarcely noticed his surroundings.

The path ended where the placid stream emptied into a fast-moving river. Ethaniel fell to his knees on the grassy bank. There was no bridge as far as he could see in either direction. The water appeared deep, and he didn't want to risk being caught in the current.

First, he lay on his stomach and cupped water into his hands, drinking his fill. Then he stood and wiped his hands on his homespun tunic.

He stared at the fabric, and more consequences crushed the wind from his lungs. All his life, he'd taken for granted the food he ate, the clothes he wore, the mat he slept upon in his father's cottage.

How would he live now?

Fighting down panic, Ethaniel followed the river downstream. He listened to the sounds of the forest with new ears. Myriads of birds sang and called to one another in the trees overhead. What did they eat? Seeds? Insects? Wouldn't they be considered meat, since insects were living creatures? He'd never eaten meat in his life, since it was forbidden by the law of the Brethren.

Ethaniel studied the vegetation he crushed under his bare feet. He knew to watch for sheep's bane, because it was poisonous for them to eat. Old Reuel said what was good for sheep was bad for humans, and vice versa. Could he eat sheep's bane, then?

The lengthening shadows of late afternoon brought him back to full awareness. To his utter surprise, the edge of a bluff appeared, and with a roar, the river cascaded over its lip, transforming into a waterfall. Once the foaming waters at the bottom calmed, the river pooled between rocky banks and finally emptied into a large body of water.

Was that the sea? Or the beginning of it? For Ethaniel had heard the sea was endless, and this was not. A land mass was visible across the expanse of water, more craggy cliffs with scraggly trees clinging precariously. To the west, the body of water continued, widening as the opposite shore grew farther and farther away and finally disappeared.

To the east, however, the cliffs came together in a plateau of good solid land. Toward that Ethaniel headed, keeping well back from the edge of the bluff. He had not yet reached the point of despair that he would knowingly plunge headlong over the edge.

By the time full darkness fell, he had not reached the plateau. Though more exhausted than he'd ever been, Ethaniel pondered continuing through the night, but the roar of a river dragon sounded close by, and he looked for shelter instead.

Ahead, a large dead oak blocked the moon's light, and Ethaniel cautiously approached. He listened intently for sounds of life, but heard only the soft hoot of an owl and the rustling of small creatures in the grass and fallen leaves.

With his eyes adjusted to the dim light, Ethaniel spied a hollow place in the trunk high enough to be out of reach of any river dragons. Feeling for handholds, he climbed up. Before venturing inside, he broke off a small branch and poked about, dislodging a snake. Then he pulled himself into the hole, curled up, and fell asleep with his head pillowed on his arm.

Ethaniel awoke when the rising sun warmed his face. He opened his eyes, suddenly remembering where he was and why. To his astonishment, two pairs of yellow eyes stared at him. Forcing himself to remain still, he studied the two tree dragons who continued to stare, unblinking.

"Good morning, little dragons," he said softly. Though he and Peniel had tried to catch them when they were small boys, tree dragons were too swift. This was the closest he'd ever been to one.

The nearest dragon's tongue slid out, the forked ends testing the air.

"I won't hurt you." Ethaniel crooned as he would have to a skittish lamb and slowly moved his hand closer. With a hiss, the tree dragons backed away.

"Don't leave, please!" Without meaning to, Ethaniel shifted his numb legs, and the little dragons disappeared.

With a sigh of disappointment, Ethaniel sat up and worked the kinks out of his muscles before climbing down. There was no sign of the tree dragons or any other wildlife. Ethaniel had never felt so alone in his life. Even when he spent many nights out in the pasture with the sheep, at least he had their warm presence about him.

His parched mouth reminded him how thirsty he was, so he trudged on until he came upon a small brook also headed for the sea. Ethaniel cupped his hands and drank until his thirst was quenched. Then he gathered clover growing along the bank and stuffed his mouth. He ate enough to dampen the pain in his empty belly, but he knew he'd need something more, and soon.

By midmorning, he reached the high plateau. Looking back, he could see far enough to tell the lay of the land on either side of the large arm of the sea. Did this represent more than one land? He'd never known much about the world outside the Brethren village. All he'd been told was the Village of Peace kept to itself, that all without was violence.

So far, the only violence he'd encountered had come from a river dragon, and it was only following the urgings of its hunger. Ethaniel better understood that urge now.

The plateau led to a drier land of striated rock formations, without trees or much vegetation of any type. Was there water? Ethaniel had to have water to survive. Shading his eyes against the glare of the sun, he spied an outcropping of rocks, at the base of which grew some kind of plants. He would walk that far, and if he found no water, he'd return to the brook before night fell.

The sun rose higher while the formation grew larger and more details became visible. It appeared empty of life, and Ethaniel imagined making a stronghold there in which to live. He had to eat, though. Even if there was water, he needed food, too.

When he reached the looming rocks, the sun had risen to midday. Ethaniel slowed his pace, studying the layout for a way to climb up and view his surroundings. He startled when a cascade of pebbles tumbled from a nearby overhang.

A reptilian head peered out from a gap in the rock formation, and the slit-pupiled eyes narrowed. When the creature brought up a bow and nocked an arrow, Ethaniel turned and ran.

The arrow sped past his ear so close, he felt the air of its passage. A sob escaped him, and he stumbled on the uneven rocks, falling painfully to his knees.

Then a roar even louder than a river dragon's sounded from above. Ethaniel jerked up his head in time to see a shadow block the sun. A blue dragon, wings spread wide with a long tail snaking behind, flamed the place where the archer had been. Another roar, this one of pain, reverberated on the rocks. Ethaniel pushed himself off the ground and hobbled away. There was nowhere to hide from the dragon.

A rush of sulfurous air above made Ethaniel drop to a crouch, protecting his head in vain with his arms.

"Go ahead, dragon, but please, make it quick." Ethaniel squeezed his eyes shut, making his last thoughts of Melody.

Make what quick? A deep voice sounded in his head, dispelling the image of Melody's face.

When nothing happened, Ethaniel peered up. The dragon landed beside him and snaked his long neck closer. The sparkling eyes studied him, and the nostrils widened, exhaling smoke.

"My death, of course." Ethaniel lowered his arms, more perplexed than terrified. "You're going to flame me now, aren't you?"

If you wish. The dragon rose up and inhaled.

Ethaniel jumped to his feet, waving his arms. "No! Please! I mean you no harm. I'm a pacifist, after all."

A pacifist? With a puzzled frown, the dragon turned his head and coughed, sending up a puff of smoke and sparks. *What by the shell is a pacifist?*

Ethaniel opened his mouth, but nothing came out. He'd never had to explain pacifism before. "Someone who doesn't believe in hurting anyone else," he finally said. "Even those who might hurt him." Frowning, he realized for the first time how difficult it would be to purposely let someone hurt him without trying to protect himself.

Hmm, the dragon said. *I thought a human's only purpose was to hurt each other and us dragons.*

"I'm sure some do, but not all." Now Ethaniel frowned at the dragon. "How can we understand one another?"

The dragon sat on his haunches and cocked his head. *I do not know. I have been told some humans can understand us, but they must be descended from someone called Alden.*

"Never heard of him." Ethaniel nodded back to the rock formation. "Thank you for saving me from that—creature which tried to kill me."

The creature is called a Mohorovian. And you're welcome. The dragon dipped his head in quite a civilized manner. *I am Flavatorix.*

Remembering Melody's name for him, Ethaniel realized this was a chance to begin a new life apart from the Brethren. He straightened and said, "I am Ethan."

The dragon showed Ethan his cave high in the rock formation. Ethan wondered why Flavatorix would be so friendly to him, until he learned the other dragons had banished his new friend for refusing to flame a couple of humans who had trespassed the dragons' holy place.

"Then why were you willing to flame me?" Ethan asked with a frown.

I was testing you. Flavatorix snorted, and it sounded like a laugh. *Even if you asked me to kill you, I could never take the life of another sentient creature.*

"Sentient?" He'd never heard that word before.

You have intelligence, and a good heart. Flavatorix sat in the middle of the cave and curled his long tail around him.

Like you. "So we were both banished by our people." Though Flavatorix radiated heat in the small cave, Ethan felt a chill. He never in his wildest imaginings expected to find a kindred spirit in one of the great dragons. "How long have you been here?"

Three journeys of the sun, a little more than twelve seasons, though this barren land does not mark the passage of time as does our holy place. Flavatorix hung his head and closed his eyes. *It feels like much, much longer.*

Ethan reached up to touch the warm, smooth scales of Flavatorix's cheek. "You miss your home. I am sorry."

The dragon's eyes opened, glowing, and Flavatorix stared at Ethan. *Thank you. You must miss your home as well.*

"Not all of it." Other than his friend, Peniel, and Melody, who was forever lost to him. And the sheep. Ethan had to admit, he missed those dumb sheep.

He threw off his melancholy. "It's time for me to find a new home."

Flavatorix gestured with a claw on his front foot. *Why not stay here? There is room, and I will share my kill with you.*

"Kill?" Ethan's gorge rose at the thought of eating meat, which was forbidden by the Brethren's Oath of Peace. "What do you kill?"

Out here, there are only conies, small and tough. But I fly to the forests every seven days and bring down a deer. Once, a wild pig.

"You eat them raw?" Ethan stared at the piles of bones in the cave's corners.

Sometimes. But when I have to flame them, they are no longer raw. Flavatorix pushed at something on top of the nearest bone pile. *Like this deer I flamed yesterday. There are a few scraps clinging to the bones.*

With his stomach twisting from revulsion and hunger both, Ethan reached out and felt the nearest bones, the ribs of an animal a little larger than one of his sheep. How could he eat this when it had been forbidden all his life?

But he hadn't had to kill it. The Brethren's law said, *Do no harm.* What harm would it be to eat the meat of an animal that was already dead?

Then his head began to pound. He'd been banished from the Brethren village and was no longer obligated to keep the Oath of Peace. His hands shook, and he clenched them. He had to make a decision, whether to eat meat and live or slowly starve to death trying to stay true to a law that no longer applied to him.

The odor of the meat was not unpleasant. Ethan's hunger made the decision. He pulled a piece of flesh from the rib bone and put it in his mouth. Its texture was unfamiliar, but the flavor was good enough. He only gagged once as he swallowed, already reaching for a second piece.

Thank you, Flavatorix, he said in his mind while chewing, not expecting the dragon to hear him.

You are welcome. Flavatorix's mouth widened in what looked to Ethan like a dragon smile.

An underground stream bubbled up in a deep rift at the heart of the rock formation. The water had the taste of sulfur, but it was drinkable, and so Ethan made his new home with Flavatorix the great dragon.

Once a week, the dragon flew back to the forest to catch their food, and in between, they explored the area beyond the rocks. Ethan envied Flavatorix's ease of traveling the vast expanse of the plains, while he learned to run at a faster pace than he'd ever needed to before.

Ethan marked their time together by scratching lines into the wall of the cave with a sharp rock, even though he honestly was not homesick, now that he'd found a friend. Before he knew it, three months had passed, and the days grew shorter. When the wind blew from the north, it brought the chill of autumn, and Ethan wondered where he would find some warmer clothes. He never thought he would miss the soft wool of his sheep and the wool cloak hanging on a peg in his father's cottage. Was it possible to construct clothing from deer skins? He'd have to ask Flavatorix if he could leave the skin of his prey intact.

The dragon had gone foraging, leaving Ethan alone for a few hours. The wind had died down, so Ethan took advantage of the warm day to clean out the cave. He chucked out the newest accumulation of bones into a hole, retrievable if needed later, but giving them more usable space in the cave.

After the last bone clacked against the others, Ethan returned to the cave, expecting silence. But the clacking noise persisted, coming closer, and Ethan stopped to listen more carefully.

The sound came from two directions, faint but growing nearer. Ethan clambered to the top of the rock formation for a better view.

A dozen Mohorovians, the reptilian creatures like the one who shot an arrow at him, climbed the rocks, surrounding him. He could see their entire bodies now, and his heart began to pound erratically. They were larger than a man, muscular and nimble. Each of the creatures was armed not only with a bow and arrows but with long, sharp claws on its hands and feet and a mouthful of sharp teeth.

Flavatorix! Our cave is under attack!

But the dragon was too far away to hear him. What could he do?

On the topmost rocky shelf, a small boulder balanced precariously. Ethan had always avoided touching it lest he accidentally dislodge it. But one of the creatures approached directly beneath it. Could he push the rock in the right direction so it would hit the creature? And if he did, would the others fear and run away?

A memory came unbidden, of the day he'd taken the Oath of Peace, swearing upon his life never to harm another living creature. But these creatures would not hesitate to kill him. It couldn't be wrong to defend oneself, could it?

Ethan sucked in a startled breath when the newer memory replaced the old one. He'd been banished from the Brethren; the Oath no longer bound him.

With new resolve, Ethan climbed down to the ledge and sidled over to the big rock. Bracing against the wall behind him, he measured the distance and angle and then pushed against the rock with his feet, knocking it over the edge and nearly sending him over with it. He clutched the ledge while he watched the rock tumble down, down, heading directly for the creature.

Hearing the sound, the Mohorovian jerked up its head, tried to move in time, and couldn't. The rock smashed into him, knocking him off the rock formation and to the ground far below.

Ethan held his breath, waiting for the rest to run away scared, as he would have done. But they continued climbing as if nothing had happened.

"What can I do?" Ethan wailed. "Oh, Flavatorix, if only you could hear me!"

I can hear you, Ethan. I am coming now. What has happened?

In a rush of thoughts, Ethan told Flavatorix what was happening. He was so focused on relief the dragon was near, he almost didn't duck fast enough when the nearest creature shot one of its arrows.

Hurry, Flav! Ethan sidled along the ledge to a scant shelter between two boulders.

Roaring, the mighty dragon dove down with a gout of flame, so close Ethan felt the intense heat. When Flavatorix flew past, two of the nearest Mohorovians fell from the rock formation, their flesh charred. Again and again, Flavatorix dove and flamed at the creatures. Ethan worked his way down to watch his friend, admiring his grace and power. One by one, the Mohorovians fell. Surely there were no more?

Then Flavatorix roared in pain, and Ethan clapped a hand over his own head. He'd *felt* the dragon's agony as if it were his own. He couldn't see him, but he heard the clatter of rocks as another of the reptilian creatures fell to its death.

What happened? Ethan stood still at the entrance to their cave, scanning the sky. Finally, the dragon appeared, and Ethan moaned. An arrow protruded from one of Flavatorix's eyes.

"No," he shouted. *Come here, my friend, and I will try to remove it.*

It is too late. Flavatorix landed beside Ethan, panting. *Their arrows are poisoned, and this one pierced my only vulnerable place.* He stared at Ethan out of his other eye, which was glazed with pain. *I am not long for this world and must take you to a safer place.*

What? Tears flooded Ethan's eyes. How could Flavatorix *die?* He was one of the great dragons; he should be invincible.

Sadly, even we have our vulnerabilities. Flavatorix turned his sinewy neck and nodded at his back. *Climb on, and I will fly you to the forest.*

His thoughts as blurred as his vision, Ethan scrambled up the dragon's scaly shoulder and straddled his back between two of the ridges. He found a notch to hold onto just in time, for Flavatorix lifted into the air with an audible groan.

With the wind whipping his braid, Ethan crouched low. He marveled at the beauty of the dragon's flight while his heart wept at the tragedy of his impending loss.

Far below, the terrain changed abruptly from desert to forest. To the north lay a stone fortress, and Ethan even spied the wooden palisade of the Brethren, but it looked tiny from this height.

For a moment, Ethan considered asking Flavatorix to fly out over the sea so that when the dragon lost his strength, they could both plunge into the water and drown together.

No, Flavatorix said, his voice more commanding than Ethan had ever heard it. *You must not waste the gift of life so dearly bought.*

Forgive me, my friend. Ethan leaned his cheek against the dragon's back ridge. *If only I could die instead of you.*

Then the dragon struggled to breathe, and his wings faltered. With a gasp, Ethan held on more tightly, willing his feeble strength to support his friend. A large meadow opened below them, and Flavatorix circled to land, angling swiftly down.

Instead of the graceful landing Ethan had watched him make a hundred times, Flavatorix crumpled into the tall grass, jarring Ethan so hard that he lost his balance and pitched headlong toward the ground. Even in his dying, the dragon was aware of him, for he broke Ethan's fall with the pad of his front foot, setting him down beside his head.

Ethan scrambled to his feet, seeing the accursed arrow up close for the first time. Already Flavatorix's color had faded from a brilliant blue to an ashy gray. Ethan clenched his fists, barely holding back a scream of rage. How he hated those Mohorovians!

Flavatorix opened his uninjured eye, which had grown cloudy, and fixed his gaze upon Ethan.

Do not let anger and hatred rule you, my friend. They will poison your heart as surely as this arrow has poisoned me. The dragon's shallow breaths became more labored. *Promise me, please, Ethan.*

Ethan placed his hand on the dragon's cheek. His heart tightened, but with sorrow, not anger. *I promise.* Tears flooded his eyes. *I will never forget you.*

The great eye closed, and Flavatorix let out a long sigh. At first, Ethan thought the dragon was just relieved, and then he realized it had been his final breath.

He curled up beside the still head, weeping without shame.

Ethan did not know how much time had passed, but he heard human voices and sat up, peering over the dragon's neck ridges. A large group of villagers approached, and Ethan was torn between running away and standing guard over his friend's lifeless body.

"See? It's dead," a woman said. "Just fell from the sky, like I told ya."

"Are you sure it be dead and not injured?" a man asked.

Rising to his feet, Ethan faced the villagers. "The dragon is dead." He wanted to say more, but his throat tightened.

The people halted and stared at Ethan with surprise.

Several murmured between themselves, but Ethan heard one word over the others: *Dragonslayer.*

"No, no." He held up his hands. "It wasn't me. A Mohorovian shot the dragon, and he carried me to safety before he died."

"A Mohorovian?" the man in front asked. "What is that?"

"It's a c-creature," Ethan stammered. "It looks like a giant lizard but can shoot arrows. And they're poisoned."

"Poison?" Another woman shrieked, backing away. Others began to panic.

A big man wearing a blacksmith's apron stepped forward and held up his hands, calming the crowd. "I've heard of Mohorovia. It's a long way from here. Whatever killed this dragon won't be bothering us."

"Then the boy isn't a dragonslayer?"

Ethan couldn't see who asked the question. "I would never kill a dragon." He wanted to say more, to tell them about Flavatorix, but he didn't get the chance.

The villagers rushed forward, ignoring him now to study the dead dragon. One man used a stick to open Flavatorix's mouth, and others poked and kicked the once-blue scales.

"What are you doing?" Ethan grabbed another man's arm when he pulled out a knife and started to cut out one of the dragon's teeth.

"What's the matter with you, boy?" The man shoved Ethan to the ground. "This is the greatest trophy ever seen in these parts."

Others swarmed around, ignoring Ethan now in their eagerness to cut out a tooth or a claw or a scale. Tears of helpless rage spilled over Ethan's cheeks, and he scrambled to his feet and backed away, toward the nearest trees.

I'm sorry, Flavatorix. I can't fight them all.

He turned and ran, but before he lost sight of the clearing, he looked back once more. The villagers were now piling branches around the dragon's body. To burn it, he supposed. Disgusted with their behavior and his own inability to stop them, Ethan stormed into the forest.

He hadn't gone far when he came upon another meadow. A sight met him there, so familiar it made his heart ache. An elderly shepherd struggled to bring his scattered flock together. What could have panicked these sheep?

"Oh," Ethan said. Could they have seen Flavatorix in his last desperate flight?

At a bleat nearby, Ethan jerked his head toward the sound. A ewe and her lamb ran toward him. Without thinking, he approached them, holding his arms out wide.

"Now, now, my beauties," he crooned. "All is well. Follow me."

The sheep stopped and allowed Ethan to herd them back to the shepherd. When he neared the older man wearing ragged homespun, Ethan saw how gnarled was the hand holding the staff. Deep lines in the man's face mapped a long and difficult life.

"Is the dragon dead, lad?" the shepherd asked in a voice rusty with disuse.

"Yes," Ethan croaked. He cleared his throat and straightened. "He died saving my life."

The old man nodded. "A true friend, then."

Ethan's mouth opened in astonishment. "How did you know?"

"I saw you on its back." The man smiled, revealing merry eyes. "You have a way with animals, lad."

Ethan started to say Flavatorix was not an animal, but how could he ever explain in a way the old man would believe? He shrugged instead.

"I was a shepherd at my old village." He indicated the man's sheep. "My name is Ethan."

"And I'm Gandy." His dark eyes bore into Ethan's. "Are you looking for work, then?"

Ethan studied the flock, larger than the one he'd tended at the Brethren village. "Yes." Then he met Gandy's gaze again. "What place is this?"

"Yonder village is Eli's Crossing, in Southmoor." Gandy smiled. "But I don't see it much. Prefer to stay out with the sheep."

"Me, too." Ethan's nostrils caught an acrid odor. When he looked back, smoke rose into the air beyond the trees. At least no one could defile Flavatorix any longer.

"Are ye one o' the Brethren, Ethan?" Gandy's rough voice caused him to turn around again. "You have one of those braids."

Ethan blinked back tears. He would always mourn Melody and Flavatorix, but he couldn't afford to live in the past. His new life began today. "Do you have shears? Or a knife?"

Gandy opened a leather bag at his waist and pulled out a pair of sheep shears. He handed them to Ethan, who held up his braid, sucked in a steadying breath, and clipped it off.

He stared down at the wooden hair clasp on his unraveling dark braid, a pine cone painted on a green background. Though the Brethren called their home the Village of Peace, Ethan had not found peace there. If he and Flavatorix could have lived away from all others, Mohorovian and human, perhaps they could have found peace. He sighed and tossed the hair to the ground.

After staring at it for a moment, Ethan bent down and removed the hair clasp. He could keep this small memory of the family he'd once had. With another sigh, he handed the shears back to the shepherd.

"No, sir." He straightened and spoke the truth. "I am not one of the Brethren. But I will be your apprentice, if you'll have me." *And I will keep my promise to you, Flavatorix.*

Gandy nodded once. Understanding shone in his wise eyes. The old man turned to herd the sheep, and Ethan gladly followed.

The events of "Dragon's Oath" take place a generation before the birth of Mercy d'Alden, the title character in He Who Finds Mercy, *a YA Christian fantasy series. Readers of* Mercy's Prince *might recognize a couple of characters briefly mentioned in this story, which was written to answer a plot question in a new series,* Mercy's Children.

For more info about the author and her books, please visit katyhuthjones.blogspot.com.

The Hallway of Three Doors

a fairy tale

D. G. Driver

The seer tapped the teacup as Seta drank. "Drink it down. All of it." The seer took the empty cup back from Seta and poked her fingernails into it.

Seta had heard stories about Annelle Brugher. Supposedly, Annelle had foreseen the war and had predicted the drought. That's why she had stored away plenty of water for the village's survival. Seta wondered how much of that was true or just coincidence. She also wondered if the rest of Annelle's house was as maudlin as this windowless workspace draped with lavender and gold curtains.

"I see horses," Annelle said at last.

"My father raises horses."

"Of course he does," Annelle said. "But what do the horses represent to you?"

Seta shrugged. "That's where our livelihoods come from. Or used to, anyway."

"Think about it," Annelle urged. "Travel? Adventure?"

"No, that doesn't sound like me," Seta said. "I think the horses you see are the ones I mentioned. Do you see anything else?" She didn't want to talk about the horses and how she had convinced her father to sell them to the army. That had been a long time ago, when she thought the income would help the village. What it did instead was make the town a target for enemy cannon fire.

"I see a jar full of money."

"Ah, that would be the jar where I kept my life savings before my intended husband stole it."

"It does not represent future prosperity? Allowance?"

"No."

"Destitution? Rejection?"

"Maybe. I don't know. You really have to dig to get that."

"That is the point," Annelle said.

"Oh, I guess I didn't realize that." Seta slumped back in the high-backed chair.

This was not going well at all. She didn't need a seer to tell her that she had chosen the wrong man. Anyone could have told her that she'd been a fool to tell Gabriel about her secret dowry. "Do you see anything else? Anything helpful?"

"A road."

Seta shook her head.

"It could mean many things…"

"I don't think you're getting it." Seta crossed her arms. "I don't want to know who I am or what you see that represents me. I want to know what to do with myself. I want something I can use."

Annelle put the cup down on the table. "I cannot tell you what to do with your life. No one can make those kinds of choices for you."

"But that's what I'm paying you to do."

"I can only help you understand yourself, and then you can use that understanding to make your choices."

Seta stood. "Obviously, this was a mistake. I already understand myself. Only, I've always made the wrong choices when it comes to other people. Now I want to make some right ones. Maybe your skills aren't good enough to help me with that."

"Perhaps not," Annelle said, standing up as well. She followed Seta to the door and stopped the younger woman from opening it. "I don't know of a seer who can help you, but I do know of a place. A place I've never told anyone about before."

"What kind of place?" Seta asked, dubious.

"The Hallway of the Three Doors."

No one wished Seta farewell or safe journey. Those who saw her ride out of town on a horse stolen from what was left of her father's stock had spit at her. There hadn't been any point in saying goodbye to her father. He'd have packed her bags for her.

Mother dead. Brothers off fighting. Seta had no reason to linger about. She'd ride until she found those doors, and if there were no doors, she'd ride until she was far enough from her responsibility to the village to forget about it.

Two weeks later, Seta and her stolen mount stopped in front of the castle Annelle had described. Her doubts about the castle containing an enchanted hallway multiplied when she took in the desperate state of it. The building was ready to collapse. A bombing had displaced many of the bricks and stones in the foundation. If there ever had been a magical hallway, it probably didn't exist anymore. If she tried to go inside, the whole building could crash down on her.

If she didn't go inside, she would never know if the answers she sought could be found. There existed a dim promise of betterment inside those fragile walls. The hallway might show her a life where the choices were made for her instead of by her.

So she went inside, gingerly stepping on floors that she didn't trust to hold her weight. One room led to the next. Daylight poured into every room from bombed walls, tattered roofs, and bashed windows, revealing blackened tapestries and scattered chunks of furniture.

The light around her dimmed as she stepped into a dead-end room no wider than her arms outstretched and no longer than ten strides of her feet. Unlike the rest of the castle, this room was completely intact with hip-high maple paneling and red, crushed velvet wallpaper.

To her right were three doors. None of them alike.

The first door had no handle. The plain, wooden door needed none since it was propped wide open. Beyond it, Seta saw a city full of merriment. Banners flew, and people danced in the streets. Yet, above the city, clouds gathered, dark and stormy. Though the decorations of the place were bright and lovely now, Seta knew that it wouldn't be long before the silken banners became heavy with rainwater. The party would have to turn indoors.

That door tempted her. All seemed comfortable and easy there.

The closed second door was completely different from the first. Some fine craftsman had purposely carved intricate etchings all over the dark wood. The door handle was long and bold with a complicated keyhole.

Seta longed to discover where that door would take her. As she approached the door to pull the handle, she noticed how her hand barely covered the top knob of it. Stepping closer to the door made her overly aware of how her five-foot-two body barely reached half its height. The door seemed to be growing. Or was she getting smaller? She certainly felt smaller.

Seta ran her fingers along the floor and through the deep grooves of the carvings but couldn't find a key to the lock. Perhaps she wasn't meant to see what was on the other side.

The final door was poorly made. The door wasn't sanded or painted. Splinters poked out from it, ready to attack her fingers. It was clearly constructed hastily. Though it had a doorknob, Seta doubted that it would turn. The door looked as though it was jammed into its spot and merely needed a shove to knock it down.

Despite the carelessness of its design, the builder did see fit to include a window, a peephole level with her eyes and made of rose-colored glass. Through the window she could see a world devoid of people. For miles in every direction, she could see natural resources of every sort.

Seta put the pieces together and understood that beyond this third door was a world she would have to build on her own. Alone, with no help. That world made her apprehensive. True, what choices she made in that world would affect only her. On the contrary, however, was loneliness. A high price to pay for peace of mind.

Loneliness. She had to laugh at herself for even thinking of that as a deterrent. All she had was herself anymore. She could hardly go back home where everyone despised her. Anywhere else she went she would be starting anew. Alone.

"But there's the possibility…"

Of what? Of finding love? Whether lover or friend, what kind of person would it take to end her regrets and give in to the pure joy of connection?

Seta trembled with the doorknob of the third door filling her palm. Was this the right door? What about the other two?

Then it came to her. The point of this hallway was not to plague her with new choices but to show her the way. Seta closed her eyes and walked in a circle four times. Whichever door she saw first when she opened her eyes again she would go through.

A hand grabbed her upper arm, interrupting her spin and tugging hard enough to pull her off balance.

"Come on," a woman's cheery voice called.

Seta opened her eyes and followed the high-pitched laughter until she could see the full head of blond hair bobbing up and down in front of her as the woman ran, dragging Seta along toward a mansion lit brightly and filled with people.

Behind her, Seta saw the first door slam shut and vanish. She wanted to stop and run back to it. This wasn't the world she had chosen. Or was it exactly how she had wanted it to be? The decision made for her.

Seta was in the City of Frivolity. That's what Larissa called it, anyway.

"We simply must get you primed because everybody from the City of Frivolity will be here."

Larissa, the very same giddy woman who had dragged her though the door, had taken her to a dressing room to be adorned in a golden satin gown, have her cheeks powdered with blush, and have her lips smacked with gloss. Now she was knotting Seta's hair into a hairstyle that made Seta's neck lengthen gracefully. All the while, she gossiped about who would be seen at the party downstairs.

"Of course Madame *Weary* is the hostess. She must be eighty years old, but she pins her hair so tightly that her skin stretches around her skull. I think she's trying to look younger, but she looks more like a painted corpse."

Larissa gave her no opportunity to speak, not that Seta had anything to add.

"The youngest prince will be here, too. I call him Prince *Drudgery*. He's so incredibly boring. The third born, you know. He doesn't have to be charming. Whoever he marries won't be the next queen. All the same, he could try to be entertaining. The only single prince left, and all he does is sit and play violin with the musicians all night. What is that all about? What kind of example does it set for the Workers?"

On and on Larissa rambled until both of them were dressed for the party. Seta's mood had been elevated by all the talk. She could hardly wait to see all the people who had been mentioned. Her only fear was that she would call people by Larissa's wicked nicknames rather than by their real names, none of which she knew.

Their presence made a stir when she and Larissa were announced. Men's eyes left their dance partners to stare. Women gossiped behind their fans. Feeling beautiful and exotic for the first time in her life, Seta held her head high above it all and proceeded to greet the hostess.

The hostess was all that Larissa had described and more. An older woman with flaming red hair, Madame Wielder—not Weary—wore a gown too tight and young for her. In her hand, she held a nearly empty glass of wine. The rest of the wine she breathed out with her hello. Arms open wide, the hostess hugged her newest guests warmly and presented Seta to all of her friends.

Everyone took turns petting Seta and speaking kindly to her. All of it tickled her pride until she observed that when the hostess swayed her attention elsewhere, those same friends turned their backs and chortled vicious comments about the hostess and Seta both. They were hardly discreet about it either. Almost as if they wanted Seta to hear them.

Seta hoped Larissa might introduce her to a few people before running off. Not to be. The woman disappeared into the crowd. Seta meandered to the catering table to fill herself with tart pastries and sweet wine. Tasting such food was a luxury nearly forgotten after years of famine. Here in the City of Frivolity, rich food was the entrée. In fact, Seta didn't see a single healthy morsel on the table. To add to the plush array of goodies, Seta observed that the table never emptied of treats. Every pastry she loaded onto her napkin was replaced immediately with another fresh from the kitchen, brought by ever-diligent servants.

Unable to eat another bite, Seta sat on a bench against the wall near the orchestra. Infected by the tempo, Seta tapped her toes so continuously that her shins began to ache. Only then did she realize that the music never slowed down, never paused between songs, never relaxed into a romantic slow dance.

Seta turned her attention to the peppy group of players on the stage. She observed that as members became tired, other musicians appeared from a back room, instruments in hand, and would simply slip into place, mid-song, mid-note even. Seta wondered if there were an endless supply of musicians in the back room alongside the pastries and wine.

Everyone smiled and laughed and drank and ate and danced. Seta enjoyed the high spirits for a while. Laughter hadn't rung in her ears in many moons. All the same, after a while, the noise gave her a headache. The smell from the catering table caused her mouth to feel sticky and dry. The peppy polkas pounded on her nerves.

An hour after midnight, all the guests ran outside to the fountain to relieve themselves in one way or another from their drink. The musicians continued to play without any dancers in the room. Cautiously, Seta crept toward the conductor. She wiggled a finger to let him know he should bend over to hear her speak into his hair-covered ear.

"Please. While everyone's outside. Could you play a ballad?"

"A ballad?" He said it as if he didn't know what she was talking about. He raised his arms and cut off the music. The instant silence made her head thrum. "A ballad?" This time, he said it to the orchestra with a shrug.

To the dumbfounded faces, Seta tried to explain. "Like this." She hummed a lullaby her mother had taught her. The musicians stared at her blankly.

A man's voice spoke up from the violin section. "Wait!" Seta couldn't see who had spoken. "How about something like this?"

His one lone bow ran across the low strings, holding, holding, then moving slowly from note to note as though the player were making it up as he went. It was hauntingly beautiful. Seta closed her eyes and breathed in the music. She let her body sway to it as she moved onto the empty ballroom floor. Before she knew it, she was twirling across the floor, letting every ounce of remorse spin out of her. The rush. The dizziness. It all felt so joyously heart-wrenching.

One couple came back too quickly. Seta didn't know it until the violinist ended his progression with a tuneless squeak. Seta stopped so suddenly from her dance that a bolt of pain ran up her spine. The couple straightened their clothes and aimed for the wine decanters. They hadn't noticed her. The rest of the crowd trickled back into the room, and the music returned to normal.

Seta slinked back to her spot.

Two hours after midnight, the guests fell drunk to the floor and the orchestra packed up their instruments. The hostess bustled everyone off to guest rooms until only one handful of guests remained, which included both Larissa and Seta.

Madame Wielder came down the stairs and discovered the group sprawled out all over the bottom steps. "Oh dear," she said, raising a manicured hand to her pinned-up cheek. "I didn't realize there were still people here. Oh dear, oh dear."

In a voice both slurred and deep, a voice so unlike the one that chattered so freely in the dressing room hours ago, Larissa said, "I hope you're saying 'Oh dear' because you're so excited that you have extra people here."

One of the men in the group added, "Or that you're alarmed that you've made us wait so long."

Madame Wielder apologized. "There are simply not enough rooms. You'll have to take a carriage to find lodgings elsewhere."

"At this time of night?" A dark man groaned from the bottom step.

"Couldn't we simply sleep here in the ballroom?" a plump-faced man said. Everyone frowned his way.

A small woman holding a flute case between her gloved hands asked, "Where will we find a carriage?"

The hostess smiled at that, happy to have at least one solution. "I'll loan you my carriage and driver." She held her skirts tightly to her legs as she pressed between the unmoving outcasts. At the bottom of the steps, she said, "I'm so glad that you came tonight. Let's do it again tomorrow." With that, she fled through the servants' door and was not to be seen again.

The group stumbled outside to the carriage that awaited them. Seta saw that the door to the carriage had similar carvings to the second door from the magical hallway. Like that door, the carriage door made her feel unwelcome. When the group tried to organize seating arrangements, Seta happily chose to sit next to the driver, with two men—one grumpy, the other round with a pleasant grin—and the mousy flute player sitting behind her. Larissa and two other men sat inside.

The driver pulled his shoulders up around his ears and clicked for the horses to go.

"Hello," she said to him. When he didn't reply or even nod her way, she tried, "My name is Seta. What's yours?" Again, he didn't answer. "I appreciate your driving us at this late hour."

He said something then, but all she could make out of it was "...over with as soon as possible." To make his point clear, he drove the horses hard, whipping them constantly while not managing to get them to go any faster than their fastest speed. Seta sat on her hands to keep from pulling the whip away from him. Nothing about his manner made her feel that he would take too kindly to her interference.

Seta twisted her body to see how the people behind her were reacting to this cruel treatment. The mousy woman covered her face with her hands. The grumpy man had his back turned to it, his head cocked as if sighing about the loss of a good bed back at the house. The round man patted the woman on the shoulder to reassure her. As he did, his eyes met Seta's. She nodded toward the driver, and he winked conspiratorially.

Leaning over the driver's left shoulder, the round man said gamely, "Hey there, friend. Have you got any carrots tucked away on this carriage? For the horses, I mean. Not for myself, of course. Ha ha! I've found that tying them to the end of the whip and holding them before their noses makes them run very fast."

The driver muttered something about "...middle of the night."

"You know," he tried again, "none of us are in a particular hurry. We've got all day to sleep."

"Yes," Seta joined in. "I don't even know *where* I will sleep let alone have to worry about getting there quickly."

His temper increased. "Don't care where you're going, do you? Don't care when you get there, huh?" the driver ranted, whipping the horses harder than before. He pulled on the reins to force the horses off the road. The turn was so sharp, the carriage balanced momentarily on two wheels, tipping dangerously to the right. Shrill screams came from inside the coach.

Smoothing out his hair, the grumpy man shouted, "Where do you think you're going?"

The driver lowered his chin farther into his cloak and fumed. "Oh, another one, eh?"

The grumpy man didn't put up with the driver's attitude like Seta and the other top passengers. He shoved the round fellow out of the way. "Where are you taking us?"

The driver didn't answer, and the grumpy man didn't bother to ask again. Instead, he reached out and grabbed the whip near the base just above the driver's hand. With both hands, he yanked the whip across the driver's throat. The driver let go of the reins in an attempt to pull the whip free. The grumpy man kept his grip tight as the driver struggled to breathe. When at last the driver's energy ran out, the grumpy man dragged the driver by the whip over the left end of the driver's bench and let go.

In horror, Seta peered over the side to see the driver sprawled out in the grass behind them. He did not move.

"You killed him," she spat at the murderer.

He only shrugged in response and went back to his original seat.

Thinking quickly, the round man pushed his way forward to the driver's bench and grabbed the reins. It took a great deal of huffing and straining to get the horses to slow down.

"Aren't you going to turn around so we can get him?" Seta asked.

"No."

The murderer up top smiled and smoothed his hair again. The mousy woman buried her head in her lap. Inside the carriage, the merry voices of Larissa and her friends peaked to a frenzy as though they were enjoying a thrill ride.

"Don't you know what just happened?" Seta screamed through the shutters at them. They didn't act as if they heard her.

"I want to be with the fun people." The murderer groaned.

Seta listened closer to the conversation seeping out from below her.

"After eating like a pig, she just sat by the wall all night," Larissa said.

Then another laughed. "Sounds like she'd be a perfect match for Prince Drudgery."

The first driver had taken them into the grasslands behind the city, and now the horses had lost them in the forest. Turning the jumpy horses around proved too difficult for the round man to manage, and he merely succeeded in confusing himself about which direction they had come from. Trying to make light of the situation, the round man spouted legends about the forest. He talked endlessly, getting louder with each subject he recalled until he was loud enough to disturb the riders inside.

"Shut up already," one of the men whined.

"We've heard enough," the other man agreed.

"You should be looking for a place for us to stay," the murderer grunted from up top.

The round man stopped talking, but he fumed beneath his breath. "Ungrateful... No sense of decency..."

Seta offered him a sympathetic look, but he kept his eyes straight ahead and missed it.

"He should be a jester, really." Larissa laughed. "He's as fat as a clown, even without the costume."

It was finally too much for the man trying so hard to stay pleasant. He shouted, "I've had enough!"

There was a gasp and an "I've had enough of *you!*" before a gloved male hand swung out through the window and jammed a knife into the round man's shoulder. In pain, the man let go of the reins. The carriage rolled over a stone, causing him to lose his balance and fall from the bench.

Seta couldn't look back at the poor man to see if he had survived. She had to grab the reins before the horses ran into a tree or ditch. No one else made any effort to stop the carriage from disaster. They merely giggled, whined, and complained, and the mousy woman threw up over the side.

A dense fog settled in, wrapping around the carriage like a moist blanket, smothering them, hiding the trees, scaring the horses. Finally, Seta had to bring the horses to a dead stop.

Shouts of protest came from inside the carriage.

The murderer growled in her ear, "What do you think you're doing?"

Larissa opened the shutters and stuck her face out. "What's going on out here?"

To answer, the murderer jumped to the ground and pointed his thumb back at Seta. "She stopped."

Seta held the reins tightly so that at the slightest physical threat from one of her companions she could trigger the horses to run. Taking a long, deep breath to steady her shaky tongue, she explained, "I don't know these parts, and the horses can't see through the fog. I thought it would be safer to wait until the fog lifted. Unless one of you...?"

Larissa snorted. "I hope you're not suggesting one of us should drive."

"I can't drive these horses. Look at them."

The horses could barely stand still, their perked-up ears hearing sounds from the forest that human ears couldn't begin to pick up.

"Then what do you suggest?" Larissa questioned. "It's cold and I'm ready for bed."

Seta would have preferred to wait out the sunrise, but she feared that these angry people with no concern for the value of human life wouldn't agree with her plan. "I... I could lead you out on foot. I might be able to retrace our tracks—"

"On foot?" One of the men balked. "I wouldn't dream of it."

The murderer leaned toward her. "I expect you to come up with something better." Then he opened the carriage door and squeezed himself inside, his right leg hanging out the half-open door.

Decision maker again. She'd come into this world specifically to avoid making decisions, especially the kind that had to deal with life and death. Back home, she had failed in her choices. At least then she had cared for those people. Now she had to worry about these horrid people who would kill her if she led them incorrectly.

A creaking and rocking beside her accompanied the mousy woman as she slipped down to the driver's bench to keep Seta company. She shivered terribly under the long-sleeved gray dress she wore. Seta had only the capped sleeves of her ball gown beneath a lace shawl covering her, but since anger seemed to be keeping her blood hot, she offered the shawl to the girl.

"Oh no," her shaky voice replied. "You'll need it."

"If I get too cold, we can share it."

The girl took the shawl and wrapped it tightly around her. "Thank you." Her shivers did not decrease.

Seta whispered so that none of the others would hear. "I bet it will be warmer if we can find some trees or boulders to shelter us."

The girl nodded, and the two of them stepped off the carriage platform as quietly as possible. She led the woman to some rocks and told her to wait there. As she walked back to the horses, she glanced over her shoulder and saw that the woman was praying.

In order to keep the horses from bolting off, Seta unhitched the horses and strapped them to a low-hanging branch. Then she and the flute player pressed their bodies close to each other for warmth and waited without conversation. It could be hours before they would be able to see clearly enough to travel.

A wolf howled close by. Another howled. And then another. The group in the carriage tittered nervously. The mousy woman trembled and asked what they should do.

"We should run—fast."

They hitched up their skirts to go just as something large bounded past them. The fog curled from the gust of air like curdled milk. A pack of wolves rushed to the spot, all avoiding Seta and the mousy woman in favor of the horses.

The poor animals strung to the trees whinnied in fright, then screamed, then were silent. Seta's heart sank, knowing she'd prevented the poor animals from hope of escape.

The feasting wolves didn't hear the click of the carriage door as it closed behind the four travelers. Amazingly, the voices of the people had finally been hushed.

Without speaking, it was assumed that Seta should lead. She didn't want to, but by the way everyone hesitated in front of her it was clear that no one else had the inclination to take charge. As soon as they were far enough to not be able to hear the wolves anymore, the man with the dark hair and bloody glove began to whimper. He wrapped his arms around his head as he walked. Larissa hung her head and cursed, the dolt stumbled along, and the murderer lagged behind the others, grumbling about the state of things. By Seta's side, the mousy woman whispered more prayers between chattering teeth.

Seta followed the sound of bubbling water and was dismayed that the stream she had been hoping for wasn't much more than a leaky brook. Nevertheless, crossing it would help eradicate their scent somewhat, so she related the plan to her dependents. The usual barrage of complaints rang out.

"You don't expect me to walk through a stream in my gown and satin shoes, do you?"

The men agreed with Larissa. No ruining of shoes. Or socks. Or pant cuffs. And the water would be too cold for their bare feet.

The wolves howled.

"Oh no." The mousy woman moaned. "They've finished with the horses." In a panic, she launched into the water, positioning her body across the width of the stream.

Seta tugged at the mousy woman's shoulders. "Get up! Get up!"

"NO!" the woman screamed. "We've got to cross the stream or we won't be safe! Tell them to use me as a bridge."

Seta looked up at the quartet on the bank who pointed their fingers and snickered at the two women getting drenched.

"Don't do this for them," Seta said. "Get up and go to the other side yourself. If they don't want to ruin their shoes, then so be it."

"You don't understand," the woman said, lying down on her stomach, holding her head out of the water to speak. "They'll never cross otherwise, and I can't let it be on my conscience if they die."

Seta put out her hands again to help the lady up, but she refused. Instead, she lifted her flute case out of the water. "Please hold this for me."

"I won't tell them to walk on you."

The woman raised herself up and yelled back over her shoulder, "Use me as a bridge. The water isn't deep, so my body will elevate you enough to keep your shoes dry."

Seta stepped out of the water toward the four people already lining up to use the woman's body as suggested. "If you're going to do this to her," Seta begged, "at least take your shoes off."

"No time," the murderer said. "You heard the wolves."

"All that lacing?" Larissa laughed. "I would still be undoing them when the wolves pounce."

"And then what good is the poor girl's offer?" the dolt added.

The man with the bloody glove was already crossing. Seta tried not to watch, but each stifled cry of pain from the woman made her eyes return to the spectacle. Still dark and foggy, Seta could barely make out the woman's form beneath the boots and thick clothing of the quartet, but the crunch of her backbone snapping allowed Seta's mind to envision more than she needed to see.

When the last pretty shoe touched ground and disappeared into the fog on the other side of the stream, Seta lowered herself onto her hands and knees and crawled to the bank. She didn't want to cross. For the moment, the others couldn't see her. For the moment, she was alone. Silently, she pulled the woman's body out of the water. She dragged it to the base of a tree and tried to conceal it between a large boulder and the tree trunk, spreading dried leaves and pine needles over it, the closest thing Seta could do to a proper burial. A religious woman like her deserved a prayer and a grave marker. Seta didn't have time or know how to do that for her.

Seta considered leaving the flute but decided against it. She could better remember the woman by learning to play it.

"Girl! Oh, girl!"

"Girl! We need you over here!"

Seta didn't answer. There was a choice she had to make—to save them, if she could, or leave them behind. Stepping up on the rock beside the body, she reached for the lowest branch on the tree. The ball gown restricted her agility, but a seam popped here or there wouldn't matter now. She climbed past three times her height. Nestling against the trunk for warmth and balance, she considered waiting there all night, hoping to avoid the decision, hoping the fog would lift, wondering if the wolves would come and make an end of it for her.

The four people whined. The four people complained. The four people grunted angrily. The four people cried desperately.

Seta recalled the expressions from her neighbors as she rode out of her village two weeks ago. The anger. She'd failed them so badly. No one back home was asking for her help anymore.

Seta understood then, for the first time, that it wasn't the making of choices that she performed badly. It was taking responsibility for those choices. She had run away from her people rather than try to make amends for all the suffering she'd caused. Fate's idea of fair play had put her back into a position of responsibility again. To test her. To teach her.

She would not fail again.

By convincing herself that the evil quartet was as vital to her own self-worth as the village of loved ones she'd abandoned, she came up with the only solution she could offer.

"Climb the trees!" she called out to them. "The wolves can't reach you if you're in the trees."

As usual, Larissa balked. "Climbing trees will rip my dress to shreds."

"And I have on my finest trousers."

Seta laughed bitterly. "I didn't think you'd do it. But I will tell you this, if you don't climb the trees and the wolves find your smell again, you'll die. The wolves won't care about mucking up your clothing. Up high, they might snarl and jump at you, but you'll be safe."

"But to climb trees?"

"Could you come help us get up?"

Seta refused to help anymore. She had done her part to help them, and she felt better for it. Now if they died when the wolves came hunting for their perfumed dessert, she wouldn't be to blame.

She lowered herself to the ground, landing like a cat, feeling strong and lithe. To the fading sound of the others going on about their plight, she dashed along the stream's edge. Their voices faded after a time. The fog lifted. It was morning.

At the edge of the forest, she took in the sight of a new world spread out before her. The rising sun put a rosy glow on this barren world full of raw materials lying in wait for someone to come and make use of them.

"The third door," she whispered.

Seta knelt to scoop the soil into her hands. It crumbled easily and left her hands moist and smelling of well-tended gardens. Though the sun shone steadily, the temperature didn't make her sweat or shiver. The stream bubbled straight across the land, widening and disappearing into the horizon. Wood was plentiful in the forest, and plants with thick stalks grew in clumps here and there.

She could live easily in this world. A whole society could rebuild here. Yes. That was it, wasn't it? If there were a way to bring her village here, rebuild here, start again here, wouldn't they at last have a chance to survive?

Seta turned toward the forest. Dark clouds loomed above it. The storm from the City of Frivolity was following her.

"No," she said to the storm front. "You may not come here."

As if in reply, a great blast of thunder rang out.

Seta sighed. "All right, you've had your say. Now I want you to hush up. I need to cross back through that forest and find my way back to the door that brought me here. I don't need rain and mud to slow me down."

The rain didn't stop. Patiently, she sat on the ground, cross-legged, staring down the storm clouds as if sheer will could force them away. It didn't work. All it did was make her tired and hungry. For a while, she did sleep, catching up for all that she had missed the previous night.

She woke up near sunset, knowing it was time to find shelter or begin her trek through the forest in the rain. Both choices displeased her. If only there were a door to her world somewhere nearby.

There *had* to be one. In the hallway, one of the doors had led directly to this land. If only she could remember what the view had been exactly. The forest had not been in the view, so perhaps the door was hidden amongst the bordering trees. She plodded from tree to tree, her arms feeling the spaces between them for any hint of a camouflaged door.

Night settled in before she had even covered a third of the distance required to successfully eke out the door. Seta was so engrossed in her search she didn't see the horse until her back bumped against its hide. It whinnied.

"Where did you come from?" she murmured as she moved around to the animal's face. The horse was bridled. A large pack was hooked to the back of the saddle. Seta felt her pulse quicken.

"Who do you belong to?"

A crunch of nettles on the ground to the left of her sent her flying to the nearest tree. She crouched behind it.

"Don't be afraid," a man's voice spoke gently. "I'm Prince Dawson of the house of Ellison. I'm the third son of the queen who rules what most people call the City of Frivolity." He paused. "You may have heard me called Prince Drudgery." There was a lilt to his voice as if he wasn't sure whether he found his nickname amusing or hurtful. When Seta still didn't reply, he continued, "I played the violin for you last night. Will you come out from behind the tree so that we might meet properly? I've come a long way to find you."

Dawson had ready-to-eat food. He had supplies for a tent, but he didn't know how to assemble it. Seta did it for him and started a fire. When the meal was over, Dawson began to pick at his violin strings. He'd pulled it out when Seta showed him the flute she'd scavenged off its player.

"Did you know her?"

"Lorna? Yes." His top lip was larger than his lower lip. It seemed even larger to Seta because of the way it stuck out ever so slightly in the middle, like a sheet folded over to cover the satin lining of a blanket. "She was a Worker. It doesn't surprise me that she sacrificed herself. That is the thinking of Workers. They're not paid to work. Their religion teaches them to work for the good of all."

"And the rest of you take advantage of them."

"If they're willing to work…" To her surprise, he cut himself off, perhaps realizing what he was saying. "I try to help when I can. I learned to play the violin." He raised the instrument to his chin. Seta stopped him before he began to play.

"Playing the violin is very nice," she told him, "but it is no good to anybody unless you play it with a purpose."

Dawson pressed the violin against his chest. "Like your ballad." He pronounced the word carefully, waiting for her nod to see if he got it right.

"Not just ballads," Seta said. "Music serves emotion. All your orchestra plays are dances. The players are Workers. Slaves. Playing only so people can dance. That is not what music is about."

"Playing so slowly was…invigorating. And your dance… Beautiful! I was enraptured."

Seta hoped the fire would camouflage the redness of her cheeks. "I wanted something from the heart."

He moved toward her on one knee. "That is why I'm here. Your music moved me. I believe that I feel something in my heart, too. Love. For you."

Seta stood and turned her back. She didn't want to hear about love. She most certainly wouldn't accept love blooming from a silly dance at a ridiculous party.

"That's not what I meant about coming from the heart."

"Then teach me. Come back to Frivolity with me. Marry me."

Now he was on his feet, standing behind her, his fingers hovering above her shoulders. The tingling sensation made her body ache with longing. She turned around sharply to face him. He lowered his hands.

"I don't want to teach you about music. I don't want you to love me because I dance to your violin playing."

His petal-shaped eyes wilted. "I had thought you might feel something for... I came looking for you because I thought you were the only woman in Frivolity who might appreciate..."

"Prince Drudgery," she finished for him. He nodded. "You are hardly what I would call dull."

That brought a smile to his funny lips, and that in turn made her relax.

They sat back down by the fire. She told him about Gabriel. How he'd professed his love. How he'd stolen her money. How he had broken her heart. Then she told him about the horses, the army, and the war. He listened eagerly and asked many questions. At last she said, "I saw this land and thought it would be perfect for rebuilding. I need to bring my people here to start again. Can you understand that? I owe it to them."

Dawson in all seriousness said, "I would like to help."

Seta shook her head. "I don't see how Frivolity could be helpful to us at all. We want to build a real society, not a slave society." He winced.

They were both silent for a while.

"Dawson?" He looked up from the fire. "Do you know anything about three magical doors that lead to other worlds? I came in through one of them back in Frivolity. There's another in these parts. I'm sure of it."

"Magical doors?" he repeated thoughtfully. "There have always been stories. It's legend that our great-great-grandmother came from another world through a door in an enchanted castle and founded Frivolity. The story goes that her world had become too bleak for her, so she came to a world where things could be happy all the time. If I remember the stories correctly, she came back and forth many times to choose people to bring with her and supplies. Then unwanted people began to follow her in search of her secret door. She sent friends to find a remote, unwelcome place and build a new door in the hallway that would deter people. It stands to reason it would lead to this empty land."

"Do you think you could help me find it? Tonight?"

Dawson frowned. "Couldn't we wait until morning?"

Seta pointed toward the sky. "It'll be raining by morning. I'd say it's due to rain within the next hour or so." She looked around playfully. "Where do you plan to sleep tonight, Dawson?"

His eyes moved to the open flap of the tent, but his mouth said uncertainly, "Out here?"

"Well," Seta said, "if you take me to that door now, you can spread out *inside* that dry tent all night long."

Clearly this wasn't the plan he'd hoped for, but he agreed. They doused the fire and headed for the forest border again.

As they walked, Dawson explained what they were looking for. "It might be hard to see at night, but what we'll find are unsightly gashes on several clustered trees. The door was built from the wood of those trees. Only a hundred years or so have passed, so the damage might still be evident. I would also venture a guess that the trees would be easy to get to, because it was built in a hurry."

"It is a poorly made door."

"She wanted it to look uninviting. So people would see the two doors in the hallway, thinking nothing of them, and turn away."

"But the door has a window."

"That was added later," Dawson said. "After the queen's death, the people of Frivolity desired new people to come to the city to make it interesting again. When visitors could see what little existed here, they opted to go to the city."

Seta walked past him and kept studying the bark of the trees. To the left of her some of the deep brown bark gave way to a pumpkin color. Ever alert, she moved toward it and found that, yes, these were the tampered-with trees. Fit snugly between them, nearly invisible, was the third door.

She put out her hand to open it. Dawson put his hand over hers to pull her away. "Come home with me. It would be easier than this. You'll have responsibility for nothing. I could take care of you. Your people will survive without you. You don't even know if they'll accept your help."

"Dawson," she said. "Tell me about the middle door. Where does that lead?"

"A middle door? I only know of two doors."

"It is dark, huge, and features the same intricate carvings as the carriage doors in Frivolity. And it's locked."

"It sounds like a door I've seen in our castle. I've never seen anyone come through it. Why?"

Seta took her hand from him. "I didn't like that door."

She pulled the door open and saw some of the familiar red velvet wall.

"Come back," Dawson said. "I'll wait for you."

"I'll be back, but I make no promises."

And she stepped through the door, leaving the easy life behind her.

The reception at home was hardly warm.

"Back already?" were her father's words when she entered the front door of their house. No questions about the tattered golden ball gown she still wore under the fringed blanket she'd found in the castle and was using as a cloak.

The journey back had taken much longer than the journey out, for her horse had either run off or was stolen.

Her father sat in the only chair. "Why did you come back?"

"I found something to help everyone I've hurt."

"Nothing you can do will ease their hurt," the widower said.

That hushed her right up. She headed for her bedroom, once crammed by her and her brothers, now full of empty beds and dust. She put on a practical dress. Taking a deep breath, Seta left her room, intending to head past her father and out the door without another word.

He stopped her with a question she hardly expected.

"What did you find?"

Seta's heart lurched. Could her father actually be interested in hearing what she'd discovered? Would he want to be part of it? Trying to conceal both her excitement and the tears threatening to fall, Seta took a step toward him.

"I found a place where we could start over."

Her father brushed a hand across his face, waving her words away. "There's no such place. If there were, it would've been taken by now."

"No one knows about it but me," Seta insisted. "Come with me. I'll show you. You can help me convince the townspeople to come, too."

"I won't do anything of the sort."

The hope fled. Seta straightened up and brushed her hair out of her face. "I know I can make things better."

"You're a fool," her father told her. "You're going to tell the people here to abandon this village for nothing. What's left of their homes will be ransacked. What's left of our land will be plundered. And what about your brothers? Who will be here for them when they return?"

It was painful to say, but say it she must. "Do you really think my brothers are going to come home?" Few soldiers ever returned to their families after fighting in this war.

Her father bit his lower lip and looked away.

"I'll be coming back for the horses," Seta informed him.

"Those horses belong to the army." The man coughed. "I'll tell them where you went."

"No, you won't. You want our people to be safe again as much as I do. You'll help us at least that much."

"They'll kill me."

One last time, Seta offered, "Come with us then."

Her father shook his head. "No." The word was as quiet as the dust landing on the shelves.

She walked back into the heart of town to confront a mob of angry villagers.

"Kill her! She'll only cause more harm!"

Rocks flew as soon as she was within range.

The voice of Annelle Brugher rang above the din. "Stop! Stop! She's come here with a vision! For your own sakes, stop!"

From what people told Seta afterward, Annelle had stepped in front of the crowd and raised her hands to the sky. Some rocks hit her before people realized she was there.

"You throw stones at the people who help you," she accused.

One man stepped forward. "We're sorry if any of us hurt you, Annelle. But the girl…"

Again, voices rose in anger at Seta, but the rocks stayed in hands.

"The girl has come back to tell us something," Annelle said. "I sent her to find a place. A place few know about. She wants to bring you there."

"Why should we do what she wants? Her ideas have only brought doom on us in the past."

Annelle leaned over Seta's still body. "Because she's going to take you to a better life."

It had taken many words, and words continued to be needed as the group moved farther and farther away from the village. To motivate people into stealing horses from the ranch, knowing that they could be shot by archers, Seta had had to describe the natural vitality of the new world repeatedly, each time with new verve. To implore people to pack only their most necessary belongings and leave homes and memories behind, Seta had to preach about the new beginnings and fresh histories to be made. To drive them onward despite the army tracking them, Seta had had to tell them the story of Prince Dawson's great-great-grandmother, who had made the journey and begun a whole new society. And finally, to get them to enter the fragile castle, horses and all, Seta had had to remind them that once they crossed through the door, they would bar it from the inside so no one else could get in, and they would never have to go out again.

When, at last, they stepped through the door into the free land that awaited them, Seta was lifted upon shoulders and hailed as their leader. She became queen of what they named the Land of Renewal.

The people of Renewal remained so busy building their village, tending to their crops, and learning the cycles of the weather that they hadn't had time to explore the forest. Seta ordered her people to stay far from the City of Frivolity, and they had. That's why, when a carriage punctured the green wall of the forest and drove onto Renewal's main avenue, general panic ensued.

"What is all the shouting about?" Seta asked the seer, getting up from the desk in her parlor to look out the window.

The people were so tightly packed around the carriage it was barely visible, and the driver seemed to be missing.

"I've got to stop them before they hurt someone."

"You know the carriage," Annelle said.

"I know it's from the City of Frivolity," Seta answered. "That gives me a pretty good idea who might be inside it."

"If you're going to marry him, you ought to keep him from being murdered first."

Seta's jaw dropped. "Marry him? What an absurd thing to say."

Annelle smiled slyly. "Hurry."

"People!" Seta hollered as soon as she stepped outside. She pushed her way through the crowd. "Control yourselves!"

At the touch of her commanding hand, each person pivoted to see who had the audacity to interrupt their rioting. When they saw that the hand belonged to their leader, they backed away.

"This is inexcusable!" she shouted at her public. "Where is the driver?"

Jake Fell, the cobbler, grimaced. "I knocked him off the bench. Alex hauled him over to the water trough and dumped him in."

Seta took in the sight of the Frivolity driver struggling to get out of the trough and sighed. "Get him out and make sure he's all right."

"Yes, Your Highness."

She stepped toward the carriage door. She heard the sharp intake of breath from the people circled around her.

"It's all right. This carriage came from the City of Frivolity." In a voice darker than she intended to use, Seta said, "I recognize the door."

This time, she did not let the door intimidate her. She put her hand on the long handle and pulled it toward her. Prince Dawson sat inside, calm, patient, his violin case at his side as though he'd been protecting it.

"Are you all right?" she asked him.

"Quite, thank you," he returned. He brushed back his dark hair and smiled without showing his teeth. That thick top lip of his was pressed down like a duck's beak. "I don't suppose you'd be interested in escorting me through this convocation, would you? I have a dim inkling that they respect you."

Seta laughed slightly. "Believe it or not, Prince Dawson, I've become Queen."

"I suspected as much. I suppose I should bow."

"Oh no," she said, offering him a hand to assist his exit. "No formalities between us."

"I'm glad you feel as I do," he said, taking her hand and kissing it.

Not much in the way of work was done in Renewal that day. Most people stood in the street outside Seta's grand house, hoping to catch a glimpse of the prince through the window. Already, rumors passed about the handsome prince come to take their queen away. In a fine uniform of navy blue, buttoned with gold and cuffed with red, he looked quite dashing indeed. She could see why her people might feel concern.

"Why the uniform?" Seta asked after tea had been served.

With a twinge of embarrassment, he said, "My eldest brother fears that your people will invade. He decided we should have an army."

"An army? In Frivolity?" Seta couldn't imagine it at all. "Who would fight?"

Dawson stammered, "No one really. It's a fake army. Looks only. A lot of the men like the idea of uniforms, but no one wants to take the time to learn how to plan defense strategies or even to shoot a firearm."

Seta took a sip of the tea to prevent her smirk from being seen. "We're not going to attack you, but I must say that it doesn't seem wise to come here and tell me that you have a fake army protecting your city."

Dawson grinned and nodded. "I know that. I tried to convince Michael that your intentions were not on conquering us, but he said I had to prove it by bringing you back as my wife. Allying our lands. Mother agreed with him and the decision was made, not to my distaste, mind you, since it had been my intention all along." Dawson placed his teacup and saucer on the table beside him and leaned forward, taking Seta's free hand in his. "Frivolity can't fear attack when it knows that I am married to Renewal's queen."

Seta had heard enough. It was one thing for Dawson to propose marriage when it sounded like love might exist; it was another to suggest a marriage for political advantage. She'd had everything stolen from her by a fiancé before. Why should it be any different this time?

"Frivolity might think that Renewal then belongs to Frivolity. Isn't this marriage a convenient way to usurp my land? Don't you think the lazy, slave-owning people of your society would love to come over here and take advantage of my hard-working citizens?"

Seta stood and walked toward the window. Looking at her people out there, so interested in what she was doing, Seta couldn't help but feel her responsibility to them.

Dawson followed her. "You don't understand..."

Seta responded, "I spent a night with your people. It was enough to convince me never to return to your city. Let your family know that I despise the City of Frivolity and all it stands for. I will not attempt to stake claim on it. What would I do with a land full of slovenly, indulgent people?"

"We're not all lazy," he tried. "Some of our people work very hard."

"Harder than they have to and with no reward for their service. Your Workers, as you call them. Think how much easier their lives would be if your elite learned to tend for themselves." Seta motioned to the window with her thumb. "Tell me. Who carved the door to your carriage?"

"A Worker."

"Does he have a name?"

Dawson shrugged. "I don't know it. Why?"

"What did he get for making that intricate door, that door that represents your home? Did he get paid? Did he get food to eat? Did he get so much as a thank you?"

"He got the satisfaction of a job well done," Dawson said.

Seta was amazed with the ease Dawson had at explaining away exploitation. "Why didn't you make the door yourself?"

As she suspected, Dawson couldn't answer. He stared at her blankly, not understanding. After a moment, he returned a question, a challenge.

"Did you help build this luxurious house?"

Seta smiled. "As a matter of fact, I did." She put her hand on the drapes pulled back from the windowpane. "I sewed these." She pointed to the desk and chair. "I built and polished those." She did a small twirl with her arms wide about her. The people outside might have thought she was dancing. "I helped raise the walls. I painted the floral pattern on them. I—"

"I get it," Dawson interrupted, sitting back down.

Seta knew she had gone beyond what was needed to explain herself and allowed humility to creep back into her demeanor. She too sat and resumed drinking her tea.

To break through the uneasiness, Seta said, "I see you brought your violin."

"I had thought we might play some music. Some ballads." He pronounced the word carefully. It softened her face. His remained downcast.

"I haven't had time to learn how to play Lorna's flute as yet."

He sat up sharply. "It doesn't matter."

"Dawson, I…"

Alarm filled her. He was going to leave now, right after she had told him she hated everything he stood for. But she didn't hate *him*. In fact, she felt rather attached to him. She'd be very glad if he stayed.

That was it. If she could keep Dawson from Frivolity, then he could learn her ways. He could create. Make music.

And they could be together.

"Dawson," she said. Her heart beat ferociously. "Please stay here. Don't go back."

"My family will think you have killed me or imprisoned me."

"Then return briefly to tell them you are coming here of your own free will."

"Are you asking me to stay here as your husband?"

It would have been easy to say yes, but Seta had a responsibility to her people. She could not marry until she trusted him. "No, Dawson. I'm not asking you to marry me." His head drooped. "In time, maybe," she offered, meaning it. "I do care for you."

"Without certainty of marriage, I can't stay here," he said. "What reason would I have? My people wouldn't understand."

Seta didn't know how to convince him. This was much harder than convincing her people to follow her into unknown lands. They had nothing and were persecuted. Dawson had everything he could want. Words failed her.

Dawson stood. He picked up his violin case and held it to his chest. "Do you really believe that you and I could have a future together?"

Seta nodded. "Just not now," she said quietly.

"How can I show you that I love you and will be who you need me to be?"

Seta put her hand on his cheek and stroked it lightly with her thumb. Before she could speak, Annelle Brugher banged the doors open and entered. She approached them and bowed sharply. As she raised her head, she locked her eyes on Dawson. "If ever you come back here, Prince Dawson, Seta will know the instant she sees your carriage whether you and she are ready to be wed." With that, she turned and exited the room, leaving them both at a loss for words.

As the sky darkened, Seta watched Dawson help his injured driver into the carriage. The prince from Frivolity sat on the driver's bench, picked up the reins, and drove the carriage back to the forest. The gestures of caring and self-reliance did not go unnoticed.

Years passed. Though many citizens of Renewal made the trip across the forest to visit the City of Frivolity, none stayed long. Often, they returned with Workers who longed to be part of the community spirit of Renewal. No war was ever fought between the two cities, for neither had ever organized a real army, and it was clear early on that the two societies could exist without one another.

Seta spent most of her days alone since Annelle died. The loss of her confidant and spiritual guide hit Seta hard. Despite the fact that everyone in Renewal relied upon her, Seta had no one with whom she could share her time.

The man she wanted had never come back to her. Annelle had promised that he would. That had been the only premonition the seer ever made that Seta didn't believe. She swore that Annelle had only said it to appease her.

Seta stood at the window in her parlor. Always her favorite room. The curtains still held the aroma of Annelle's incense. The flute she'd finally learned to play rested on the end table next to Dawson's empty teacup. What she liked most about the room had always been the noise from the street below that trickled through the window. The occasional laughter and greetings being passed warmed her heart and reminded her of why she had brought them here.

The sun was setting, disappearing gradually behind the forest, making the sky glow in all shades of yellow and orange. From the place where the avenue ended and the forest began came a carriage. It was bright, as if the sun was pushing through one last burst of light between the tree trunks. The crudely constructed carriage made of raw wooden boards, neither painted nor sanded down, creaked as it rolled on its uneven wheels. The one horse leading it swerved back and forth to make up for the rocky load.

Seta giggled as the carriage came closer. Who had made this atrocity? How the thing held together at all, Seta couldn't imagine.

The carriage stopped below her window. The driver hopped down from the bench, but he did not open the carriage door to let out any passenger. Instead, he took off his hat. He ran a hand through his brown curls and turned around to face her window. He smiled at Seta, opened his arms wide to present the carriage, and then raised one arm to her.

"Dawson!" she squealed.

"Come down here, Seta, my queen! Come down here and marry me!"

Seta flung wide the window panes and leaned out into the fresh air. "Did you make that thing?" she asked, laughing and crying all at once.

"With my own two hands," Dawson said. "I built a house of my own, too, but I wouldn't suffer you to live in it. I thought I could come and stay here with you. Make myself useful. If you'll have me."

Seta wanted to jump right out the window into his arms. She could hardly stand the thought that she'd have to wait the extra few moments it would take to run down the stairs and out the front door.

"Wait! Don't move!"

Seta rushed through her house, fixing her hair and face as she tripped down the steps. In moments, she was pressing her trembling lips to his. When she looked up into his eyes, Seta knew her next choice had already been made.

D. G. Driver is thrilled to have another story in an FOF anthology. Her favorite genre to write is contemporary fantasy, but she dabbles in romance, contemporary, and horror (such as her story "Mother's Night Out" in Fantastic Creatures*). She likes to write about female characters finding their strength, such as the teen activist who discovers mythical creatures in The Juniper Sawfeather Trilogy or the bullied sister of an autistic brother in* No One Needed to Know*. If you enjoyed "The Hallway of Three Doors", you will also enjoy her brand new romantic fairy tale novella* The Royal Deal.*

www.dgdriver.com

Door Number Four

Bokerah Brumley

Chapter One

"All doors lead to purpose." — *Colonel Mzuzi Blackfox, C.C.C., retired*

It was testing day at the Academy of Future Creature Caretakers.

Fourteen-year-old Rase Flannigan closed the front door behind him and started down the walk. His mother beamed at him from the window. He didn't have to turn around to appreciate the busting warmth of it.

He wasn't looking forward to disappointing her.

He'd heard all the rumors. Students said the testing rooms contained engineered scenarios in artificial worlds.

Rase didn't know what to believe. He sighed. Not that it mattered. The corridor of doors stood between each cadet and an invitation to the C.C.C.

Real or not, he suspected he'd get the bad news tomorrow: he'd flunked out of the program. He knew it right down to the magic in his bone marrow, but his footsteps still ate away the distance between his parents' home and the school.

Overhead, the mint green sky shimmered with a Weather Keeper's magic, and a handful of spots developed. A moment later, the specks grew to fluffy pink clouds. The apprentice was getting better.

At the corner, his best friend, Agon, waved. The impending exam had Rase's stomach in knots, and he didn't want to talk about Amelia, Agon's latest artist crush. Instead of stopping, Rase waved back and then snapped his fingers and a single flame danced over his fingertips. He kept it alive for five blocks before it winked out. At least he was getting better at holding his spells.

A handful of other recruits collected in front of the Academy, milling about, visiting before sessions began. Most of them were reluctant to go inside, but Rase was early. He wanted to get a little more study time in before nine bells rang.

If Rase failed his final, he wouldn't be invited to join the Creature

Caretakers Corps. Only one in four recruits made it into the C.C.C. Agon had a backup plan. Rase didn't. He had never wanted to be anything other than a creature caretaker. He wanted to hear about an animal in need and rescue it. From the time he was small, the dream of joining the C.C.C. had filled him up. Helping defenseless creatures made him happy in a way nothing else had.

When Rase reached for the door, an exposed bulb above the entrance flashed red, and a warning buzzer blared at him. An eyeball, as big as his skull and hanging from a vine, dipped down between the foliage of the leafy casing and gave him a once-over. Behind him, snickers rolled through the crowd of students. A cranky voice commanded, *Announce yourself, Recruit.* The words were projected into Rase's mind.

Rase grimaced and dropped his hand. Distracted by worry, he'd forgotten to project. *Rookie mistake.* The psychic guard plant didn't recognize anyone by sight. The building was covered in it for just that reason. Shapeshifters could look like anyone. Glamours could overcome visuals, too. The security guard had been grown from an off-world cutting and recognized brainwaves and patterns. Since the C.C.C. had started using him, they'd had no cross-realm infiltrations. At least, that's what Rase had overheard in the corridors.

Rase thought of the sentient herbage structure. He projected an image of himself and his identity. *Rase Flannigan. Third-year recruit.* He thought the words one at a time. *Rhymes with shenanigan,* he added.

Ah, Rase. The crimson light turned a happy yellow. *Good luck on your test today.* The monocular withdrew, tilting and bouncing cheerfully. At least the architecture was in a decent mood that morning. It could be a mercurial plant when rules weren't observed. The entrance hissed as the precautionary sealing spell disengaged and the glass slid out of the way.

"Thanks," Rase muttered. He marched inside with his chin up and shoulders back. Maybe pretend confidence would conjure the faith in himself that he lacked. He moved into the fifteen-story open-air atrium. The Academy classrooms took up the lower two floors, administration took up one level above that, and no cadet was allowed above the third floor. The Creature Caretaker Corps took up the remaining twelve floors.

He took a right at the next corridor and slipped into Professor Blackfox's lecture hall. The dark-haired man stood at the chalkboard, writing his *Ten Commandments of Testing*, his back to the rows of student desks. Professor Blackfox had retired from the C.C.C. with honors, and he'd been teaching at the Academy ever since.

"Mr. Flannigan," he said without turning, his voice still deep and strong.

"Professor." Rase took a seat in the middle of the second row.

"Nervous about your exam?" The chalk scratched against the blackboard.

I.   *Thou shalt not cheat.*

"Something like that." Rase grimaced. It was exactly like that.

Professor Blackfox didn't stop writing. "You could apply for a fourth year."

II. *Thou shalt not waste time.*

Rase didn't answer. He didn't deserve to be there. His parents had already sacrificed enough for him. When he exhibited signs of creature talent, they packed up and moved into the capital so he could attend the Academy. He hadn't been smart enough to earn any scholarships, but that hadn't stopped them. If their son wanted to join the C.C.C., then he would. For them, it was that simple.

Yet, if Rase wasn't smart enough to make it through the Academy then *that* would have to be his answer. Maybe he could get someone else to deliver the news when he failed. Rase sighed. He didn't deserve his parents. They'd sacrificed jobs they loved so he could chase a dream.

Professor Blackfox stopped writing. "I can recommend you for a fourth year, but I don't think you'll need it, Mr. Flannigan." Then Blackfox smiled.

Rase jumped as though he'd been slapped. *Who is this and what has he done with the professor?* The man waited for a response. Rase plastered a grin on his face. "Thanks."

"In the world of animal rescue, remember that *no* attempt is far worse than attempting, risking, and getting it wrong." Blackfox held Rase's gaze a moment longer then turned back to his task, the chalk squeaking louder than before. Over his shoulder, he said, "In the C.C.C., each door leads to a new test, a new opportunity to show your skills. Use each one as though a world depends on it."

III. *Thou shalt do that which ye know.*

Rase scanned the classroom. Professor Blackfox had encouraged him and nobody was there to witness it. The man hadn't looked happy in three years.

Rase smoothed his hand over his face. He couldn't decide if the morale boost made his nervousness worse or not. When Professor Blackfox finished writing, he dusted off his hands and strolled to his office adjacent to the classroom.

Rase tugged his leather-bound textbook from his backpack but only stared at the pages. He knew most of the spells, and he wasn't about to learn the remainder of them while he was brain-bound with worry about passing the test. There wasn't anything else he could learn in the little bit of time he had left. Instead, he planned how he would tell his parents he'd failed them.

Ten minutes into his melancholy, the next student arrived. Jess, a candidate for valedictorian, waved at Rase and took a seat in the front row. She twisted her brown hair into a long strand, piled it on top of her head, and shoved a pencil through it. She turned around. "Are you ready for the big day?"

Rase shrugged. "Maybe. Maybe not." Mostly not, but he didn't want to admit it.

"I hope I get a mammal," she said.

"A good door can make all the difference." Rase dropped the tome back into his bag. No use pretending to study. The portal—the mission—could make all the difference in the world, and that fact had his stomach in knots. Rase had particular ability with reptiles and birds. Jess favored mammals. More students wandered in, and Jess straightened in her seat.

Professor Blackfox entered from the opposite side of the room. "Five minutes, students," he barked and ducked back out.

Two minutes before nine bells, a collection of disheveled students shuffled in—Jess called them the "crammers." They pulled all-nighters, cramming for their magic exams, trying to remember spells and skills and talents on half a minute of sleep. Though about half of them managed to keep a passing grade, most of them were students who had been enrolled by hopeful parents. The group took their seats, yawning and wiping sleep from bleary eyes. They'd probably been up all night preparing for the test.

At precisely nine bells, Professor Blackfox crossed to his dais and began roll call, moving quickly through the thirty-some-odd students in alphabetical order. Once completed, he placed his hands on either side of the lectern.

Rase leaned forward. He knew so little about the testing process. *Doors.* That's all he knew. Doors were the physical representation of the portals that led to each and every mission for the C.C.C.

"Remember the *Ten Commandments of Testing.*"

Race glanced at the words on the board. He didn't have to read them. In varying order, they appeared every day. All the students should have known them by heart, and he did.

"Students," Professor Blackfox went on, "this is the last time I will see your morning faces. It's been a memorable three years. Some of you have impressed me," he glanced at Jess, "and others have continued to show up." His gaze swept across the cramming crowd. He lifted the lectern top and retrieved a stack of cream-colored envelopes. "Your tests have been randomly preassigned by Dean Romero."

He stepped down off of the podium and to the right, carrying the testing assignments. He raised his free hand toward a blank wall and muttered to himself. Without preamble, the wood paneling dissolved to show a thick, red square with what looked like a steering wheel from a sailing ship in the middle.

Academy Testing had been inscribed vertically across the surface.

Everyone gasped, Rase included. They'd never seen Professor Blackfox use magic, and none of them had any idea that the testing corridor had been there the whole time. Professor Blackfox ignored their surprise and turned the large handle, spinning it around until mechanisms whirred and clicked. He tapped a circle in the middle of the locking wheel, and the door popped open to reveal an anteroom that resembled a black cube with a predominately white corridor out the other side and beyond.

Professor Blackfox marched into the space. He did an about-face and waved toward the exit. "This is your testing corridor. Please line up in alphabetical order—that would be the order of roll call—and make your way here." He pointed to the pale marble floor and a dark line appeared. He clasped his hands behind his back. "Despite what you may have heard, everything that happens today is as real as working for the C.C.C. Animals may die by your inaction."

Rase swallowed as the warning took hold. That wasn't the rumor they had all heard. It changed everything. If an animal disappeared from a planetary ecosystem, the maturation trajectory of a whole world could be irrevocably damaged.

Rase caught Jess's eye. She bit her bottom lip and then looked away.

Hushed, the students followed the instruction in orderly fashion, more in awe of their teacher than they had been in three years. It was against the rules for cadets to use magic outside of the designated areas inside the Academy, and they'd never seen Professor Blackfox use it before.

"First student, please approach," Professor Blackfox called. Jess had taken her place a few spots ahead of Rase, but she wasn't first.

Rachel Anderson had that honor. She chewed on her fingernails as she joined Professor Blackfox. He waved his hand, and a dark wall descended from the ceiling and settled between the waiting students and the anteroom. The screen effectively kept the proceedings inside private.

A few minutes later, the wall dissolved. Rachel had moved into the corridor beyond the anteroom, and Professor Blackfox bellowed, "Next!" The next student made his way forward.

Rase shifted from side to side. He considered biting his own nails, but the habit drove his mother crazy. With each step forward, his knees got shakier and shakier. Then it was his turn.

"Next!"

He darted into the room and almost lost his balance on the slick floor. Professor Blackfox waved his hand and the privacy screen lowered. The students outside disappeared. Rase glanced around. The air was different, sounds beyond the cube were muffled, a world unto itself.

Professor Blackfox took an envelope from the stack. "Mr. Flannigan, you have been assigned door number four." He passed the paper to Rase. "Remember that the magic restrictions have been lifted. Remember your training, Mr. Flannigan." He leaned forward. "And everything that happens in that room came from an animal distress call. It's as real as anything that the officers of the C.C.C. encounter in actual missions. "

Rase stared at the spell-sealed paper rectangle. "Do you know what scenario is behind my door?"

"It's luck of the draw." Professor Blackfox raised an eyebrow.

"Life-or-death decisions?" He didn't need another reason to stress about the test, but there it was.

Professor Blackfox leaned away. "As previously defined, your actions irrevocably impact the universe inside that door." He crossed his arms. "Mr. Flannigan, would you like to decline testing or shall I go on?"

"Please continue." Rase swallowed. The rumors had been wrong. He lifted his gaze and nodded. The paper weighted his hand, a metric ton of responsibility.

Professor Blackfox pointed at the space ahead of them. "When the privacy spell lifts, travel down the corridor. The exits are arranged in sequential order. You will have a few minutes to read your instructions and then you must open your door. Do not dally. The portal will disappear when you close the door behind you. At that moment, your timer will begin. The gateway will reappear when you complete your task or your time runs out. Whichever comes first." Professor Blackfox extended his hand and Rase took it, pumping it up and down. "Good luck, Rase. It has been an honor serving as your professor."

The wall behind him disappeared and revealed the monochromatic testing corridor. Doors lined the length of the hall. Each scarlet door was the same as the next, each one an equal distance from the ones before and after. There must have been hundreds of them. A different number sparkled over each one. Door zero was to his left, door one to his right.

Rase licked his lips. His future was only a few steps down the hall.

Chapter Two

"The job isn't finished until you close the door behind you." — Colonel Mzuzi Blackfox, C.C.C., retired

Rase stepped into the ivory corridor. "Thanks, Professor Blackfox." Jess was nowhere in sight, but Rase hoped she'd gotten her mammal wish.

Without preamble, Professor Blackfox yelled, "Next!"

Rase glanced back to see the check-in process for the cadet who had been behind him, but Professor Blackfox and the next student in line had disappeared from view. The screen spell must function like a two-way mirror, separating Rase from the incoming student to minimize distractions.

At door number four, Rase stopped. It wasn't the first time he'd stepped through a portal, but it was the first time his future depended on what happened behind a closed door.

The carmine door interrupted the pristine corridor. It unnerved him. With trembling hands, he lifted the envelope. *Door Number Four* had been scrawled underneath his name in an unfamiliar penmanship. Must have been Dean Romero's. Whatever was inside, it would decide how the next ten years of his life would go.

Chin up. Shoulders back.

That's what his father would have told him.

Naught left but to do it.

Delaying never helped anybody. He flipped the envelope over and tore into it, no longer caring about keeping it neat. His pulse pounded against his eardrums. He grasped the thin rectangle inside and eased it from its place.

Rase Flannigan

Save the Marken-Bray.

The Marken-Bray was a huge…wild…stubborn…three-horned…rainbow-striped equine. They hated him, and the feeling was mostly mutual. He dropped his hand with a snort. He'd gotten a door that would have been perfect for Jess.

Too soon, a whimper drew Rase's attention to the end of the hall. A crammer stood there, opening his assignment at door number one. *How long have I been standing here?*

The crammer nodded at Rase. "Good luck." He grasped the knob and disappeared into his assignment. The sound of the door closing echoed up and down the hall.

Rase took a deep breath, his pulse pounding in his eardrums like thunder when the Weather Apprentice got the formula wrong. Magic was just outside of his reach. His palm tingled when he grabbed the handle.

A quarter twist and the door popped open. The salty smell of an ocean poured over him in humid bursts. He raised his hands, summoning the easiest thing he knew. Flames rolled over him without burning. Whatever was out there, at least he would wow it first.

Rase pressed against the door, moving it with his shoulder as he went. Portals were impervious to magical impact by design, so the fire Rase wore did not spread to the doorframe. Without a squeak, the door swung open to reveal a blue-sand beach, the expanse interrupted only by juts of black, volcanic rocks. A few meters from the surf, a thick jungle stretched to the right of the portal.

He stepped over the threshold and his boots sank into the sand. Heat from a red sun warmed the sand. He definitely wasn't dressed for a day at the beach. He pushed the door closed. When the latch clicked in the doorjamb, the portal disappeared.

In the real C.C.C., operatives were assigned special spells to conjure portals whenever or wherever they needed them. That magic must be taught in boot camp.

He scanned the area. Nobody. Nothing. Just him, as far as he could tell.

Rase dropped the fire spell, letting it slide off him. The flames winked out.

If the Marken-Bray wasn't on the beach, then it had to be nearby. A clue would come. With Professor Blackfox in charge, it wouldn't come unless he kept moving.

Thou shalt not waste time.

Rase started toward the rainforest. At the edge, he studied the undergrowth, looking for a path of some kind to indicate where others had gone before. Seeing none, he pressed his hands to his lips and repeated a blade spell he'd learned during the warfare unit.

His left side fluoresced, a wave of magic moved up and down the length of it until it formed a magic blade, an extension of his arm. He hacked at the leaves, some of them as big as he was. He cut into the forest, inching forward.

He burst into a clearing, the circumference made up of palm trees.

Perspiration dripped from his upper lip. His sweat-soaked uniform had grown uncomfortable. "Be gone," he said, waving his blade arm, and the magic machete disappeared. He unbuttoned his wet shirt, peeled it off, and tucked it into his belt, keeping his sleeveless undershirt. If he needed it, he could get it on in record time. Otherwise, it didn't make much sense to continue sweltering in a polyester blend.

Once done, Rase grimaced. *I let too much time go by.* "Hello?"

Something squawked, and Rase froze. He held his breath to try to identify which direction the sound came from. Another *squawk-be-gawk*.

The jungle seemed a strange place to keep a chicken. Grandmas kept chickens in yards. He'd healed one or two egg-bound hens for the older women of the neighborhood.

"Where are you? I'm here to help." Maybe the noisy bird would be his clue.

That noise again. From the other direction that time. Rase crouched down, peering through the gigantic foliage. It wasn't a Marken-Bray, but whatever it was would have to do.

An orange chicken, striped in green, stuck its head out from behind a palm tree stem. The black comb hung over one of its eyes, in the same way that Agon liked to keep his hair for Amelia. The rooster pecked at the bark then ducked back behind the big plant.

"How can I help you?" Rase's mouth twisted. Rather polite for poultry.

The chicken paused and then bolted into the clearing, moving in a jerky high step. Rase joined the anxious bird in the middle, reaching for it. Each time he almost caught it by the tail, it darted away.

It screeched at him and then launched itself into the greenwood like a sparkle-shot. That bird was the only thing remotely close to a mission that he'd come across since he'd gotten his assignment for door number four. It was almost as if they'd set him up to fail. He gritted his teeth.

Yet, Rase hesitated only a moment before he went barreling through the forest after it. Action was better than standing still. He clamped his mouth shut as a cloud of insects pelted his cheeks.

Glimpses of orange kept him going, leaping over felled trees and beneath hanging vines. On and on, the chicken ran until it came to a ravine. At first, Rase thought the bird had stopped beneath a large tree to rest, but the chicken moved dangerously close to the lip of the chasm.

Panting, Rase slowed. "What are you doing there?"

The rooster tilted its head, and its black comb flopped one way then the other. Rase eased closer, reaching out for the bird. "Don't do it, little man."

Then the chicken flung itself over the sheer rock face with a cry that sounded too much like Geronimo.

"Chickens," Rase muttered. Maybe that hadn't had anything at all to do with his assignment. He had probably just wasted his whole testing. He eased to the edge, leaning just far enough forward to see over the side and down into the valley so far below.

No doubt about it.

That door number four was much bigger on the inside.

A color flash caught Rase's eye. Slack-jawed, he stared.

A Marken-Bray lay on a rock shelf below, a nasty gash stretching across its shoulder. Purple blood had splashed onto the surfaces of the surrounding rocks. From the angle, he could tell that the creature was female. He just had to get down there, do some suturing, maybe some healing, and then get the Marken-Bray mare back up.

He'd found his assignment.

The idiot chicken had been the key.

The cliff had no vines, no rope, and no way down. He had to improvise.

Quickly, Rase removed his shirt. He tied one long arm of his shirt to a sturdy tree that clung to the rim of the canyon. He wrapped the wrist of the other long sleeve around his hand. He squeezed his eyes closed, and then he stepped off the cliff and into the air.

Backward, he stepped down the sheer rock face, glad for the added grip of his thick-soled cadet boots. In only four steps, he reached the end of his shirt. Hanging by the end of a sleeve, the distance to the ledge felt closer to a mile.

His mouth dried. His uniform didn't get him the whole way down. It barely reached a third of the way. *How could I have been so foolish?*

He'd worked with what he'd had. According to Professor Blackfox, that was admirable. Besides, he could jump the last little bit. He took a deep breath and blew it out through his nose. He combined a cloud spell with a soft spell. The result was more like a giant pillow, like something a Weather Keeper might make. He tossed the bundle of magic down beside the Marken-Bray. If he aimed right, maybe he could land on it.

Now or never.

Rase pressed his lips together and jumped, aiming for the magic landing pad, spreading his arms wide, as though it might help slow his fall. When he landed, the Marken-Bray screamed and kicked at the air. The sound echoed up and down the gorge. Her wound gushed, spewing violet gore all over.

Rase muttered a healing spell, reaching for the nasty gash. The equine pulled her leg close and snapped at Rase's fingers with her teeth. Rase jumped back and nearly off the wall and into the ravine. He floundered, swinging his arms to help pitch his weight back where it needed to be.

His heartbeat pounded in his eardrums. He had to calm the beast enough to mend her wound. A lightning thought struck. Marken-Brays weren't comfortable with anyone they didn't know. Though talking sometimes calmed them.

"My name is Rase," he offered. "I've come to save you."

The Marken-Bray mare nickered and then she groaned. The sound sent a shudder through Rase. Her chest rose and fell; her whole body convulsed at the end of every exhale. He chewed on his bottom lip. She wasn't doing well.

She groaned again, shifting on the rocky landing. She was going to die. Rase was sure of it. If he didn't do something, she would die.

No. He couldn't let that happen.

He had to help the Marken-Bray. He had to make her better. Her life depended on it and so did his future. The C.C.C. was the only thing he'd ever wanted to do. If he couldn't pass his test… He took a step closer. She kicked at him, her forelegs swinging wildly.

Rase took a hoof to the chest, and he went sailing away, upward, and into the sheer cliff face. When he hit, the sharp edges gouged his bare back, and he tried to cry out but the impact had knocked the wind from his chest. He slid down, crumpling beside the Marken-Bray. He was trying to help something that didn't want his help.

It wasn't going to work. He took a long breath and then climbed to his feet, trembling from head to toe. His back stung from the cuts that ran parallel to his spine, and the stabbing pain nearly sent him back to his knees.

He considered taking a seat until his time ran out and the portal reappeared, but he'd promised to try. If he gave up, he would never forgive himself for not giving his all. If he didn't make it into the C.C.C., it shouldn't be for that. He owed it to himself…his parents.

Thou shalt not give up.

He had to try again.

With a strand of magic, Rase reached upward, slipping the simple filament into the knot that held his shirt to the tree trunk. He worked it, pulling one way and then the other until he'd loosened it enough that it slipped from its place and floated down to Rase's waiting arms beneath.

Trying was better than not-trying. He had to get her bleeding stopped. The mare couldn't take much more.

"I'm trying to help you," Rase soothed, his hand outstretched.

The animal whinnied with a shrill voice, a mad call of a wild animal.

Rase dove at the mare and threw his arms around the injured leg. "It's my job," he bellowed. She kicked and screamed, but Rase didn't give an inch or let go.

He tied his shirt over the wound on the Marken-Bray's leg, pulling the two arms tight. The uniform started to turn purple, but he created another filament, thinner this time. He threaded it between the two sides of the wound and tugged. He repeated that again and again, sewing the wound closed. The mare convulsed, and the ground shifted.

Oh no.

Rase grasped at the air, struggling to conjure something…anything…

In slow motion, the ledge gave way.

Chapter Three

"Don't get stuck on the other side of the door." — Colonel Mzuzi Blackfox, C.C.C., retired

Rase sat beside a rushing river, his knees pulled close. They were hundreds of feet below the rock ledge where the Marken-Bray had been stranded moments ago. She hadn't made a sound when they landed.

He wasn't sure how they'd wound up in one piece. They should both be dead. Maybe the equine was. He couldn't tell. She hadn't moved since he'd been seated beside her, staring at nothing, and mostly in shock.

He climbed to his feet. No way around it. He'd failed.

Beside him, the Marken-Bray dissolved. She left no trace, as though she had never been.

Moisture flooded Rase's eyes. Grit covered him, his skin like sandpaper. He rolled his shoulders to work out the kinks. He couldn't feel it yet, but he would be sore tomorrow.

Testing or not, that hadn't been at all what he had expected. Not at all. No matter how many times he read it in books, he never believed his attempt to save a creature might kill it. He never thought it would happen to him.

He could never tell his mom the story. He'd have to come up with something else to tell her. Maybe he could just stick to the part with the chicken.

A ruby door appeared where the mare had been, interrupting his planning.

Rase turned away, swiping at his wet cheeks. He cleared his throat and tried to pull himself together for the bad news. A creature had died as a result of his choices. He had no place in the C.C.C.

The knob turned and Professor Blackfox strolled through, leading two men.

"Rase Flannigan," Professor Blackfox said, a smile on his face. He gestured to the others beside him. "This is Dean Romero." The taller, dark-haired man raised a hand. "And this is General Ito." The shorter man touched the brim of his cap. He wore the uniform of the C.C.C.

Rase studied the scuffed tips of his once-shiny boots. It was probably a good thing that he didn't need them anymore for the Academy. "Thank you for coming." He hunched his shoulders, wishing he could melt into the ground.

"Rase, you passed." Professor Blackfox sounded happy about the failure.

Then the words registered in Rase's brain. He frowned. "But we fell off the ledge. I don't know why I'm not dead and she is." His voice cracked and his chin quivered at the admission. In a weird twist of circumstance, he'd avoided the death he'd handed to the Marken-Bray. He didn't know how to tell his parents.

"That's true, but not once did that stop you from trying to help that Marken-Bray." Professor Blackfox chuckled. "I think the whole observation deck cheered when you launched yourself at that stubborn creature with no thought to your own safety."

How could his professor laugh?

There wasn't any way…

A revelation glimmered at the edge of his thoughts.

"None of it was real?" Rase rubbed his forehead, afraid to hope.

"Your injuries will have to heal, but this place," Professor Blackfox gestured, "isn't real."

"The mare wasn't really injured?"

Professor Blackfox shook his head. "I'm sorry for the lie, Rase, but we needed you to treat the test as though lives depended on your every action. The C.C.C. had to see how you might work in those real-world scenarios."

Rase opened his mouth, but no sound came out. He wasn't really responsible for the death of the Marken-Bray. The weight lifted from his shoulders.

General Ito stepped forward. "Son," he began, "I'd like to offer you a spot in the C.C.C. We need men like you."

"Congratulations, Rase Flannigan." Dean Romero offered his hand.

"What?"

"You passed. The C.C.C. is offering you a position." Professor Blackfox beamed at Rase, and Rase couldn't quite bring himself to smile back.

It was surreal. "The C.C.C. wants me?"

"We've had our eye on you for a long time." General Ito nodded.

"Let's get you cleaned up and on your way home. I'm sure your parents will appreciate hearing the news from you." Dean Romero stepped toward the door, and Rase followed.

Later, Rase lingered in the waiting area, hoping to find out how Jess had fared. He spun around when someone tapped him on the shoulder.

Agon grinned. "Didn't mean to startle you."

"It's fine." Rase crossed his arms, trying not to preen. He wanted to jump up and down. *Celebrate. Shout.* He'd been working for this moment for three long years. He hadn't needed a fourth year after all.

"How'd you do?" Agon asked, pushing his hand through his hair.

"I passed. You?"

A sheepish grin slid across Agon's face. "Blackfox said they would have to review the footage and make a judgment. They only say that so they don't have to deal with crying students on testing day. They'll send a rejection letter." He shrugged. "I won't pass."

"I'm sure you'll make it in." Rase meant to comfort Agon, but it came out trite.

"I won't." Agon squared his shoulders. "It doesn't bother me as much as I thought it might."

Rase was quiet a moment. "How did Jess do?"

"Wouldn't you like to know?" Agon winked. "She passed. She got pretty beat up, though. She said to tell you she'd be at the graduation party and she hoped you'd be there."

"Good for her." Rase's chest swelled to three times its normal size. He'd passed his test, and Jess wanted to meet him at the Academy ball. It was a day for good news.

Agon waved to an older man in a uniform, sitting on one of the city benches. "Dad wanted me to try." He snapped his fingers once, but nothing appeared over his fingertips. "Magic isn't my strong suit. I have an alternate plan. Something I've cooked up with Amelia."

"Will your father be disappointed?"

Agon shook his head. "No, I think he knew the C.C.C. wasn't for me."

The older man stood and smiled. "Agon, let's go." He tugged a pocket watch from his pants pocket. When he squeezed, the lid popped open and flashed in the sun. "Your mother will be setting supper."

Agon waved at his father. "I think I'm going to try art next." He started to leave but stopped and turned back. "It's kismet, Rase. You were meant to be here, I wasn't. I managed to get a decent education in the process. It wasn't all wasted." He nodded as though reaffirmed by the day's results. "See you around."

Rase watched the duo until they faded into the horizon, then he set his path toward home.

When he set foot on the sidewalk to his door, the front curtain shifted. His mom had been watching for him from the window. He'd been so sure of failure when he'd left that morning. His parents would be twice as happy as he was. They'd probably want to go out to dinner. He paused on the porch. The setting sun cast a rainbow across the sky.

"Rase? Is that you?" his mother called. She peeked through the window and the grin split her face nearly in two. "Did you pass?"

Rase took a deep breath and put his hand on the door handle. His heart was stuffed so full. He didn't know how to express any of it. He was about to deliver the news he never thought he'd have.

So he did the only thing he could.

He opened the door.

Ten Commandments of Testing
By Professor Blackfox

1) *Thou shalt not cheat.*
2) *Thou shalt not waste time.*
3) *Thou shalt do that which ye know.*
4) *Thou shalt not give up.*
5) *Thou shalt make educated guesses.*
6) *Thou shalt help all creatures, great and small.*

7) *Thou shalt esteem the lives of others above thy own.*

8) *Thou shalt do thy best.*

9) *Thou shalt not whine.*

10) *Thou shalt not dwell on past failures.*

Bokerah Brumley is a speculative fiction writer making stuff up on a trampoline in West Texas. She lives on ten permaculture acres with a host of creatures, five home-educated children, and one husband. She also serves as the blue-haired President of the Cisco Writers Club. Recently, she accepted novel contracts with Clean Reads Press and Liberty Island Media. She works as a part-time marketing associate for a New York press and also moonlights as an acquisitions editor for The Crossover Alliance.

http://www.bokerah.com/

Threshold

Laurie Lucking

I skimmed the last paragraph of my history assignment then flipped the textbook shut. Homework, check.

Stuffing the book into my backpack, I peeked out the window above my desk. Alexis was still out playing soccer with neighbor kids, and Mom and Dad would be engrossed in their reality show for at least another 45 minutes. Perfect.

The corners of my lips curved into a smile as I darted to my closet. After digging my flats out from under a pile of t-shirts, I tugged at the string hanging from the ceiling and lowered the heavy wooden ladder. I scrambled up then pushed open the trapdoor at the top.

A lazy breeze whirled past as I crawled through onto a patch of soft grass. I eased the door shut, sweet, floral scents filling my senses. Patches of flowers spread in every direction, interspersed with trees, shrubs, and fountains.

I loved garden days.

I took off down the path, pausing to admire a clump of lilies in an unusual shade of purple. Beyond, a collection of daisies smiled into the late afternoon sunshine.

"Heidi! We were hoping that was you."

Releasing the flower, I turned toward the high-pitched voices. Three fairies fluttered before me, their colorful dresses setting off their iridescent silver skin.

"Who else would it be?" Apparently the ground trembled whenever I crossed over from the "human world."

Shea straightened her pink skirt. "Well, the way those centaurs gallop around sometimes, the tremor isn't that far off."

I gave them a second appraisal. "You girls are all dressed up. What's the occasion?"

"The trolls are going to play for us. We get to dance." Nell bobbed up and down excitedly.

"Really? Isn't their music usually slow? And kind of depressing?"

Posie nodded. "They said this time they're working on something more fun."

"That's why we're so glad you're here." Shea yanked at my arm.

"And that we caught you first." Nell's smile was mischievous on my other side. "We're going to help fix your hair."

I ran a hand over my ponytail. "What's wrong with my hair?"

"Don't you want to do something special for the dance?"

"I—I hadn't really thought about it." Who knew Lockwood had an equivalent of prom?

"Heidi." Shawn jogged up behind us. Just under six feet tall, with tangled dark blond hair and bright blue eyes, he was the only other human I'd ever seen in Lockwood. But unlike me, he made it his permanent residence.

"Sorry, Shawn. She's coming with us." Shea tightened her hold.

Nell gave him a flirtatious wink. "She'll be all yours later."

He raised his eyebrows at me.

I sighed. "They insist I need my hair done for some dance."

"No boys allowed." Posie made a shooing motion.

Shawn fixed a pleading look on me, but I shrugged. "I couldn't reason with them either."

He laughed and raised his hands. "All right, I know a losing battle when I see one. Come find me when you're done."

"Will do."

A moment later, the fairies led me into their ring of willow trees. Lights twinkled everywhere, though I could never determine the source. The air hummed with who knew how many sets of wings fluttering in neighboring enclosures.

"Now, sit right here." Shea directed me to a stump. "Nell, would you get us some flowers?"

"I'm on it." The little fairy batted her eyelashes before flying back through the hanging fronds.

Flowers? "This really doesn't need to be elaborate."

"Sure it does." Posie removed my ponytail holder and ran her slim fingers through my hair. "Don't you think you'll be dancing with Shawn?"

"You guys know we're just friends, right?" I cursed the heat creeping up my neck. Okay, maybe I had a *little* crush on Shawn, but I wasn't about to tell that to the gossipy fairies.

"For now." Shea stuck some kind of pin into my hair. "But you don't have to stay just friends. We need to help him notice that you're not a little girl anymore."

Posie removed a pin from her mouth. "Sometimes it takes seeing someone in a different light to ignite that spark."

"I really don't—"

Nell's reappearance cut short my protest. An assortment of roses, lilacs, tulips, and some little yellow buds spilled from her arms.

I was going to look like that lady with the fruit piled on her head, only with flowers.

They chattered as they flitted around me, inserting pins and blossoms. The new unicorn baby was the cutest yet, the fairies had been busy collecting flower petals for a new mural, and Posie was spending more time with a guy fairy named Cade.

"There. Perfect." Nell flipped back her purple hair.

Shea grinned. "Come see! Come see!"

They directed me to the pond at the center of their enclosure, buzzing around my shoulders. I knelt carefully, trying not to disturb my hairdo.

My reflection was almost comical, but I didn't dare laugh. My dark hair embodied spring, all loops and braids and carefully placed flowers—quite the clash against my casual green tank top. I eased my bewildered expression into a smile and glanced up at the fairies. "It's lovely, thank you."

Posie squeaked with delight, attempting to help me up. "Just wait until he sees you."

I held back an eye roll. Thank goodness dances here were such a rare event.

They parted the willow fronds as I exited.

Shawn lay sprawled against the base of a tree. His eyes opened slowly, but then he jumped up. "There you are." He nodded to the hovering fairies. "I'll take her from here, ladies."

The air filled with high-pitched giggles before they returned to the cover of their little grove.

Shawn approached, his lips pursed. "Wow. You look very…festive."

I smacked his shoulder. "Oh, stop. This wasn't my idea."

"No, it's nice. Really." His grin faded as he plucked a pink rose from behind my ear and handed it to me. "You look beautiful."

I studied the flower, twirling it between my fingers. "Thanks. Not that I believe you."

"I mean it." He tipped my chin up. "So beautiful, in fact, that I believe I'd better escort you to the dance."

"You think so?"

"I'd hate for you to be pestered." He leaned close and switched to a stage whisper. "I understand there are trolls about."

I faked a gasp. "Trolls, you say? In that case, I'd best accept your offer."

He bowed then held out his arm with a smirk. "It is an honor, my lady."

I took his arm, smiling when he pulled me closer to his side.

We wandered the garden paths, enjoying the perfect day. Despite the fading light, the air warmed my skin, though not as much as Shawn's touch on my arm. The ripple of the fountains swept away thoughts of midterms and my upcoming tennis tournament, and every set of flowers seemed to smell even better than the last.

Music floated to us, the sounds of instruments tuning and warming up.

"They must be setting up over there." Shawn pointed to an open patch of grass just beyond the largest fountain.

Hoofbeats pounded on a side path. A group of centaurs emerged from the greenery, led by one with burnt-orange eyes and a tan vest slung over the dark skin of his chest.

"Noland!" I ran up and threw my arms around his neck. "I haven't seen you in ages."

He lowered his head, sending a wave of black hair across his face. "At times it is beneficial to take a—sabbatical, you might say."

"Well, I'm glad you're back." I glanced behind him to the others, who stomped in place. Niles and Lowry? The half-men, half-horses were such reclusive creatures that I rarely saw any of them except Noland. "Do centaurs dance?"

Noland smiled. "We appreciate music, but hooves are not best-suited to dancing."

"Fair enough."

"Enjoy the festivities, young one."

"Thanks. You, too." I stepped back to join Shawn as they filed past us. I waved at the other centaurs, who nodded in return.

Many trolls and fairies crowded around by the time we reached the clearing. Floral garlands hung suspended high above, no doubt the work of fairy magic.

"I can't believe I happened to come when there's a dance. It's almost like they knew I'd be here."

Shawn turned, his brows drawn. "I'm glad you're here for it, but it is odd. Then again, Noland always seems to know when you'll be making an appearance, so maybe they weaseled it out of him."

A group of six trolls stood on a crudely made platform. Several held string instruments of varying sizes; the others played what looked like recorders carved from wood. They fell silent for a moment then launched into a lively song.

Shawn laughed. "They really must've been practicing—I've never heard them play anything like this. Would you like to dance?"

"How do we dance to this?"

"However we want." He shrugged, a playful light in his eyes. "We're the only humans here, after all, so who's to know if we do anything wrong?"

"True. But then again, that means we're representing our entire race."

"Then let's show them how it's done." He snatched my hand and grabbed my waist before I could protest further.

We swayed, whirled, and hopped in our own made-up steps for three straight songs. The next tune was slower, and I appreciated the opportunity to catch my breath. Shawn led me in some variation of a slow waltz.

I studied the boy before me as he looked over my head to where a group of trolls spun each other around with joined hands. Despite being the only human living in Lockwood, Shawn had always seemed just as much a part of this place as the unicorns and trolls. But he never aged, never changed. When I'd first discovered the portal as a six-year-old, he'd been like an easygoing older brother, introducing me to everyone and teaching me the workings of this stunning, bizarre new land. As I grew, our relationship adapted more to friends and equals, at times partners in crime. Now, I estimated we were about the same age, though he never gave the slightest hint of his own history or how he'd come to be here.

"How do you suppose the fairies dance without injuring each other?"

I blinked and followed his gaze. The fairies swirled in intertwining circles, weaving in, out, and around so quickly their figures blurred into streaks of silver.

"Maybe it doesn't hurt when they hit each other with their wings."

He grunted. "I know I find the sensation unpleasant."

I adjusted my grip on his hand. "Maybe you're not quite as tough as the fairies."

He pinched my side, and I doubled over with a squeal. A moment later, the music paused as musicians traded places. Even more trolls wandered into the dance area. At the start of the next song, they widened into a large circle for some kind of group dance. Several glanced back at us.

Shawn huffed as we moved farther aside to give them space. "Count on trolls to be continually in the way."

"They are the ones providing the music."

His attention returned to me. "Always so kind and understanding." He tweaked my chin. "I really should try to be more like you."

The stutter in my heart rate didn't slow the heat rushing to my cheeks. "Eh, but then who would keep the trolls in their place?"

"Good point." He twirled me in a circle, moving a bit farther down the path. "You know, they've pushed us so far to the side I feel like the suitor in one of those old-timey romance novels." He waggled his eyebrows. "When he whisks the young lady away from the crowd to—"

He dropped a split second before I did as the ground collapsed beneath us. We clung to each other, our screams lost in the cavern of soil as our feet slammed into solid ground.

"What the—?"

Raucous laughter sounded above us.

"We was wonderin' when ye'd discover our little surprise." Wahl, a short troll with medium brown skin and long dark hair, peered over the edge of the pit.

Bragg, slightly taller with an impressive beard, stepped up at his side. "We're so glad ye enjoyed the dance." He grinned and swiped a tear from his eye.

Shawn growled, but I placed a hand on his chest. "We did, very much. Is this a tradition among trolls, then? For one lucky couple to get some privacy?"

I glanced to Shawn, who narrowed his eyes at me.

Bragg laughed again, more good-naturedly this time. "Nah, this was special for yer friend there. Sorry ye got caught up in it."

Shea fluttered into view. "Oh, Heidi. Just look at the mess. How will we get you out of there?"

"We'll figure something out." Hopefully before I needed to be home.

Shawn rubbed a hand across my back before pulling away to study the side of the pit. Our heads were only about a foot beneath the surface. "If I can just make some footholds…" He dug his fingers into the hard dirt.

"Here, this should help." Noland stood at the edge, a long, thick rope tied loosely around his girth. He kicked the other end down to us.

Shawn reached for it then passed it to me. "Ladies first."

Taking a deep breath, I grasped the rope with both hands. I managed to scale the dirt wall, slipping a few times. Shawn gave my feet a boost when I reached the top.

The fairies cheered as I emerged from the opening. Before I knew it, they'd whisked me to the side and buzzed around me, brushing off dirt and fixing my hair.

I looked past them toward the hole. Shawn's head poked out, and several of the friendlier trolls grasped one of his hands as he clung to the rope with the other. Noland strained forward, taking one step and another until Shawn was on solid ground.

The fairies closed in before I could reach him. "Oh, Shawn, are you all right?"

"You poor thing!"

"How could they be so cruel?"

I rolled my eyes. They clearly needed more boy fairies to shower their affection on.

A minute later, he escaped their attentions. The crowd dispersed, some returning to the dance, others wandering off into the fading light.

"Are you okay?" He held my shoulders, peering into my face.

"I'm fine. Mostly just startled."

He released a breath. "I'm so sorry you got dragged into that."

"No harm done." I shrugged. "Besides, it's not like I've never been an accomplice to any of your pranks."

The mischief returned to his eyes. "There is that."

"Heidi!" The call was faint but clear. Mom.

"Uh oh, I'd better get back. Mom's probably going to tell me it's time for bed."

Time never seemed to pass at the same rate here as at home, but the portal allowed me to hear anything happening in or near my bedroom. I even set myself an alarm on occasion.

Shawn nodded, his expression wistful. Taking my arm, he pivoted me in the direction of the portal. As we walked, I hastily undid my hairstyle, leaving a trail of flower petals and hairpins in our wake. We stopped just to the side of the handle.

He removed a few remaining blossoms from my hair. "Well, have a good night. Or week, or whatever."

"I'll come back soon. I promise."

"You always say that."

"And I always do. Or at least try to." I attempted a winning smile.

He chuckled. "I suppose you do. I'll see you next time, then."

It broke my heart to leave him like this. As a kid, I was oblivious to any pain he might've experienced in saying goodbye, but now… Noland and the others were always here, of course, but it couldn't be the same as human company.

Mom's voice rang out again from behind us. I really did need to go before she discovered me missing.

"Goodbye, Shawn." On a whim, I enclosed him in a hug before crouching down to open the trapdoor.

He stood frozen in place, a whisper of a smile twitching on his lips. "Goodbye."

I practically jumped off the ladder, careful to push it quietly back into place. Kicking off my shoes, I ran a hand over my hair and stepped out of the closet just as Mom peeked in my door.

"Heidi, there you are." She raised a brow.

"I was just picking out my clothes for tomorrow."

"Ah." She leaned against the doorframe. "And before that?"

"I was…" I scanned the room and spotted the novel on my nightstand. "Reading."

"Hmm." Her gaze followed mine to the book. "Sometimes you get so quiet up here I worry you've climbed out the window."

I hoped my laugh sounded natural. "You know me, Mom. I expect to be recruited as a stunt double any day now."

She cracked a smile. "I just hope you're not up to something."

I donned my best innocent look. "Between tennis and homework, I don't have time to get into anything." I'd tried to tell my family about Lockwood when I first discovered it, but the portal only worked when I was alone and I could only handle so much laughter about my "overactive imagination." So I kept it to myself—my own, private escape from reality.

"Well, I came up to make sure you're getting ready for bed."

"I'm on it." I ducked back into the closet to grab my pajamas.

"All right." She paused before disappearing from view. "Is Tonya's party on Friday?"

I bit my lip. "Yeah." I'd almost forgotten my best friend's birthday.

"And you're coming to my concert tomorrow, right?" Alexis poked her head in, her wet, blond hair curling at the ends. Her PJs were pink with a sparkly crown.

"I wouldn't miss it. I'll come say goodnight in a few minutes, okay, Lex?"

"Okay." She scampered off.

Mom followed, closing the door behind her. I sank onto my bed with a sigh. Apparently I wouldn't be returning to Lockwood *that* soon.

Over a week since my last visit.

I climbed faster, nearly hitting my head on the trapdoor. Hopefully, Shawn wouldn't be too mad.

Grass crunched under my hands as I crawled out. Lockwood shifted between eight different landscapes in a random order no one could decipher, changing every morning. But the creatures' homes remained fixed. Today, the rock face that housed the trolls' caves looked a bit out of place amid the surrounding forest, but the fairies' willow groves in the opposite direction blended right in. Shawn lived in a little hut farther out, and no one seemed to know where the centaurs resided. It was as though they disappeared every evening and materialized again at daybreak.

I breathed in the fresh air and set out down the path toward the lake.

A minute later, Shawn rode up on a lavender unicorn, its golden horn glinting in the light. "Your timing is perfect." He held out his hand. "Interested in an adventure?"

I grinned and grasped his fingers. "Always."

He hoisted me up to sit in front of him. I entwined my hands in the unicorn's white mane, and Shawn wrapped an arm around my waist before spurring the animal forward again. I leaned back against him as we picked up speed.

"What's the hurry?"

"The trolls are after us."

"Of course they are. What'd you do this time?"

"Well, I could hardly let their stunt at the dance go unanswered. So last week, when we had an ocean day, the fairies lured them out with a rafting excursion. Meanwhile, Nell, Shea, and I covered every surface of their caves with glow lichen. It was lit up like a Christmas tree in there when we were done." He shook with laughter. "You should've seen the look on Bragg's face when he came stomping out. If steam really could come out of people's ears, the guy would've been a whistling teapot."

"I'm sad I missed it."

"Me, too." His arm tightened around me. "Anyway, they laid low for a while, but then two days ago, it was the mountainside. I spent half the afternoon picking lingonberries, and those little tramps stole them."

"Uh oh. Nobody messes with Shawn and his lingonberries."

His chuckle rumbled through my back. "Nobody. Which is why it's time for payback. They gathered a bunch of clod mushrooms this morning, which are now in these bags right here." He indicated the sacks slung across his back. "I don't want to eat the disgusting things, so I thought I'd dump them in the lake instead."

"Hmm. Seems like a fair revenge." I shifted to glance at him. "But isn't that kind of wasteful, to throw away all that food?"

"If you can call it food." He grinned down at me. "Hopefully, some underwater slug will take an interest."

We slowed as we neared the lake then hopped off the unicorn's back. Shawn fed it some kind of rectangular gray treat from his pocket before sending it on its way.

"Quick, grab a bag."

We each took one of the sacks and tipped them over the water until every last mushroom had disappeared beneath the surface. Footsteps and grumbling sounded from the path.

Shawn kicked at the sand. "Ugh, how are they so fast on those little legs?"

"You go. I'll distract them." I handed him my empty bag.

"Are you sure?"

"Yes. They like me."

He raised an eyebrow.

"Well, much more than they like you. Now go."

He disappeared into the trees just as Bragg and Wahl lumbered into view.

"Ah, Miss Heidi. Afternoon."

I inclined my head. "Good afternoon. You two seem to be in a hurry."

"Haven't seen Shawn, have ye?" Bragg narrowed his eyes. "He's usually with you."

I shrugged. "I've been looking for him myself. I thought he might be fishing at the lake, but obviously not." I rubbed my forehead, aiming for a thoughtful expression. "Have you tried the fairies? I'm sure you've seen the way they fawn over him."

"Hmph." Bragg tugged at his beard and held a whispered conference with Wahl. "I guess we'll try that, then. But ye'd best not be caught up in his tricks."

"Wouldn't dream of it." I smiled and waved at their retreating figures. "I hope you find him."

Now to kill some time to make sure they actually left. I strolled to the shore and searched for flat stones. After skipping ten across the water's calm surface, I made my way to where Shawn had entered the tree cover.

He popped out from behind a thick trunk and squeezed my shoulders. "You were brilliant. Thank you."

"Any time." I set out farther into the maze of foliage.

He matched my pace. "To the swing?"

"If we can find it." The lake landscape always seemed to have the same wooden swing hung from thick ropes, but its location varied.

After a few steps, Shawn glanced at me. "The fairies do not fawn over me."

I snorted. "Oh, please." I affected a high, airy voice. "Shawn, you're so brave. Oh, Shawn, if only I could ride a unicorn like you do."

He punched my arm. "It's not that bad."

I raised a brow and kept walking.

"Hmm. Does it make you jealous?" He stepped closer until our sides bumped.

"No." At least, not usually. "It's good for you to have some feminine influence when I'm not around."

His grin faded. "You've been 'not around' a lot lately."

My breath hissed through my teeth. "I know. I'm sorry, I just don't know how to fit it all in. School, homework. Tennis practice almost every day. Plus, Alexis always wants me at her music events, and I need to spend time with my friends…"

"It's fine." Shawn's fingers curled into fists but then released. "Now the real question is, how do you predict the trolls will retaliate this time? I'd love to head them off for once."

I jammed my hands into my pockets. Shawn always changed the subject when real life came up, as though trying to convince himself Lockwood was the only plane of existence. "Well, they haven't gone after your hut in a while, have they?"

"No, good point. I'd better get the latch repaired soon." He pinched the bridge of his nose. "And maybe have a trap waiting for them, just in case."

We were settled onto the swing's wide bench, close to working out the details of his trap, when a cry rose from the direction of the lake.

"I guess they figured out you weren't with the fairies."

He grinned. "Ah, there's nothing so satisfying as the sounds of sweet revenge." He laid his arm behind me and clasped my shoulder. "Especially when accompanied by the world's cutest fourteen-year-old sidekick."

"Fourteen?" I sat up straighter. "I'm fifteen."

Shawn stilled. "You are?"

"Almost sixteen."

"No." He rubbed his forehead. "No, I thought we had more time. When is your birthday?" He questioned me like a lawyer in a murder trial.

"Next week. Why?"

His expression darkened a shade further.

"Shawn, what's going on?"

He blew out a breath. "Your sixteenth birthday is when the portal closes."

I reeled back as though he'd slapped me. "The portal's going to close? But why?"

"That's just how it works. Once you reach sixteen, you're closer to an adult than a child, and your portal closes so it can open up for someone else."

"But…" I couldn't vote or live on my own yet, and already I was being kicked out of childhood. "Why am I just finding this out now?"

He ran a hand over his hair. "I assumed Noland explained it to you. That's how I found out. And this isn't exactly the kind of conversation a person has just for fun."

"So what do I do?"

We swung forward and back several times before he answered. "You decide."

I shivered. "Decide?"

"You can't cross over anymore, so you decide. To stay here, or stay there."

Understanding dawned on me like a metal bat to the head. "You decided to stay here."

He nodded, his mouth forming a tight line.

"And I…" I sank back against the seat, a hand over my mouth. The delightful, ever-changing landscape of my childhood alongside my dearest companion, or my family, my friends, the entire rest of my life. One would be gone forever.

And I had a week to make my choice.

I sat at dinner that evening, pushing food around my plate. Roast beef and mashed potatoes was usually one of my favorites, but tonight it seemed so bland compared with the exotic fruits and vegetables of Lockwood. The chatter between my parents and Alexis floated around me, only snatches filtering through my distraction.

Work. Bills. Music lessons. Homework. Car repairs.

Wasn't there more to life than this? Would it really be worth giving up my adventures in Lockwood for such a boring existence?

"Heidi, are you okay?"

My attention snapped to my mom, who studied me with raised eyebrows.

"Uh, sorry. What was the question?"

"You're not eating."

"Yes, I am." I shoved a forkful into my mouth and chewed vigorously.

She sighed. "I asked how your math test went this afternoon."

"Fine." I swallowed and took a sip of water. "Not too tough."

"I'm glad to hear it." But Mom's expression was anything but glad. She pressed her lips together, as though trying to hide how much my curt response disappointed her.

Luckily, Alex chimed in with something about her social studies class. But I kept looking at Mom. My reluctance to join the dinner conversation was enough to make her sad. How would she respond if I disappeared? And Alexis, still babbling away like it was her sworn duty to fill the silence. Without me, she'd be an only child.

Even Dad. He caught my gaze and winked, motioning to his plate. I attempted a smile and took another bite of potatoes. He still tucked me into bed every night and called me his little girl. My leaving might steal that playful grin from his face forever.

I stared down at my plate, focusing on cutting up my roast. Mom was suspicious enough already—the interrogation would never end if I burst into tears in the middle of a meal.

Adventures with mythical creatures or school and a future career?

A small hut amid rotating landscapes or our comfortable house in the middle of a suburb?

Shawn, Noland, and the fairies or my family and friends?

The questions plagued me on a nonstop rotation, like scrolling movie credits on replay. Every time my mind leaned one direction, my heart pulled the other. I couldn't wait to get back to Lockwood, yet dreaded it. It wouldn't be the same now, knowing I might soon have to give it up for good.

Three days later, panic mode set in. Half my time was up and I was no closer to a decision. I skipped tennis practice, feigning illness. The expanding dark patches under my eyes made the charade believable.

My movements were heavy, stilted as I climbed the ladder. Wind whipped past my face the moment the trapdoor lifted. I heaved myself out and practically crashed into Noland.

"Greetings, Heidi." He took a few steps back, unsteady in the shifting sand. A layer of tan dust dampened the usual ebony sheen of the horse half of his body.

"Hey. Were you waiting for me?"

"I often sense your movements."

Not really an answer, but I wasn't in the mood to argue.

"You are sad today." His eyes seemed to penetrate my very soul.

"My sixteenth birthday's in a few days."

"Ah." He lowered his head. "It is a decision of great import."

"You can say that again." I trailed my foot in the sand, watching ridges and valleys form in its wake. *Wait.* Something lit my mind like a flickering light bulb. If he could predict my comings and goings... "Have you seen anything?"

He took a few seconds to respond. "In what respect?"

"About my future." I sucked in a deep breath. "Do you know what I'll choose?"

His jaw shifted. "Lockwood will soon undergo a change of great magnitude."

My lips widened into my most genuine smile in days. "Because I'm here?" It quickly faded. "Or because I'm gone?"

"Ah, young human. I'm afraid I cannot say. There is much value in discerning for oneself what one's heart wants. I would not take that away from you."

My shoulders deflated like a popped balloon. "But it's impossible. I don't know what I want."

"You, of all creatures, should know nothing is impossible. Just look at this place." He backed up, his right arm sweeping across the landscape. "Though each world holds a piece of your heart, you will make the right decision. In the end, you shall be whole."

Slightly comforting, but still not very useful.

He stepped back farther. "It's a pleasure to see you as always, Heidi, but I know I am not the one you're here for. I believe you will find him at his dwelling."

I instinctively looked toward Shawn's hut. "Thank you."

Noland bowed and trotted away. I shuffled forward through the thick sand, the heat one degree below uncomfortable. The desert landscape was my least favorite, but today it suited my mood.

Shawn met me halfway, a folded blanket tucked under his arm. "Hey, kid."

"Hey, kid, yourself. I'm probably older than you now."

He scoffed. "Maybe by a day or two." He inclined his head to the side. "Should we go find some shade?"

"Sounds good." We set out toward the mesa in the distance, and I didn't bother breaking the companionable silence. The pattern of lines leading up the sides of the rock face came into view as we drew near. Would I ever see it again?

We walked to the side opposite the sun. Shawn spread out the blanket then sat and curled his arms around his bent knees. I lay back with my hands cushioning my head.

I twisted to study his face, devoid of its usual mischief. "Do we need to worry about the trolls today?"

"Nah." He shook his head. "I've been pretty quiet lately."

My gaze shifted to the sandy hills and valleys stretched out in every direction. Like a tan ocean with its waves on pause. "You know, I've always found it odd they call this place Lockwood. I mean, it's only a forest like once a week. Nothing about *this* indicates 'wood' in the least."

"Yeah, I guess it is strange." He didn't even attempt a smile.

I tapped his leg. "In case you're wondering…I haven't decided yet."

His eyes met mine, and he nodded.

"I talked with Noland about it. Apparently he's seen my future, but he wouldn't tell me anything."

His laugh fell flat. "That sounds like Noland."

"My mind just goes in circle after circle. I don't see how I can give one up. It's too hard." Then again, *he* had made the decision somehow. "How did you—?"

His expression hardened.

"Never mind." I sighed and let my eyelids drift shut. "You'll be the first to know. Assuming I ever figure out…"

"Thank you." His voice was much nearer than before.

I opened my eyes. He'd scooted closer and was stretching out at my side. He put his arm around me and coaxed my head onto his shoulder. I curled up against him, pressing my face into his soft cotton shirt.

"I just don't know what to do."

He stroked my hair as the pent-up tears fell in an unrelenting stream. "I know."

I trudged to school the next morning, uninspired by the clouds looming like a giant gray comforter about to drop from the sky. Closing my eyes, I envisioned the desert in Lockwood. The bright sun beating down, lighting up the sand like a golden fire—warm on my skin, but never quite enough to cause sunburn.

I pulled my jacket closer and heaved a sigh. Comparisons between Lockwood and this world hardly even seemed fair, but what else did I have to go on?

By third period, the debate had all but consumed my mind. Four days left to decide. Relying on autopilot, I jerked with surprise when my desk partner greeted me in science class. I didn't even remember walking there. I dug out my textbook and notepad, if only to look busy and have something to doodle on.

Mr. Venning lectured on the structure of viruses, pacing across the front of the classroom and messing up his white-blond hair as usual. I tried to listen since I actually liked science, but soon my musings took over once more.

If I stayed in Lockwood, I'd never take a test again. No homework, no report cards. Would I miss any of this? My friends stopping by my locker, maybe. Chaotic lunches where we yelled across the table to hear each other talk then giggled hysterically when a message was misinterpreted. The days in class where something clicked and finally made sense. The idiotic boost of self-confidence when I wore a new outfit, or…

"Miss Benton, are you all right?"

I flinched and glanced up. Mr. Venning stood before me, but the classroom was otherwise empty. The bell must've rung already.

"Oh, I'm fine." I flipped my textbook shut and unzipped my backpack.

"You seem a bit—distracted."

"That obvious, huh?" I managed a tight smile.

He tugged out the chair from the desk ahead of mine and turned it around. "Do you want to talk about it?" He sat, leaning his elbows on his knees.

"But isn't this your lunch time?"

He shrugged. "I can eat my leftover pizza in two minutes flat. I timed it once. So don't worry about me." He watched me expectantly.

"Well, it's just…" It's not like I could explain my predicament. "I guess—growing up requires some tough decisions."

"Ah." He sat up, folding his hands in his lap. "You do face a lot of difficult decisions at this phase of life. What kind of career may interest you, where you want to go to school. The prospect of leaving home in a few years. But keep in mind that growing up isn't something to be feared. You'll face more choices and responsibility, it's true." He glanced out the window. "This stage in your life is all about learning and maturing. But you can't do much with it yet. It's like you're building up all this inner potential, ready to be unleashed when you're sent out into the world on your own. As an adult, it's finally *your* opportunity to make a difference."

I nodded, chewing my lip.

"That's why it's such a tragedy when a young person misses the chance to live out that potential." A shadow crossed his face before his eyes returned to me. "Do you enjoy biology, Miss Benton?"

"It's one of my favorite subjects. Right behind gym." My smile came more naturally this time. "We're in the bowling unit right now."

He laughed and slapped his knee. "That is tough to compete with. But you seem to have a knack for science, and the field needs more people like you. Sharp, driven, compassionate. You could make a real difference someday, practicing medicine or in research." He tapped his fingers on my desk. "Just something to think about. My door's always open if you have questions about colleges or career paths."

"Thank you, that means a lot. And I will think about it." I stood. "But now I'll let you take a break before your next class."

"I'm happy to help any time." He rose and returned the chair. "See you on Friday."

"See you."

"And Miss Benton?"

I paused and looked back. "Yeah?"

"Keep in mind that growing up doesn't have to be accomplished all at once. I think my collection of model trains and freezer full of microwave dinners would attest to that."

"Thanks, Mr. Venning."

His words stayed with me throughout the day. Building up inner potential ready to be unleashed. The chance to make a difference. Lockwood appeared in a whole new light. Varying landscapes, mythical creatures, adventures. But what did it all mean? I couldn't accomplish anything of significance staying sixteen forever, playing tricks on trolls and gossiping with fairies. The lack of pain and hard work would be nice at first, but could I be truly happy without a broader range of emotions and experiences?

The sun shone brightly on my walk home. I pushed through the front door, immediately tackled by Alexis with a hug because she was accepted into some new orchestra. I squeezed her back, wincing at the thought I'd considered leaving her. The choice that had been within me all along was suddenly so clear.

Now I just needed to break it to Shawn.

I surveyed the open meadows stretched out before me. I'd promised Shawn would be the first to know, but I couldn't make my feet turn in the direction of his hut.

Instead, I headed toward the fairies' clusters of willows. Best to get the easier goodbyes out of the way first.

Half an hour later I emerged, swiping moisture from my eyes. My neck stung a bit from Nell's tight embrace. Though I'd never fit in with the fairies' high energy and interest in unusual fashion, I'd miss their enthusiasm and teasing.

Movement in the distance caught my eye. Shawn? My heart half leaped, half twisted. The figure turned, revealing four legs and a horizontal back.

Noland. I ran to him, tall grasses brushing my legs with a comforting swishing sound.

"Greetings." He tilted his head. "I see your decision is made."

My mouth opened and closed without uttering anything coherent. Of course he already knew my choice.

"It is the right path, Heidi. Though you will be greatly missed."

I leaned over and kissed his cheek. "Thank you. I'll miss you, too."

"You will always have us in your mind and heart. Don't forget."

"I could never forget all of you."

He patted my shoulder. "Now, you'd better go to him. He's waiting for you."

The tightness in my chest threatened to crush my lungs. "Goodbye."

"Farewell, young one."

I crossed the meadow to Shawn's hut, pausing to wave at Noland as he galloped away. Breathing deeply, I plodded up the two steps leading to the door and knocked. The fact he hadn't come to find me yet wasn't a good sign.

The door opened, revealing a boy with bed-mussed hair and his usual nondescript t-shirt and shorts. "Hey." No surprise. No mischief.

"Hey."

He angled the door wider to let me in. I hadn't been inside the small, circular hut in years, but apparently nothing had changed. It held merely a bed, a table with two chairs, and a dresser. Shawn did all his cooking and washing outside.

I perched on one of the chairs. He remained standing. I threaded my fingers together, unsure where to start.

"You're not coming back, are you?" The sadness in his eyes punctured my soul like an axe.

"No." I splayed my hands on the table. "But, Shawn, you have to understand. I can't leave my parents, and I want to see my sister grow up."

He sank into the chair across from mine. "Yeah, I figured that's how it would be."

I had to go on before I lost my nerve. "And I had this great conversation with my teacher, Mr. Venning."

"Venning?" He jerked. "What subject does he teach?"

"I have him for biology. But I think he's only been teaching for a few years, so you couldn't have had him."

"Oh." His slow nod wasn't convincing. "I must be thinking of someone else."

"He had all these inspiring things to say about growing up and how it's really in adulthood that you get to use your gifts to make the world a better place." I drew in a quick breath before continuing. "That's why I think you should come, too."

His frown turned sardonic. "My portal closed a long time ago."

"I know. But you could use mine."

He was shaking his head before I could finish the statement. "And what, live with your family? They'd welcome the strange guy you dragged home from a different land without question?"

"I…well, I haven't thought it through yet. But I'm sure we'd come up with something."

"No. You go back to your family, your world-changing initiatives, but leave me out of it." He leaned back, folding his arms. "I've made my choice."

"But Shawn—"

"No, Heidi. The world has moved on without me, and I'm fine with that." He rose and walked to the door. "But you belong there now." He held the door open and motioned to me.

I gaped at him.

"You should go."

My chair clattered as I stood, shaking. I stomped over to him, tears stinging my eyes. "Fine. Never grow up. Avoid reality forever."

He stared at the floor and slammed the door behind me.

I paced my closet again and again. Tomorrow I'd turn sixteen. Should I try to reason with Shawn, or would the attempt just make things worse? I grabbed the rope with a sigh. Despite the somersaults my stomach performed at the prospect of facing him again, I'd always regret it if I didn't at least try.

My chest constricted as I emerged in the midst of a copse of trees. The lake scene had always been my favorite. Without really thinking about it, I set out toward the water.

Shawn sat on the beach, staring across the glassy surface. I walked until I entered his line of sight.

"Heidi." He blinked and jumped up. "You—you came back." His expression wavered, as though he wasn't sure whether it was a good or bad thing. "I felt the ground shake, but I didn't think…"

"Not for good. I don't turn sixteen until tomorrow." I approached him cautiously. "But after everything…I didn't want it to end like that."

He nodded with a relieved smile. Jogging forward, he wrapped me in a hug. "I'm so glad you came." He nuzzled his face in my hair.

I snuggled closer against his warm chest. How could I say goodbye to him forever?

He released me and paced a bit before sitting back down in the sand, elbows propped on his knees, chin leaning on his hands. I sat down beside him, sifting through my hazy brain for something to say.

Shawn glanced over. "I'm really sorry about last time."

"Me, too."

He closed the distance between us and twined an arm around my waist. I tucked my head against his shoulder. We sat in silence, listening to the peaceful lapping of the water.

Shawn's voice broke my trance. "Can we talk?" He shifted to face me.

"Of course." Apprehension curled my insides into a ball. Based on his grim expression, it wouldn't be a pleasant conversation.

"I need to apologize again for before. It wasn't fair of me to snap at you like that, especially since you don't know…" He rubbed the back of his neck.

He seemed to be planning to go on, so I waited in silence.

His brows lowered as he looked out across the lake. "When I was ten, my parents were planning to go out to dinner, but the babysitter canceled. They decided not to go, even though they were already dressed up and everything. I threw a fit, arguing that they clearly didn't trust me if they couldn't leave my younger brother and sister in my care for just a few hours. So, they went."

I dug my fingers into the sand. He'd never talked about his life in the real world before. I didn't dare ruin it by interrupting.

"A storm went through that night. The sky turned an awful green color, the wind picked up. And on their way home—" He winced, shoving his fingers into his hair. "The police found them in their car, crushed under a tree." His voice was raw, pained. "If I hadn't been so juvenile and stubborn. If I hadn't insisted…"

"Shawn." I forced my voice out through my choked throat. "It wasn't your fault."

"That's what everyone kept telling me. But I just couldn't—" A sob strangled his words.

In an instant, the last of his carefree facade disappeared. He wept, cradling his face in his hands. I held his shoulders, whispering, "It's okay. It's okay," over and over, stroking his arms and back until he calmed.

"Sorry." He frowned and looked away. "I just haven't thought about them in so long."

"Nothing to apologize for." I extracted a tissue from my pocket and handed it to him.

He blew his nose and wiped at his eyes, then tipped his head back, breathing heavily.

"I'm so, so sorry that happened." I bit my lip. "I realize that doesn't help, but—"

"There's nothing else to say. I know. Thanks." He bumped my leg with his fist, his lips quirking up into a hint of a smile. "I found the portal soon after we moved in with my grandparents. It was just what I needed—a way to escape. To almost forget." He straightened and stretched out his legs. "But a few months before I turned sixteen, Grandpa had a stroke. He was in rough shape, and Gran just couldn't do it anymore. The state wanted to put us in foster care." His voice grew hoarse again.

I slipped my hand into his, and he grasped my fingers.

"Caitlyn was going to be fine. She was only nine and so cute. She had this cheerfulness about her, in spite of everything. And Darrin, he was so good at…well, he was smart. And really grounded. I don't know how he did it, but I found myself turning to him for advice, even though I was two years older." His laugh was devoid of humor. "Then there was me, the angsty teen. Too quiet, too temperamental. They couldn't find a family willing to take all three of us, but one couple was able to foster two. They were trying to decide how to split us up, and I decided to make it easy for them."

He fell quiet, his gaze directed at the ground. I squeezed his hand. No wonder the poor guy had lost all interest in the real world.

"So you see why I can't go back." He glanced to me then out to the trees. "But I can't blame you for making a different choice. Of course you want to stay with your family. You have a bright future ahead of you." He said it through gritted teeth, but he was clearly trying to mean it.

"Thanks. I hope so." I leaned against him. Hopefully whatever my future held would be worth leaving this. Leaving *him*.

"Why do you think the portal came to you?"

I sat up to look at him. "What do you mean?"

"You're talented; you have friends, a loving family. I always thought it appeared for someone who really needed that escape, like I did."

"Hmm." I angled back against my elbows. The portal first appeared when I was so young, I'd just taken it for granted. I turned to study the boy beside me. His lips were pursed, his hands clenched. His eyes so wise and sad for a sixteen-year-old.

"I always enjoyed my adventures here, and I've certainly had my challenges. But you're right, I didn't really need it. I think maybe—" I swallowed against the sudden dryness in my throat. "Maybe it was because you needed me."

His expression warred between protest and agreement. Finally, he donned his familiar grin, though it didn't quite reach his eyes. "I guess that portal knows how to pick 'em."

Sitting up, I traced the backs of my fingers across his cheek. "I'll miss you."

"Yeah." A muscle tensed in his jaw. "I'll miss you, too."

I tried to memorize his face as we stared at each other, but it would never be enough. How could I capture every moment, every expression? After who knows how long, I swallowed and rose. "I should go. I don't know specifically when I turn sixteen, and I don't want to risk…"

"I understand." He stood and brushed off his shorts. "I'll walk with you."

He twined his fingers with mine and led me down the grassy path.

At the portal entrance we stopped, facing each other. I threw my arms around his neck. "Take care of yourself, Shawn. It's been such a gift. You, this place…it all made my childhood so magical. And you've been the dearest friend I could've asked for."

He pulled back and smoothed the hair from my face. "Try not to grow up too much, okay?"

My laugh turned into a half-sob. "I'll try."

He nodded. "Goodbye, Heidi." Leaning forward, he pressed a kiss to my forehead.

"Goodbye." I ran my hands down his arms, squeezing his fingers before I let go.

I opened the trapdoor behind me and stumbled through, keeping my eyes fixed on him until it shut with a decisive thud.

Morning light filtered into my bedroom. I sat up and stretched, a yawn tugging at my mouth. My eyes felt coated in cotton, the lids stiff and puffy. I winced as the realization hit me square in the chest. I'd said goodbye to Shawn last night. For good. Sighing, I leaned back against the headboard.

Something near the far wall caught my eye. A boy, his dark blond hair disheveled, leaning his head on his bent knees.

"You're here!" My voice came out as a whispered squeak. He raised his head as I untangled my legs from the sheets and took off across the room. He'd just risen to standing when I launched myself at him, the force of my hug propelling us both against the wall.

He laughed and circled his arms around me, one hand rubbing up and down the length of my back. "I'm here."

I squeezed him tighter. Shawn was *here*. Solid and real and smelling of spearmint. When I thought I'd never see…

Gasping, I stepped back. "I turn sixteen today."

His grin came slow. "So you do." He bopped a finger on the tip of my nose. "Happy birthday, Heidi."

"But the portal." I dashed into my closet and scrambled up the ladder, panting. The trapdoor tipped open, revealing stacks of musty boxes surrounded by plastic bags full of old clothes and coats.

A kick to the ribs would've been less painful.

Tears rimmed my eyes as I descended. I padded back out of the closet, no longer hurried. "It's gone." I stared at the floor, numbly making my way to the edge of my bed.

"It's okay. I know." He perched beside me on the mattress. "That's why I'm here."

"What?" My eyes probably bugged out like a cartoon character's. "You mean, you chose to come back? For good?"

He shrugged with a rueful smile. "So it would seem."

My grin widened then faltered. "But what will we do with you? I'd love for you to stay here, and we may be able to convince my parents for a while, but—"

He waved a hand, cutting me off. "Don't worry about it. I have a plan." He studied his lap, refusing to meet my gaze. "I should've told you when I first made the connection, but it was just such a shock."

"Told me what?"

He shifted to face me. "Mr. Venning, your science teacher. He's my brother."

"Mr. Venning is your brother." I massaged my temples. "Your *younger* brother? Are you sure?"

"Positive. Venning is an unusual last name, the age seems about right, and science was always his favorite subject." He shrugged. "Plus, your conversation with him had Darrin written all over it. Even ten years later."

Mr. Venning was his brother. I studied Shawn's profile in the dim light. His hair was a few shades darker than Mr. Venning's, but they had a similar shape through their nose and chin.

Brothers.

"Wow. That's just crazy. You think he'll take you in?"

"I sure hope so." He crossed his ankles. "I left him a note when I went through the portal the last time. I'm hoping he'll understand."

"You can walk with me to school today. We'll have to sneak you out first, and then you can meet me down the block or something." I bounced in place, my excitement growing. "How incredible—to see your brother again after all this time."

"Ha, yeah. It'll be weird...but really good."

"Is that why you decided to come back?"

"My brother?" He angled his head, considering. "That was definitely part of it. But..."

He took my hand in both of his, tracing lines across my fingers and palm. I shivered as a wave of tingles coursed up my arm.

He raised his head and searched my eyes. "When you left, nothing was right. Nothing made sense anymore. It wasn't the same without you." Releasing my hand, he cupped the back of my head and pulled me closer until our foreheads rested together. "I realized I'd rather grow up with you than stay in Lockwood alone."

"But another portal should open up now, right? So someone else would—"

"I don't want someone else."

My insides turned to jelly.

He tilted his chin forward until his lips found mine. Warm. Tentative. Searching.

I caressed his cheek, ran my fingers through his hair. Relished being close to him, our existences no longer separated by a portal. Shawn came back to the real world. For *me*. I wanted the perfect moment to last forever, frozen in time.

Then again, I couldn't wait to see what our futures would hold.

An avid reader practically since birth, Laurie Lucking discovered her passion for writing after leaving her career as an attorney to become a stay-at-home mom. She writes young adult fantasy with a strong thread of fairy tale romance and co-founded Lands Uncharted, a blog for fans of clean YA speculative fiction. While brainstorming "Threshold," she drew inspiration from Peter Pan *but wanted more romance and a happily ever after! Her debut novel,* Common, *takes a Cinderella-type love story between a maid and a prince and adds a secret friendship, a plot against the throne, and a group of unusual nuns.*
        www.laurielucking.com

Idiot's Graveyard

Arthur Daigle

A gorgeous summer day was coming to an end as Dana Illwind and Sorcerer Lord Jayden led a small merchant caravan. They'd protected three wagons for eleven days, a task Dana had been certain would have been boring. After all, they were far from hostile borders and nowhere near wilderness areas that could harbor threats. To her surprise (and no one else's), they'd had to earn their pay guarding the wagons.

"I still don't get what they were thinking," Dana said. She was a woman of fifteen, wearing a simple dress, fur hat, backpack, and leather boots that came up to her knees. Dana had a knife and was giving serious thought to getting a better weapon. She had brown hair and brown eyes and was pretty enough that men working the caravan had been a bit too friendly for her liking during the trip. She'd told two of them to stop and drawn her knife on a third.

"Bandits aren't known for clear thinking," Jayden told her. Jayden was a walking contradiction. He wore expertly tailored black and silver clothes and had long blond hair that was perpetually messy. Jayden carried no weapons, but as the world's only living Sorcerer Lord, he was dangerous even empty-handed. He was handsome, confident, skilled, and a wanted man for constantly harassing the royal family and their supporters. Smart men avoided him, which should have made their guard duty as dull as dry toast.

Dana counted off fingers, saying, "They recognized you. They knew about the manticore you killed single-handed. You gave them a fair warning. And somehow they still thought attacking was a good idea."

"They were likely desperate, stupid, drunk, or some delightful combination of the three," Jayden replied.

The caravan's owner winced from where he sat on the lead wagon. "And now they're not anything."

"You'll find the road safer with their passing, as will your fellow merchants," Jayden replied. The fight with the bandits had been brief, one-sided, and exceedingly messy. Dana had been repulsed by the consequences of the battle, but she couldn't disagree with Jayden. Those men would have gone on to hurt others if he hadn't stopped them.

That was the problem with being around Jayden. Dana liked him, in a sisterly sort of way, but he dealt harshly with foes. She'd decided to join Jayden on his journeys partly in gratitude after he'd risked his life for her town, but also to limit how much damage he might do.

And he'd done a lot of damage. Jayden had been the end to many threats in the three months they'd traveled together. Bandits preying on travelers, wolves and bears preying on livestock, and monsters that preyed on everything, he'd faced them and won. But Jayden had an intense hatred of the king and queen, one Dana didn't fully understand and he wouldn't explain. It had taken all her efforts to keep him focused on defeating dangers to the common man rather than going after the royal family like a starving dog after a bone. So far, she'd guided him down the right path, but it was a constant effort.

The caravan owner stood up and pointed at a dim light in the distance. "That's the town of Jumil. I'm afraid it doesn't have much to offer. The inn is cold and cramped. Their blacksmith specializes in mediocre work. Salt is an exotic seasoning. And the residents, well, they try hard."

"Yet you wish to go there," Jayden remarked.

"They pay well for spices and produce good furs," the owner replied. "I'll make a fair profit here even with your ten percent share of the cargo."

"Why don't other merchants come here if it's so nice?" Dana asked him.

"They used to, but the roads have been a nightmare ever since the civil war."

Shocked, Dana said, "That was twenty years ago!"

"I wouldn't lie to you," the man replied. He tipped his hat to Jayden and said, "No offense, but you're not the first to clear this road. It's been done many times by many men, but monsters and bandits keep cropping up, drawn in by the chance to rob farmhouses and travelers."

Jayden yawned as he walked. "Keeping the roads safe is supposed to be a job for knights. It's a shame they're too busy getting ready for war to care what happens to their own people."

The caravan owner chuckled without mirth. "As far as they're concerned, we're as far beneath them as livestock."

The town of Jumil was if anything less impressive than the caravan owner's description. The houses looked sturdy enough and properly maintained, but there were no decorations, no boardwalks to keep people from walking in the mud, and pigs wandered the streets rooting through garbage thrown out windows.

If the town wasn't pleasant, the residents were another matter. A cheer rose up when the caravan approached, and men ran out to greet them. Most of them were shopkeepers and homeowners eager to buy a share of the cargo, while some men came hoping to sell what goods they had. Still more people came to see the newcomers. It took Dana a moment to realize that a caravan's arrival was a spectacle for them rather than an ordinary occurrence.

"You're the first strangers here in a week," a town guard told them. He studied Jayden's odd clothing with some concern.

"And we are indeed strange," Jayden replied. "Nevertheless, we come bearing only the best of intentions."

The guard frowned. "You, ah, you're the Sorcerer Lord, aren't you? There are wanted posters for you in every town with more than fifty souls."

"Is that going to be a problem?" Jayden asked. He looked relaxed, even bored.

More guards came, but only to escort the caravan inside town limits. The first guard made no effort to alert them, instead saying, "If you cause no trouble then there will be no trouble. No bounty is worth dying for."

That cheered Jayden for all the wrong reasons. "Pray tell, what's my head worth?"

"The price on you goes up by the month. The latest bounty is five hundred silver pieces."

"Five hundred?" Jayden looked at Dana. "It's offensive. A cow fetches twenty silver pieces. A plow horse is worth fifty. I've bedeviled the crown for five years, robbing them, humiliating them, yet I'm worth only ten plow horses. Clearly, I have to improve my performance."

"Helping caravans and towns in need might bring the price down," Dana countered. Jayden's smile showed how little that mattered to him. "Settle up with the merchant and I'll see about getting us a place to sleep tonight."

"Agreed."

Dana spotted the town's inn and slipped through the growing crowd to reach it. She had to work fast. Jayden got bored easily, and when that happened, his thoughts turned to harassing the king. She had hours at most to find something, anything, for him to do that would bring in cash and possibly magic.

The caravan's owner had summed up Jumil's inn quite well. It was clear they got little business with their few rooms and would be totally unprepared if more than twenty visitors came to their town. There were a few men drinking at a table, so the inn wasn't totally deserted. The innkeeper watched the caravan through an open window while a boy swept the floor.

"Hi there," Dana said cheerfully. "My friends and I need rooms for the night."

The innkeeper pointed at Jayden, still outside and happily talking with excited children. He did love attracting attention. Sounding more curious than worried, the innkeeper asked, "You're with him?"

"Yes."

"Listen, we don't want trouble."

"You already have it. We were attacked by bandits on our way here."

One of the men drinking set down his mug. "It happened again?"

"It happened for the last time," Dana corrected him. That cheered the men if not the innkeeper. "It was a paying job, and one that helped your town. We don't have another job lined up after this one, though, so I thought you might be able to help. My friend is interested in old ruins, the older the better, but he's open to other opportunities. Are there threats nearby? Monsters, bandits, problems you'd like to go away and never come back?"

The innkeeper's brow furrowed. "There's an old stone tower north of here. We don't go near it, what with the howling at night."

A man at the table waved for Dana to join him. "We know places you could earn some coins and do us a good turn. Innkeeper, get the lady a drink and put it on my tab."

The next hour proved better than Dana had hoped for. The innkeeper provided directions to the tower and a history of the place going back three generations. More potential jobs came from the other guests. They had a litany of complaints, including thieves, highwaymen, walking skeletons, and a wyvern responsible for eating cattle. They also knew of a nearby mayor fond of confiscating cargo from passing merchants. It was a good list that would keep Jayden busy and profitable.

Speaking of Jayden, the Sorcerer Lord was noticeable by his absence. Dana looked outside in the growing darkness and saw Jayden chatting with the guards. It was odd to see them so friendly with a wanted man, but she'd seen that people in isolated towns like Jumil took a relaxed view of the law. They worried about their families and neighbors. Anything happening outside their little world was beyond their control and of little interest.

Dana had been the same not long ago. Her father was mayor of a small town, and she knew firsthand how hard people worked just to put food on the table. If some injustice or disaster fell on people a hundred miles away, there was little they could offer besides their sympathy. And if a stranger came with a dubious past, men were willing to overlook it provided he behaved and had something to offer.

Jayden had a lot to offer. He'd learned the magic of the long dead Sorcerer Lords, and in a kingdom with few wizards that made him a rare and precious commodity. He could handle big threats, like when he and Dana destroyed the Walking Graveyard a month ago. If a man was desperate, had some gold saved up, didn't mind property damage, and had no connection to the royal family, he could hire Jayden. That might be what was happening outside.

It was so dark that stars twinkled in the night sky when Jayden finally entered the inn. The caravan owner and his men came next, laughing and with coins to spare. Their wagons were already loaded with furs and safely stored in an empty barn. The innkeeper cheered at the increase in business and readied rooms for his guests.

Dana and Jayden shared a table near the back of the inn's common room.

Smiling, Dana told him, "I found places we could go next, all within five days' walking distance."

Jayden smiled back. "Two hours in town and you're already sharing girlish secrets with the ladies?"

"I spoke with men in the inn." She frowned and added, "I don't get along with other women. They're always so catty, like my being there is a threat."

"I imagine it has to do with having husbands with wandering eyes. You are efficient as always, Dana, but there's a matter I have to attend to first."

Worried, Dana asked, "What kind of matter?"

"We'll discuss it on the road tomorrow. For now, eat, drink, and enjoy what little this town has to offer."

The next morning brought a sparklingly bright day. Jumil's people were still giddy from having the road open to traffic and trade, and the innkeeper brought out a simple but filling breakfast. They were still eating when an older and visibly drunken man staggered into the inn.

"What brings you, mayor?" the innkeeper asked.

Dana prepared for the worst. Jayden's reputation meant there was no telling what sort of reception he'd receive, and the mayor might have come to arrest him. But the man brought no weapons or guards, and in his inebriated state, he was a threat to no one but himself.

Steadying himself against a wall, the mayor took out a scroll and unrolled it. "This came last night by royal courier. It…you need to hear it."

Reading aloud, the mayor announced, "By decree of His Majesty the King and his beloved wife the Queen, from this day forth there is a tax of one copper piece per person per day staying at an inn, hostel, or hotel, to be collected and sent to the capital each month."

"Mercy, you'll bankrupt me!" the innkeeper protested.

Still reading from the scroll, the mayor said, "Furthermore, the owners and operators of these establishments must record the names and destinations of all customers, to be reported to the capital on a monthly basis and at the owners' expense."

The caravan owner and other guests at the inn edged away. If the king knew who you were and where to find you, he could tax you. Rates started at twenty percent and went up from there. The king could also take offense at where a man went and who he did business with, resulting in fines, arrest, imprisonment, and possibly execution depending on royal whim.

"Hold on, now," the caravan owner began.

He needn't have worried. The mayor rolled up the scroll and said, "So for legal reasons none of you were ever here. Just, you need to know what's going on, and that other mayors might obey this foolishness." The man looked despondent as he left, muttering, "I used to like this job. I'm sure I did."

"Every innkeeper in the kingdom just became an informant for the crown," Dana said.

One of the men at the table grimaced. "This wouldn't have happened before the king remarried. He's not the same man he used to be before that wench and her clan got their hooks into him. The kingdom's been a dark place since the old queen passed away and her son was exiled, and it's growing darker by the day."

"Truer words were never spoken," Jayden said. He smiled in genuine friendship rather than his usual sarcastic grin. "It pains me to leave such good company, but we've work to do. I bid you good day, gentlemen, and wish you luck."

Dana followed him out onto the streets, where he headed north. "Jayden, you said you'd tell me what this was about when we got onto the road. Where are we going?"

"I accepted the job to help those merchants for a reason I didn't share with you before. I'd heard of a company of infantrymen marching the same road we took to reach Jumil. I want to know where they're going and why they were sent here. I spoke to the town guards last night. They confirmed the company's arrival two months ago and which road they departed on."

"We're going after an entire infantry company." Dana put a hand over her face. "Jayden, you're strong, but you can't fight eighty men. It's insane!" Nearby people turned and stared when she shouted. Lowering her voice, she said, "I like you. I respect you and know what you can do. I don't love the king any more than you do, but one man taking on a kingdom is insane. You're going to get killed."

"Possibly. Dana, the king and queen are planning a war of conquest against neighboring lands. Why would they send away troops they're going to need? Why send them to a part of the kingdom that's more or less safe?"

"Less safe than more," she told him. "There are monsters in the woods."

"So many they need eighty men to defeat them?" They left the town limits while Jayden spoke. "I'm not an idiot, contrary to all appearances. The adventures and opportunities you've found for me all take me away from more civilized parts of the kingdom, places where I could strike at the king and queen. I don't mind, as your leads have produced gold and two inscribed spells of the

Sorcerer Lords that enhanced my strength. But my goal has not changed. I intend to either bring down the throne or hurt it badly enough to prevent it from visiting the horrors of war on other lands."

"This isn't a good idea."

Jayden shrugged. "The alternatives are worse. You are, of course, not obliged to join me. I'm sure your parents would be glad if you returned home."

"I'm trying to save your life!"

"I know." Jayden was uncharacteristically polite. "I appreciate your concerns and the risks you've taken on my behalf. No one else has done the same, and I have helped many in the same way I did you and your town. It nearly cost you your life when we fought the Walking Graveyard."

"That thing only ate my shoes," Dana said. "I liked those shoes."

"It could have taken your feet. You remained with me after that happened, and I'm grateful. Dana, if I'm right, then something is dreadfully wrong and could get much worse. I'm not sure I can prevent it, but I must try."

Dana hated this. She'd tried her best, but Jayden was dead set on taking on the army, a force far worse in character than it once was. The kingdom was short of manpower ever since the civil war, so short that citizens were only obliged to join local militias rather than become soldiers. The king got around that by hiring mercenaries from other lands, brutal men whose loyalty depended on monthly pay.

"So where are we going?" she asked.

"The men went north to an unpopulated and isolated region."

Dana stopped in her tracks. "Wait, north? There are ruins of a stone tower north of here. The innkeeper said nobody's gone near there for decades because of weird noises."

Jayden rolled his eyes. "I normally don't hate being right."

Dana and Jayden traveled the entire day, leaving farmland far behind and entering rolling hills and forests. The road they followed was narrow and winding, but there were fresh wagon ruts and countless boot prints in the dirt. Men had come through in great numbers.

"The innkeeper said the tower is all that's left of a larger ruined settlement,"

Dana told Jayden. "It was always in bad shape, but long ago, there was a flood that took out everything but the tower. People used to go there to scavenge bricks for their houses. They stopped when they heard weird noises with no source."

"Have livestock or people disappeared?"

"Nobody got close enough to risk it. They've been shying away from this place for generations. The only men who came close were fur trappers, and their traps stayed empty no matter how long they were out, the bait drying out instead of being eaten."

Jayden frowned. "The duration of the problem suggests powerful magic is involved. Whatever it is, it hasn't been freed yet, a blessing indeed. If these mercenaries dig up the source of the power, they risk causing devastation across a wide area. Thousands could be in danger."

"Could this be magic from the old Sorcerer Lords?" she asked. The original Sorcerer Lords had died out over a thousand years ago, torn apart by internal divisions and finished off by the elves of old. Long gone they might be, but they'd left behind ruins, artifacts, and monsters that survived their creators' passing.

"Possibly. They produced horrors the likes of which this world hadn't seen before, and some of their evil lives to this day. Such willingness to commit terrible deeds is far from unique. Many have perpetrated equally foul acts since the fall of the original Sorcerer Lords and could be responsible for this problem."

The countryside became ever more wild, with tangled weeds and trees twisted in unnatural shapes. At the same time, there were few animals present and no signs that men lived here except the road itself.

"We'll leave the road and travel near it for the next few miles," Jayden said. "That way we may miss sentries posted by the mercenaries."

Dana worried she might pick up ticks in the tangled brush, but she found insects and vermin just as absent as larger animals. Marching through the brush slowed their progress and left a trail even an idiot could follow.

"What do we do if they found whatever caused the trouble?" she asked.

"Steal it if possible, destroy it if necessary, or run for our lives if it's as dangerous as I think." Jayden smiled at her and added, "I dislike running, but it's best when the alternative is dying. I'd like to put that off as long as possible."

"I'd never guess," Dana said dryly. The going was tough with the thick underbrush. It didn't help that there were no animals to eat it, and it looked like dead briars and brambles weren't rotting, either. She practically needed an axe to force her way forward. Casually, she asked, "Jayden?"

"Yes?"

"Do you think the man behind that tree is trying to hide from us?"

He glanced to their right. "The one behind the oak?"

"Yes, him."

"I imagine so. It would be impolite to ask, but then I've never been accused of being good-mannered. Hello!"

The raggedy man broke from cover and ran for the road. Now that he was in the clear, he looked like an escaped slave or prisoner. His long brown hair was tangled, his clothes torn and dirty, and he had fresh bruises. Jayden walked after him at a leisurely rate while speaking arcane words that formed a black whip in his hand. He swung it and the whip stretched wildly until it reached ahead of the fleeing man. The whip burned through the underbrush, hacking through curling trees and twisted brambles, finally cutting through an oak. The man skidded to a halt in front of the shredded plant life.

"I see you like a captive audience," the man said in a polite tone. He held up his shackled hands and rattled the chains running between his wrists.

Jayden and Dana walked over to the man while the whip retracted and disappeared. Smiling, Jayden said, "Now then, what's a fine-looking gentleman like yourself doing on a lonely road?"

The stranger smiled back. "Trying not to die. It's a full-time job as of late. I suppose introductions are in order. I'm—"

Dana marched up to the man and poked him in the chest. "You're Jeremy Galfont, the grave robber! My father has a wanted poster with your picture. You've desecrated graves across the kingdom!"

"I, madam, am an asset recovery specialist," Galfont replied. "In my defense, the wanted posters got my bad side. I'm quite handsome when I'm allowed to shave, bathe, and eat regular meals."

Jayden cast another spell, forming a sword of utter blackness edged in white light. He pointed it at Galfont's throat, making the man sweat. "That answers one question and demands another. You look like someone whose past caught up with him, but we found you on the road with no guards or men chasing you. Care to explain your situation?"

"Certainly, but would you mind pointing that sword somewhere else? It makes me nervous." Jayden answered Galfont's request by lowering his blade from the grave robber's throat to hover between his legs. "That's not much of an improvement."

"It wasn't meant to be. Answer my question."

Galfont gulped before he began. "I'd like to start by saying this isn't my fault. The lady's description of me leaves a lot to be desired. I recover riches that would otherwise be of use to no one and reintroduce them into the economy."

"You rob graves!" Dana yelled.

Galfont rolled his eyes. "Must you put a negative spin on it? My profession requires patience and skill. I do hours of research to learn which graves have valuables to recover. I've never hurt a man nor beast, and I always spread the wealth."

"Jayden, can I hit him?"

"If his story doesn't progress, then yes."

The grave robber sighed. "No one appreciates the hardships I go through.

Three months ago, I was spending hard-earned coins in a tavern when a very polite young man came to my table. He said he was interested in hiring me. Despite the young lady's poor opinion of me, I don't hire to anyone. Employers either want the profits of my hard work, or they want me to do something dangerous and repugnant."

"Like rob graves?" she asked.

"If I may continue," Galfont asked peevishly. "The man knew a lot about me, never a good sign in my line of work, and promised a reward for my services. I thanked him for his offer, threw my drink in his face, and ran out the back…where I found a number of men with swords. I was arrested and told my reward would be keeping my head and neck close friends. My work was to help dig up a treasure in an ancient ruin."

"The stone tower north of here?" Jayden asked.

"The same. I was taken there with eighty mercenaries, men without any sense of humor, I might add. I work best alone, but they insisted on staying with me night and day. We spent months digging and sifting through the ruins. I told them it was pointless! It was clear to any with eyes that these were elf ruins, and elves don't bury their dead with anything, not even clothes."

Dana tried to imagine that and blushed. "That must make for awkward funerals."

"Closed caskets are required," Galfont told her. "The ruins were trapped with magic wards, old and very powerful ones. I got around them with one part skill, one part experience, and eight parts blind luck, but early yesterday morning, I found a hidden room in the tower containing a silvery box three inches across. My captors recognized it and were very pleased to get it."

Jayden lowered the sword and pressed closer. "This is very important. Did they identify it?"

Galfont shrugged. "They called it Vali-something or other. I'd never heard the word before."

"Validendum?" Jayden asked.

"No. It was harsher sounding than that."

"Valivaxis?"

The grave robber snapped his fingers. "That's it! Wait, you knew the word. Oh dear, that's not good for me, is it?"

"It's not good for anyone. How did you escape?"

"I was tied up and thrown into a wagon while the mercenaries broke down their camp. They'd only just started when there was a terrible scream. Something, and I'm glad to say I don't know what, attacked their camp. I heard its death cry, a ghastly sound, and I heard them pile wood on the body and burn it. I gather they lost a lot of men. They got back to breaking down their camp and were ready to leave. This time, I saw one of the men carry the Valivaxis. It got all glowy, and a shiny door opened in front of him. This, I'm sorry, I can't describe it without using the word 'thing,' came out and attacked. I broke free and ran."

Frightened, Dana asked, "What happened to the men?"

"Some tried to fight and others fled. The ones who ran lasted longer. I know a few of them got away because I heard them stumbling around in the dark the same as me. There was a terrible screaming sound, so I think the second monster was killed."

"We're in trouble," Dana said.

"We are, as is the town of Jumil and everyone else within five hundred miles," Jayden said. "We have to close the Valivaxis before anything else escapes from it."

"I doubt I'd be much use in my current condition," Galfont said. He wasn't lying. The man was unarmed and had obviously suffered during his incarceration. He held up his shackled hands and said, "I feel I've been of some use in this matter. Might I be so bold as to ask for payment, kind sir?"

Jayden cut through the shackles with his sword and allowed the black blade to vanish. The grave robber bowed and, before leaving, said, "I'd tip my hat if I had one. Wizard though you are, sir, I'll wish you luck, because magic alone won't be enough."

"Wait, you're letting him go?" Dana demanded.

"We can't turn him in for the bounty money given my own wanted status, nor would I want to considering the tortures he would receive. That means we either kill him or let him go, and I choose mercy when possible."

Galfont made a hasty exit while Jayden walked onto the road and headed for the stone tower. Dana followed him and asked, "Jayden, what is this thing?"

"I'd read about the Valivaxis long ago. It dates to the Ancient Elf Empire, one of the many magic artifacts that survived its collapse. Its more common name is the Idiot's Graveyard."

"A grave for idiots? It must be full to overflowing."

Jayden smirked. "The name refers to the royalty buried there. In elven society, it's considered a heavy blow for an enemy to desecrate the graves of your ancestors. Elven emperors were very worried about the loss of face they'd suffer if their dead were disinterred. They built the Valivaxis, a gate to an inhospitable world where they placed their dead."

Puzzled, Dana asked, "Why is it called the Idiot's Graveyard if that's where they put their leaders?"

"The elves never got over the fall of their empire. They had to blame someone, and the emperors were a popular choice."

Dana snapped her fingers. "The monsters that attacked the mercenaries came from the Valivaxis. They were meant to defend it, weren't they?"

"This is why I like traveling with you, Dana. Yes, the ancient elves knew if someone stole the Valivaxis, they could use it to dig up the former emperors. As a further safeguard, they stocked it with their wizards' failed experiments, monsters created with powerful magic and too unstable to control. Elf wizards placed those abominations in a magical slumber, neither moving nor aging, wakening only if triggered to be a final guard against attack. Opening the Valivaxis is easy, but there is a specific way to do it to avoid waking its foul defenders. The mercenaries did it wrong and paid with their lives.

"And it remains open. The Valivaxis has only been opened once before, releasing monsters twice a day until it was correctly sealed. That one horrible mistake cost the lives of many good people before it was closed, however that was done. Now that it's open again, it will continue releasing its guardians, horrors created by an ancient and debased people, and they will attack any and all they meet."

Worried, she asked, "How many monsters are in there?"

"No one knows, and I'd rather not find out."

Dana jogged in front of Jayden and asked, "But why would the king and queen send men to find it? What good are graves with no treasure and monsters no one can control?"

Jayden scowled. She knew him well enough to know he wasn't mad at her asking the question, but instead at the answer he'd have to give. "There are two equally disturbing possibilities. The first is they didn't know that the emperors were buried without even the clothes on their backs and hoped there were riches to recover. Vulgar as that is, I wouldn't put it past them."

"And the second?"

Jayden stopped walking, seething in anger. "They knew there is no treasure and want the monsters. Such an uncontrollable force can be a benefit depending on where they are released. Suppose a spy working for the king sneaked into an enemy country with the Valivaxis and opened it. The monsters would attack the first people they met, sowing destruction and discord, costing countless lives. The royal couple could then send in their armies to finish off whoever survived and claim land now conveniently devoid of people."

Dana felt a cold, empty feeling in her stomach at the thought. "They wouldn't be blamed for it, either. No one could link them to the monsters."

"I don't know how they discovered the location of the Valivaxis. Perhaps they found some ancient texts describing where it last was, or they hired a wizard or seer to locate it. Once they knew the location, they seized Galfont to help recover it without heavy loss of life. It was a brilliant if revolting plan that would have worked, except one of their men must have accidentally opened it. And now we have to close it if we're to save Jumil and all the towns nearby."

Jayden and Dana spent the rest of the trip in silence. Dana was terrified of what they'd find. Two monsters had been freed from the Valivaxis and then destroyed, but eighty men had died to do it. She'd been worried how Jayden could fight so many mercenaries, but how could he defeat monsters that were able to win such a fight? Jayden, confident as ever, marched to a battle he might not win.

The land became ever more desolate as they progressed. The soil was rocky, so much so that boulders jutted up from the ground. Thin soil supported few plants, and even those were thin and sickly. By and by, the road grew steeper until it took a lot of effort to climb up. Eventually, the road leveled out and brought them to the ruins.

"I was wondering how a flood could destroy an entire ruin," Dana said.

"This would do the job," Jayden agreed.

The stone tower was on the very edge of a gorge going sixty feet down to a dry, rocky riverbed far below. Stone tile roads led to the edge of the gorge, showing where the rest of the ruins had been. Some long distant flood had weakened the ground so much that it had gone down the gorge as a rockslide, taking with it whatever buildings and roads had survived until that time. Now only a stone tower fifty feet tall and twenty feet across remained alongside freshly dug pits.

There were new additions to the ruins courtesy of the mercenaries. Flattened canvas tents littered the ground next to crushed wagons, smashed crates, and broken wood barrels. Snapped spears and bent swords were scattered about. There were charred remains of two bonfires, one cold and the other smoldering with glowing embers. Dana spotted a ribcage three feet across in the older fire, and a mound of large, blackened vertebra in the second. Here and there, some of the mercenaries' property survived by luck or good planning. The pits still had intact digging tools in them, as if the owners would soon be back.

And there were bodies. Most had been placed in the pits and covered with a thin layer of soil. A few remained above ground. They'd suffered serious wounds, many crushed to death as if a great weight had fallen upon them.

"I've no love for mercenaries, but no one deserved this," Jayden said as he walked along the edge of the pits.

Dana shied away from the fallen men. "I'd heard from my father that some of them had come from as far away as Skitherin Kingdom. Imagine traveling so far just to die."

Jayden pulled open a destroyed tent and searched through it. "We have to work fast. The Valivaxis could open again at any time."

Dana picked a spot far from the dead mercenaries and looked for the silvery box. "The grave robber said some mercenaries escaped. How long until they bring reinforcements?"

"The closest towns have small garrisons, too few to help." Jayden found a pouch of coins and tossed it aside. "Gold. Any other day that would be a worthy find. Nearby town militias are too poorly trained to be of much use. Surviving mercenaries will have to travel for days to reach the nearest town big enough to offer help, then spend days further bringing them here. This assumes they don't simply flee the kingdom after such a loss. No, we don't have to worry about mercenaries in the near future."

More searching turned up a host of loot. There were coins, rings, weapons, some armor, and plenty of tools. Dana might be a mayor's daughter, but her family was still of modest means. A pile of valuables like this would be worth a fortune to the poor people back home. But no matter how hard she looked, she didn't find anything resembling the Valivaxis.

Dana found a handsome blue cloak and bundled treasure into it. It bothered her to take things off a battlefield and made her wonder if there was really a difference between this and what Galfont the grave robber did. True, he disturbed graves and left families of the dead traumatized, while she was taking what was freely available for any who walked by. She could live with the distinction.

"Some of these silver coins are tarnished black," Dana observed. "I think the mercenaries found them while digging for the real treasure."

"I've come across other antiquities," Jayden told her. "There's nothing of great value and no magic, but it's still more than I expected. I'd thought all the remnants of the Elf Empire were long since looted."

"How long do we have until the Valivaxis opens?" she asked.

Jayden overturned a damaged wagon and sifted through its contents. "The legends said it opened twice a day when activated."

That news made Dana stop working and stand up. "Galfont said two monsters already came out, and that was yesterday."

"Which means either another one has already been set loose or will be so soon. Keep looking."

Dana searched with a renewed vigor. They had to find the Valivaxis for their own sake and for the people in Jumil. She could only imagine what would happen if a monster tough enough to fight a company of infantrymen attacked such a small town. It would be terrible!

Wait, what was that glittering in the bottom of one of the pits? Dana had missed it earlier because there was a body in it and she hadn't wanted to touch it. Gingerly, she climbed down and shifted the dead man aside. "Jayden, this might be it."

Jayden ran over and climbed down beside her. The Valivaxis was in the hands of a younger man once handsome to behold and dressed like an officer. "This must be the man who arrested Galfont. He found his prize and paid for it."

"Can you close it?" she asked.

Jayden took the silvery box and studied it. "The good news is it's safe to touch. Once opened, the Valivaxis has no further defenses. The bad news is it will remain dangerous until closed, which I don't know how to do."

"Bad news seems to understate the problem."

Dana and Jayden left the pit and sat down. Jayden touched a small panel on the Valivaxis and slid it over. "It's a puzzle box. Arranging the panels in the right pattern will close the gateway to the other world."

Jayden slid panels across the box from one position to another. Somehow, the panels could move from one side of the box to another without coming off. Dana saw two panels together form a word in elven, but Jayden separated them and moved them into new positions.

"There is a pattern to it," he said. "The dragons represent years, months, and days, while the words list specific elf emperors. I believe the dates match important events for the emperors, birth, death, or coronation. The problem is many of these dates don't correspond to any of the three."

This was far outside Dana's training or experience. She left him to the box and kept an eye on their surroundings. After all, Jayden might be wrong about the mercenaries leaving. Survivors could return to reclaim their prize if they were scared to come back without it. There could also be a monster about, whether from the Valivaxis or one native to the kingdom.

"Why do you think people living nearby heard noises?" she asked. "I mean, the box was sealed and the monsters were asleep."

"Sleepers stir in the night, and no door is ever entirely closed," he replied. "Those noises might have been what alerted the king and queen to the presence of the Valivaxis in their land. Let's see, slide this one here...no, that's not right. Emperor Clastisin wasn't born for another century."

It had taken most of the day to get here, and even summer's long days had to end. The sun began to set and clouds turned a lovely shade of orange. Dana rummaged through the destroyed camp and found food and water. She was eating a late dinner when she saw a glint far down the road.

"Someone's coming."

Jayden's attention remained on the Valivaxis. "Tell them to wait or, better yet, to leave. When was Emperor Laskimaxil born?"

The last rays of light struck the approaching figure. As it neared, Dana could make out a man wearing a suit of silver plate armor set with jade panels, easily the gaudiest armor she'd ever seen. As the man neared, she noticed elaborate etchings on the jade. The knight was unarmed and moved without haste.

"Someone weird is coming," she warned.

Still looking at the Valivaxis, Jayden asked, "How weird?"

"His armor has jade on it."

Jayden set down the Valivaxis and stood up. Studying the approaching knight, he said, "That *is* a strange suit of armor. It looks ceremonial with the jade. Wait, elves favor green jade above all other precious stones. They call them eternal leaves."

The jade knight reached the edge of the ruins and destroyed mercenary camp. He stopped walking well away from Jayden and Dana but stood facing them. A sour, acidic smell permeated the air.

"Name yourself," Jayden called out.

The jade knight answered with a shriek no man or animal could make. His shoulders shifted forward, and a sickening cracking sound rang out. Eight oozing green tentacles sprouted from his back and stretched out thirty feet to grab intact swords and spears. Armed, the hideous knight advanced on them.

"The Valivaxis must have released this abomination before we arrived," Jayden said. He backed up and cast a spell to form his black magic whip. "Get behind me, and whatever you do, don't let it touch you."

Slime dripped from the jade knight's back as he walked into battle. Dana ran to the left, and from there she saw a crack running down the horrible creature's armored back. Those tentacles sprouted from the crack, and inside it, she saw what looked like pulsating organs.

"I'm not trying to enter the Valivaxis," Jayden told it. "I'm trying to close the gate. You can help me do it. We can close the doors and keep the emperors' graves safe. Do you understand?"

"Burning, changing, twisting, winding," it hissed and swung three swords at Jayden. Two blades came from the right and one from the left. He ducked two swords and struck the third with his whip. The whip burned through the sword and cut off the tip of a tentacle. The jade knight howled and backed up, but only for a few seconds. It grabbed a shovel with the disarmed tentacle and attacked again.

"I'm not your enemy!" Jayden shouted.

"Twisting words, bending thoughts, burning minds, winding ways." The jade knight was totally mad, its mind as warped as its body. It pressed the attack with swords and shovel coming straight down. Jayden ran from it and swung his whip again. This time, he caught a tentacle and the whip wrapped around it. There was a hiss as the whip burned through the tentacle. The jade knight howled again but didn't flee. Instead, it ran at Jayden and swung its remaining weapons with wild abandon.

Jayden took cover behind a damaged wagon while the hideous knight dropped down on all fours and scuttled around it. More cracks appeared on its armor, this time on the legs and arms, and still more tentacles stretched out. It lunged at him, swinging a host of weapons, and Jayden barely dodged the attacks. He cut a spear in half and leaped over a sword aimed at his ankles. Jayden lopped off another tentacle, forcing the jade knight back. It dropped its weapons and grabbed the damaged wagon with its tentacles, then lifted it up and threw it at Jayden. He hacked the wagon in half and ducked when the jade knight jumped fifteen feet and sailed inches over his head.

Quite by accident, that jump brought it close to Dana.

"Run!" Jayden ordered.

Dana grabbed a shovel, the only weapon at hand, and headed for the tower. The jade knight scuttled after her, its arms and legs splayed out like a lizard's. Its tentacles swung at her and she swatted one aside with the shovel. When another grabbed her around the waist, she drew her knife and slashed it. The tentacle spurted yellow ichor and let go.

Jayden caught up and stabbed the jade knight in the leg. Black sword met shining armor, and the magic blade pierced deep. The jade knight howled and ran off fifty feet.

"Pay attention to the man with the sword!" he yelled at it.

The jade knight gibbered and howled, a frightening mix of random words and animal noises. Its tentacles grabbed tent poles, shovels, picks, anything it could use as a weapon, and it charged Jayden again. He ran to the left and it followed, leaving Dana safe for the moment.

This would be a good time to run for her life, but that wasn't an option when this abomination was faster and tougher than she was. If it beat Jayden, it could come after her and there was little she could do to stop it. She took a step closer to the stone tower, wondering if there was anything in it that might help. That thought ended when her right foot got so hot she jumped back and cried out in surprise. She looked down to see that she'd stepped into the remnants of the second bonfire. Her leather boot was blackened where it had touched the still-hot embers.

Thinking fast, Dana scooped up red-hot embers with her shovel. The jade knight had its back to her while it was fighting Jayden, and she saw those wide openings in its armor where the tentacles emerged. She ran after it, and just as it was attacking Jayden, she threw the shovel's contents straight into the hole in its back where those freakish tentacles sprouted.

The jade knight screamed a high-pitched screech of agony. It threw its weapons aside and flailed about, knocking Dana to the ground. It clawed at its back, trying to dig out the embers burning it from the inside. Jayden rushed in and drove his sword through the panicked beast's chest, impaling it and lifting it off its feet. The magic blade winked out, and he let the jade knight drop to the ground. It twitched and squirmed for a few moments, then became still.

Jayden ran over and helped Dana up. "Are you hurt?"

"Bruised, but I'll live." She stared at the abomination shaped like a man. It was dead, a blessing, but many more could soon arrive. Even now, it disgusted her in the way it parodied a knight yet had those awful tentacles growing from its body...growing longer. "Jayden, the tentacles you cut off, they're healing! It's getting better!"

The jade knight stirred. Its wounds began to seal shut, and it tried to get up. It got on its hands and knees before falling back to the ground. Dana realized now why the mercenaries had burned the other two monsters. Hard as it was to hurt them, they could recover if they fell in battle and had to be completely destroyed.

Jayden pressed his hands together and began chanting. The jade knight hissed and sat up. Its tentacles slithered about until they found idle weapons to grab. A tiny spark formed within Jayden's hands and he continued chanting. The jade knight struggled to its feet just as Jayden finished his spell. The spark flew off and slipped inside the monster's armored body through the crack in its back.

"Get in the pit!" he shouted. Dana jumped into the nearest pit and Jayden leapt down beside her.

BOOM!

The spark expanded into a fireball twenty feet across. When the flames subsided, Dana got up and saw that the jade knight had been consumed by the blast. Only shattered bits of jade and melted scraps of armor remained. Nearby tents and wagons were burning, as were some weapons.

"That's a new one," Dana said as she climbed out of the pit.

"It's actually the first spell I learned," he replied. He followed her and leaned against a broken wagon, this one not on fire. "I don't use it often because it takes so long to cast. Enemies are rarely obliging enough to let me complete it."

Something glowed to their right. Dana and Jayden turned to see the Valivaxis shine and its many panels slide about.

Dana stared at it. "You have got to be kidding me."

A glowing door appeared ten feet in front of the Valivaxis. Dry, cold air spilled out of the opening, and they heard a multitude of growls. The magic door was only four feet across, but it widened as some new horror pressed forward.

"Can you close it?" Dana asked.

Jayden ran over and snatched the Valivaxis off the ground. He slid the silver panels on the little box, but the moment he took his fingers off the panels, they immediately started moving again. "No! We've got another one to deal with, and soon!"

Countless clawed hands grasped the edges of the magic door. At first, Dana thought it was a large number of monsters coming through at once, but as the slavering green horror kept pushing forward, she realized there was only one creature. The dozens of green, slimy, wide-jawed monsters were connected, with limbs fused together to make a single abomination. The many heads had no eyes, only gaping mouths, yet they turned to face Jayden and Dana.

Jayden threw down the Valivaxis and remade his black whip. To Dana's surprise, the magic door moved when he dropped the silvery box. She shouted, "The door is linked to the Valivaxis! It goes where the box does!"

"What?"

There wasn't time to explain. Dana grabbed the Valivaxis and ran for the gorge. As she ran, the magic doorway moved with her, carrying the monster along. The monster kept coming out, more and more horrible bodies like an entire crowd. She didn't know exactly how big it was, but it kept crawling out of the magic door. She'd nearly reached the gorge's edge when the monster figured out what she was doing. It grabbed at rocks and ruined wagons, trying to stop. Jayden struck it with his whip and it let go, allowing Dana to keep running until she was at the edge of the gorge, and the magic door was ten feet over the lip.

The monster tried to pull back into the magic door, but there was too much of it through already, and it fell screaming to its death.

Jayden looked down at the creature at the bottom of the dry riverbed below. "Dana Illwind, you are without a doubt my favorite person in the world."

A full day had passed since their battle, yet Dana and Jayden had not left the ruins. Dana had gathered up a respectable pile of treasure while Jayden had covered every square inch of dirt with formulas and math equations. He'd spent the entire night and all of today trying to find the right combination of panels to seal the Valivaxis. He wiped a patch of dirt clean and scratched new numbers on it, and then scowled.

"Any luck?" Dana asked.

"That depends on your definition of luck. I have three configurations that might close the Valivaxis. The problem is there's no way to know which one will work until it tries to open again."

She walked alongside him and frowned. "What do we do when we close it?"

"Take a boat three days out to sea and throw the Valivaxis overboard. I see no alternative."

"How soon until it opens again?"

"Two or three minutes, assuming this configuration is wrong." He stood up and stretched his arms. "We're running out of time. We have to be long gone before the king's men come. Still, this is the best place to close the door without endangering others."

Dana looked over the edge of the gorge at the two ash piles at the bottom. Jayden had cremated the first monster Dana had dumped over the gorge, and then the next one that had appeared around breakfast time and plummeted to its doom. Would the Valivaxis open again and another monster fall to its death? They'd know soon enough.

The sun began to set, and to Dana and Jayden's frustration, the Valivaxis started glowing. But this time something was different. The panels didn't move across the box and a magic door didn't form. The glow came from one side of the box and then another, as if it was searching for a way out. Finding none, the light died away and the Valivaxis fell silent, releasing no new walking atrocity upon the world.

Jayden gingerly picked up the Valivaxis and wrapped it in a cloak once owned by a mercenary, then stowed it in a backpack with treasure he'd found in the camp. "Come, Dana, let's be on our way. We dare not stay longer when the king's forces could soon arrive. I'd tell you this is over, except our lives are in danger until the Idiot's Graveyard is safely hidden where none can ever find it."

"Whoever put it in the tower thought it was safely hidden," Dana said, highlighting how hard their task would be. She followed him from the camp with all the loot she could carry. "Life's never dull around you, Jayden. It might be short, but never dull."

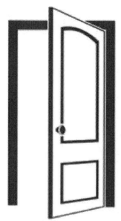

Arthur is the author of five books, William Bradshaw King of the Goblins, William Bradshaw and a Faint Hope, William Bradshaw and War Unending, William Bradshaw and Fool's Gold, *and* Goblin Stories. *These books were almost inevitable given that Arthur has been a fan of science fiction and fantasy since he was old enough to walk. Major influences include the works of the puppeteer and filmmaker Jim Henson and*

the British artist Brian Froud. Expect more books in the future, as all attempts to stop Arthur from writing have failed.

https://www.booksie.com/portfolio-view/ArthurD7000-131311

Cosmic Cravings

AJ Bakke

"No chocolate!" Bree wailed. Dramatically, she threw her little paws in the air and flopped on the floor of the candy shop in despair.

Something loomed over her. She looked up in time to see the tread of a shoe. Bits of debris from the street stuck to it as it descended.

Suddenly, an intervening cat blocked the impending doom. Fluffy, white fur filled Bree's view.

She heard the man utter a wordless exclamation. Stomping sent vibrations through the floor, bouncing her. She could easily envision his arms flailing as he hopped around, trying to simultaneously regain his balance and avoid stepping on the cat. A common dance in the city of Promise.

Usually a cat would eat a mouse instead of protect it, but Bree was no ordinary mouse. The cats of this city were particularly fond of her—once they got past the initial instinct to pounce.

Anyway, Bree had more important things on her mind than whether or not she might be crushed by an unwitting foot.

She jumped to her paws as her human friend, Amiah, helped steady the stranger.

"Go ahead," Amiah encouraged him to move ahead of her in line. She stooped down and, before anything else, pet the cat as was proper. The feline arched and then turned to saunter away, tail in the air.

Bree tilted her head, one pink eye squinting accusation at the world in general.

"Come on, get off the floor, Bree." Amiah offered a pudgy hand.

Bree sighed dramatically and crawled onto Amiah's palm. "But you don't understand. This is a cosmic emergency!"

Amiah transferred Bree to her shoulder. "Uh huh." She didn't sound convinced.

Bree hopped aboard and held onto a bit of golden brown hair. It hung thick and wavy, all the way to the woman's waist.

"I can't even even!" Bree cried.

Amiah chuckled. "That's not a viable phrase, not here on Deart, nor on Earth."

"What's Earth?" a nearby orc child asked. It had taken Bree and Amiah some time to become accustomed to the extremely different races living in Promise. But by now, seeing a green complexion had become common. The young girl looked cute with dark pigtails, wearing stylish trousers and a long shirt with a broad belt around her waist.

"Oh…" Amiah paused, trying to come up with an answer. "Some place far away." Accurate enough.

"That's not important!" Bree waved her paws around as if she could dismiss every other subject from existence and make everyone focus on her plight. "There's no chocolate on this planet."

The little girl quizzically tilted her head. "What's chocolate?"

"Exactly!" Bree cried.

"Hey!" The girl pointed at Bree. Her pigtails bounced as she jumped in excitement. "It's Bree the Mouse-Mage!"

Amiah laughed, round cheeks rosy. "Yes it is. Would you like her autograph?"

"Yes!" the girl squealed. "Let me find something." She began to search through her carry bag.

Mages were loved, certainly, but no other mage was a mouse like Bree. So far, the novelty of a mouse-mage had yet to wear off.

The girl's father, who loomed nearby, stooped to hand her a piece of paper from a notepad. "Here you are, dear."

"Thanks, Daddy." She handed the paper to Amiah, who in turn held it up to Bree.

Bree tried to muster up a cheerful veneer. She didn't want to disappoint a little girl, after all. Pictures of chocolate-covered coffee beans danced in her head as she placed her paw on the paper.

It burst into flames.

Amiah yelped and dropped it.

The girl squealed and jumped, clapping her hands.

"Oops!" Bree exclaimed. "Sorry!"

Amiah stomped on the paper with the heel of her boot. The blue skirt of her dress swished.

"Magic and I are not getting along today." Bree sighed.

"Do you have another piece of paper?" Amiah asked.

"I do," the father said with a grin bordered by large tusks.

The little girl giggled and passed another piece of paper to Amiah.

"Focus," Amiah cautioned as she held it up to Bree again.

"But I want chocolate!" Bree cried. However, she scrunched up her whiskery nose, beady pink eyes narrowing on the paper. She carefully placed her paw on it again.

The need for chocolatey goodness intruded on her mind. Chocolate ice cream. Chocolate candy bars. Chocolate truffles. And most importantly, chocolate-covered coffee beans.

A flare of fire consumed the paper.

"Please don't burn my hair," Amiah said with a laugh. "Maybe a pen would be a better idea."

"No way," Bree squeaked. "Pens are for loser authors. Magic is the way to go for a mage autograph."

About twenty-six pieces of paper later, Amiah handed the child an intact one with the lightly singed shape of a paw on it. "There you go."

The girl smiled brightly as she took the autographed paper. "Thank you, Miss Mouse Mage!"

"You're welcome," Bree chirped.

Amiah wished them all a good day and left the shop. Bree clung to her shoulder as she set off down the sidewalk. Noise enveloped them. The streets bustled with activity. Horns occasionally honked, but they didn't belong to cars. Like chocolate, the world of Deart didn't have cars. Deart had bicycles, carts, carriages, horseback, and one's own two feet for transportation.

And magical devices, but it was such a huge expenditure of power to use magic to travel that it wasn't worth it for the general populace. The cost would be astronomical.

"I could do it that way, though," Bree said.

"Eh?" Amiah asked since she hadn't heard Bree's thoughts.

"Travel with magic," Bree said, perking up. "That's what I'll do! I'll make a portal back to Earth."

Amiah's round features pursed in a wince. "I'm not sure that's such a great idea."

"It's a perfect idea! I'll bring back lots of chocolate. And chocolate plants. That way Deart can have chocolate!"

"For all we know, they might have it already."

Bree scowled at the side of Amiah's face. "Promise is the biggest, most advanced city in all of Deart. If they had chocolate on this world, then it would be here already."

"Does chocolate even come from plants?" Amiah wondered.

"I don't know," Bree said. "It has to come from something. Coffee comes from plants."

"And here I thought lattes and chocolate bars grew on trees," Amiah said jokingly.

"Still a plant!" Bree pointed out.

Amiah laughed. "So do you want to try another candy store?"

"It will only lead to disappointment," Bree said. She pointed toward the slow rise of the land. In the distance perched the impressive structures of the Promise of Magic Industries. "Let's go back. I have work to do."

"Remember how you incinerated all those pieces of paper when you meant to only put a paw print on them?" Amiah asked.

"So?"

"So, don't you think a portal might be a bit…much?"

Bree made a face. "I'll have the fairies to help me."

"Maybe you should talk to Landon."

"No way!" Bree flicked her tail. "Just 'cause he's the head mage doesn't mean he knows everything. He'll just tell me that chocolate is a silly thing to blow the planet up for."

"Well…"

Bree threw her paws in the air. "I'm not gonna blow the planet up!"

Amiah shrugged, upsetting Bree's balance. She scrambled wildly to hang on.

"Oh, sorry," Amiah apologized, leveling her shoulder.

"No worries," Bree responded perkily. Now that she had a foolproof plan, her mood improved significantly. "Besides," she continued the argument, or discussion, whatever it was, "what better place to keep the risk of blowing the planet up to a minimum than the Academy?"

"You got me there," Amiah conceded.

As she followed one of the paths through massive, sprawling lawns within the gates of the Industries, Amiah stooped down for the thirteenth time to pet a cat.

"Hurry up!" Bree cried.

"I'm sorry, it's just that they all want attention."

"There's hundreds, thousands, of cats here," Bree said. "You can't stop and pet all of them."

As the sayings go, "Cats are attracted to magic," and "Where there is magic, there are cats." Either way, Promise held one of the largest feline communities due to the high number of mages collected there. Cats dotted the area, lying on the lawn, sitting on benches, climbing on sculptures, chasing after butterflies, and getting underfoot.

"You're stalling on purpose, aren't you?" Bree poked Amiah's ear with an accusatory paw.

Amiah giggled, her neck twitching. "I like this place. I'd rather not see it blown into oblivion."

"You're confidence in me is overwhelming," Bree said dryly. "Now hurry up. I must find a way to get chocolate! It's more important than anything else!"

Alyn bent low over his dragon's back as they flew toward home. Colossal towers jutted high, protected by pools of boiling hot water. Arching bridges of stone connected the towers of differing heights. Each plateau provided vast space for Lidran living.

Sunlight gleamed on Shade's dark blue scales, bringing out hues of purple. Alyn peered over the side of her neck, watching clouds of writhing steam pass by below. Wind whipped black hair in his face, but he ignored it.

The six crow-sized dragons and their even smaller riders descended toward the dragon tower. Shade backwinged, stirring dust as she landed. No sooner had her taloned feet touched rock than Alyn deftly leapt from her back.

Leathery wings settled as he unbuckled the harness. He fondly patted her shoulder, trying for some normalcy in the face of a dire situation. "Good flying today, love," he told her.

Shade nudged him with her snout and he managed a chuckle, though tension nearly made him choke on it.

"Talical," he addressed their flight leader. "You need me in for the report?"

She shook her head as she slung a leather harness over her shoulder. "Not at this time. I will have you summoned if necessary."

Alyn offered a respectful salute, tapping the palm of his hand to his forehead. "Very well, then. You know where to find me."

Talical's thin mouth quirked toward a humorless smile, her silver-skinned face pinched with worry. She strode away, a collection of auburn braids swinging against her back.

The other riders dispersed after their dragons had been turned loose.

"I feel entirely too small to deal with anything like this," Alyn muttered as he watched Shade amble away to join a dragon buddy sprawled on the warm rock, soaking up sunshine.

Alyn turned to make the long trek across the tower to one of the stone bridges. Exhaustion weakened his strides. He was thankful that he didn't have to make the report. He couldn't think of a sufficient explanation for the glittering anomalies that had appeared in the sky while he and his flight were out on a routine scouting mission.

"No doubt we'll be sent out again with mages to collect more information," he mumbled to himself.

Katrina dashed out into the landscaped lawn with her newest treasure tucked under her arm. She ducked beneath the drooping boughs of the Whispering Tree. Some of the stringy branches dangled leaves as far as the ground.

Even as familiar as she was with her small kingdom, it always felt magical to duck past the Gate of Whispering Leaves and enter the sunlight-speckled shadows.

"Now, where should you live?" she asked the new fairy door she'd brought with her. She used her free hand to pick a leaf out of her hair that had recently been braided into cornrows. Her scalp ached slightly, but it always did after her hair was done fresh. The end of each braid sported a bright butterfly clip, following the colors of the rainbow. Just beyond the clips, the rest of her ebony hair floofed out, thick and free.

Leaves rustled, drawing her attention to the Gate as a plump, orange cat sauntered inside her domain. His tail lifted with a curl at the end.

"Mew?" he inquired curiously.

"Welcome, Sir Pumpkin, Knight of the Dewdrop Realm."

"Mew?" Pumpkin flopped down in his favorite spot of grass near the trunk of the Whispering Tree.

"Look! We have new citizens." Katrina held her new acquisition out for Pumpkin to see. Dark wood and vines bordered a lovely, purple door. "Where should they live?"

Pumpkin's golden eyes half closed as if in thought. The tip of his tail formed a cute curlicue near his feet. After a few moments of pondering silence, he offered a high-pitched, "Mew?" with a hint of a purr.

"You have the funniest voice," Katrina teased him with a giggle. "But I agree. They should live over here."

A small hill rose on one side of her kingdom, decorated with a variety of fairy doors. She carefully dug an indent in the dry moss coating it and then set the door in place. She jiggled it until it sat firmly.

More doors were scattered throughout the area, set against the trunks of trees or balanced carefully in branches, sometimes secured with a nail or string. Katrina knew the names of every individual, couple, or family who lived behind each unique doorway.

"Oh no!" Katrina cried. "Look out, Pumpkin! The dark fairies are here!"

Pumpkin's eyes narrowed, appearing to contemplate this new threat and what to do about it while Katrina scrambled for her butterfly net. She snatched it up and swung it through the air.

"Oh no, you don't! You won't harm the citizens of the Dewdrop Realm!"

The raucous caws of crows filled Alyn's ears as Shade dipped to avoid them. The crows far outnumbered the small flight of dragons.

"Wretched crows," Alyn muttered as he bent close to Shade's neck. "We have enough on our hands as it is."

Magical anomalies were complicated all by themselves, but they also confused animals in the vicinity.

Shade swerved to one side as a crow swooped toward them. The gust from the bird's wings sent the dragon careening farther than intended.

Alyn's long, black hair fluttered as Shade attempted to correct her balance. Sharp beaks, claws, and feathers filled Alyn's view as they ran right into a flurry of crows flying around in angry confusion.

He heard dragons shrieking and riders yelling somewhere in the background. Separated from most of his comrades, he fought to keep his cool.

Glittering shards of light suddenly burst through the panicking crows. They screamed and scattered.

Shade backwinged hard, but the currents were all over the place, especially with the emergence of more unstable magic. Somehow, despite every thought and instinct screaming against it, they ended up diving right into the magic instead of away from it.

Katrina spun, swinging her net out in a circle, watching the sheer fabric form a conical balloon.

"I got you, dark fairies," she announced her victory.

A flash of light blinded her. Weight suddenly hit the net. She stumbled around, confused and blinking spots from her eyes.

"Pumpkin?" The long, thin handle bounced in her hands. She let the far end rest on the ground, afraid she'd tangled the cat in it.

"What was that? Why can't I see?" She dropped the net entirely and rubbed at her eyes. The spots finally cleared and she cast a quick look around her kingdom.

She had expected to find Pumpkin in the net, but instead, he was nowhere to be seen. All that remained of him was a Pumpkin-shaped impression in the grass.

"Pumpkin?"

Something struggled in the net.

Katrina stared at the translucent, white fabric as something dark squirmed beneath it, uttering strange sounds. Warily, she tiptoed toward her unexpected catch. Whatever the thing was, it made a pitiful keening that broke her heart. She could almost feel the creature's distress.

Dropping to her knees, she carefully untangled it. "I must have somehow caught a bird. Good thing Pumpkin ran away."

But what she found when she finally separated the net enough to see the creature caught inside was not a bird. Not only that, but there were two creatures! One little doll-sized girl and a—

"Dragon?" Katrina squeaked. It felt like her eyes might pop out of her head with surprise. "Did I really catch a dark fairy?" She gently helped the girl stand and then realized that she wasn't a "she." He was a he. She'd assumed female since he had a long tangle of black hair, but his features and body were masculine.

He looked very confused. So did the dragon as it snaked its head around, hissing at everything. It mantled its wings, trying to be intimidating.

"It's okay," Katrina tried to reassure it. She reached to gently pet one of its little leathery wings.

It bit her finger with a viper-fast lunge and needle-sharp teeth.

"Ow!" Katrina shrieked and jerked her hand back. She stared, aghast, at tiny drops of blood welling up. Tears stung her eyes.

The little man held his hands up in a placating gesture, speaking in soothing tones. It seemed like he addressed both of them, trying to stop an argument.

She couldn't understand the words. Wiping her eyes with a corner of her frilly dress, Katrina cleared her vision enough to get a better look at him.

His skin was dark silver. That definitely meant dark fairy. His black hair hung past his waist. He fiddled with it, trying to get tangled parts out of his face. She caught a glimpse of a tiny, pointed ear. He had sharp features, very much like she would expect on a fairy, or maybe an elf, but he was far too tiny to be an elf. His clothing was also what she might expect on a fairy: leather and cloth armor of some kind. It looked very nice on him, if a bit worn.

The dragon hissed at her and she realized that she had started to lean in closer as she examined the fairy. She quickly sat back.

With nothing else available, Katrina put her finger in her mouth to get rid of the blood. Then she looked at the bite again. She could almost count the tiny dots of red, forming a perfect dragon-mouth shape.

"She's only a child." Alyn tried to calm Shade's viciousness. He didn't blame his dragon for defending them. He was grateful for it, but as large as the human was, he had quickly observed a youngness about her.

He didn't often see humans. Lidra avoided them since they seemed more inclined to squish them than talk to them. He could only hope that this one didn't do that. So far, she seemed more curious than malicious.

Shade hissed again and then followed that up with a pained squeak.

Alyn tried to keep an eye on the human while he moved around to get a good look at his dragon. It didn't take long to find the injury. A leathery part of one wing had been badly scratched. Blood dripped from the wound.

"How did that happen?" Alyn wondered.

Shade growled at him when he tried to get closer.

"Hey now, love," he gently chided her. "You know I have to examine it." He sighed. Too many things needed attention all at the same time. The girl. His dragon. What had happened. Where he was now...

Alyn straightened and cast a quick glance at the scenery. The plants were similar to what he saw on scouting forays. He could have somehow ended up in one of the human establishments, but the nearest one would take at least a week to get to, dragon-back.

He tensed when the girl leaned in close to peer at Shade. Her face might have been huge, but he could still read her expressions well enough. She didn't seem to be a danger.

"Stop glittering at me!" Bree waved her paws, trying to shoo the sparkling cloud of magically engineered fairies away.

They giggled, the sound a musical tinkling like itty-bitty bells.

Bree flopped back on the bed. Since the Academy didn't have rooms for lidra-sized folk, much less a mouse, her furniture was fashioned for goblins, which made her bed the equivalent of what might fit a human three-year-old.

Bree used to be a Lidran mage back in the day, but she had turned herself into a mouse and had remained such for years. She couldn't figure out how to turn herself back.

"You'd think that at a place full of mages, we would have figured that out by now," she muttered to herself.

She couldn't even remember what she used to look like.

"I don't blow as many things up as I used to. So that's something." Bree bounced to her feet again.

The cloud of fairies restlessly changed shape. She couldn't make out individual expressions, but there was an air of expectation in the bundle of tiny, colorful sparkles.

"I've been trying and trying!" Bree cried. "Why isn't a portal happening? I'm sure I can do this." A Crossworlds Patrol lady had brought her to Deart. Supposedly, the woman was some kind of demigod, but if she could make a portal, so could Bree.

Even if Bree wasn't anywhere near demigod status.

"They told me I could be anything, so I'm going to be a demigod," she announced.

Visions of chocolate-covered coffee beans bounced tantalizingly through her mind. She thought she could actually see them, floating across in front of her. She licked her lips as a sliver of drool stretched downward.

"I need more kaffey." She bounded over the bedspread and jumped onto the side table where a large mug of kaffey had gone cold. Kaffey was Deart's version of coffee. "Since they have this, they should have chocolate."

Hind paws clutching the edge, she leaned down into the mug, trying to lap up the last inch of liquid.

She may not have gotten much sleep lately. Sleep only got in the way. She had been casting spell after spell, focusing with all of her might on Earth and chocolate, but with no success.

She heaved a large sigh which unhooked her feet. They slid as she scrambled wildly before falling into the kaffey with a squeak and a splash.

A gasp susurrated through the fairies as they darted to hover above the mug.

"Don't just float there, staring!" Bree cried. "Help me out!"

The fairies simply shimmered and tittered at her instead.

"You guys are useless!" She shook a soaked paw at them. "You're supposed to be helping me with this project."

The cloud of glitter somehow contrived to look innocent.

"I don't believe you." Bree slumped, white fur covered in liquid brown. "Oh well, now I can reach it better." She slurped it all up, licked her fur clean, then climbed out of the mug, ready to try again.

Katrina crept into the house. She peeked around, making sure the coast was clear. It looked safe. She sneaked to the pantry and grabbed a can of cat food.

"I hope dragons like cat food." She figured it might like the canned stuff better than dry. Pumpkin surely did.

As if summoned by magic, Pumpkin mewed by her feet, the sound filled with desperation.

Katrina nearly jumped through the roof. "Ah! Pumpkin! You scared me."

"Kat," came from the doorway.

Katrina clutched the canned food as she turned toward her mother. Unlike

Katrina, her mother's skin was pale. They had adopted Katrina when she was a baby.

"Oh, um, hi, Mom. I was just getting canned food for Pumpkin. I…um…was going to take it to the kingdom…for a feast?"

Her mother raised an eyebrow, probably wondering why she acted so nervous about taking some canned food. It was a perfectly normal thing to do.

Pumpkin mewed loudly, rubbing against her frilly dress.

"Okay, that's fine, honey," her mother said with a smile. "Did you want some human food as well? It's about lunch time."

Katrina tried to act normal as she smiled brightly. "Sure." The dark fairy probably didn't want to eat cat food anyway.

"I was going to make some raviolis." Her mother turned to go into the kitchen where she started heating a pot. Her blond hair was pulled back in a ponytail.

Sometimes, Katrina envied her mother's hair. It seemed much less painful to get it to cooperate, but as her mother always pointed out, she couldn't do the cute things with her hair that she could with Katrina's.

"Auntie Candy is coming to visit this weekend," her mother mentioned as she emptied a can of deliciousness into the pot.

Katrina winced. A jolt of fear shot through her. "Oh. Okay." She knew it wasn't nice to not like someone, especially if they hadn't done anything to deserve it, but her aunt Candace made her queasy whenever she was around her. Katrina didn't understand why.

"She's going to stay for a couple of weeks," he mother went on, oblivious to Katrina's unease. "Maybe we can all go to the zoo. We'll also go to the Saturday market and we can see that movie you wanted to go to. What was it called?"

"Attack of the Killer Rutabagas." Katrina perked up. That movie looked like a lot of fun! She might not like her aunt, but it wasn't as if they would have to interact during a movie in the theater.

Once the food finished heating, her mother filled a bowl for her. "Don't spill it on your dress." She handed Katrina a handful of napkins.

"I won't," Katrina promised. She carefully carried her food and the can of cat food downstairs and slipped through the gap she had left open in the sliding glass door.

Pumpkin followed, worry clouding his golden eyes.

"Oh, I'll give you food," Katrina told him with a laugh as she nudged the sliding door closed with an elbow.

Trepidation clenched her chest as she approached her kingdom. Maybe the dark fairy and his dragon weren't real. They might have left while she was gone. She hoped not.

She ducked between the dangling curtain of leaves and breathed a sigh of relief to see that her visitors were still there.

"I brought you food," she quietly announced.

The dragon hissed at her.

She scrunched her nose. "Don't be that way."

Thanks to a first aid kit, the dragon's dark blue wing now sported a band-aid. It made that portion bend a little funny when the dragon folded its wings.

The dark fairy warily moved away from a door he had been inspecting. He sidled to stand near the dragon.

Pumpkin mewed desperately, rubbing against her legs. He hadn't spotted the new arrivals yet.

"Can you see them, Pumpkin?" Katrina asked. She tried to nudge him toward the pair, but every vestige of the cat's focus was pinned on FOOD.

Giggling, she opened the can. She used the lid to portion some of the meat and gravy out onto a doll-sized plate. "This isn't for you." She quickly took it away and stuck the can on the ground. Pumpkin practically dove into it.

Then she sat down and cautiously placed the plate as close to the dragon as she dared. "There you go. That's for you," she invited.

The dragon sniffed at the food. It looked hungry, judging by the gleam in its blue eyes.

The dark fairy stepped forward and crouched next to the food before he poked a finger in it and then tasted it.

"No!" Katrina exclaimed, trying to stop him with a sweep of her hand. "That's not for you. People don't eat cat food."

The man nimbly leapt backward in alarm. The dragon hissed and flared its wings.

Katrina quickly sat back, contrite. "Sorry," she said, keeping her voice quiet. "I didn't mean to scare you. Here." She put a single ravioli on another doll plate and then set it in front of the man. She stuck a tiny fork and knife in it. The utensils had never been meant to be used, perhaps, but hopefully they would work.

"This is for you," she said, nudging the plate toward the man.

The dragon looked between its food and the dark fairy's food for a second before it ambled over and began voraciously eating the ravioli.

Katrina's eyebrows lifted in surprise before she shrugged. "Well, okay. I mean, I guess there's no rules about dragons eating pasta."

She scooted the plate of cat food to Pumpkin. "More for you!" She served another ravioli onto a plate for the dark fairy.

He retrieved his utensils and settled down to eat.

"Be careful, it's hot," Katrina warned.

As far as she could tell, they both liked the raviolis. She sat back to eat her own portion. "I wish we could understand each other," she said between bites. "I want to know where you came from."

Katrina spent as much time as she could get away with in the Dewdrop Realm with the dark fairy and his dragon. She slowly gained their trust by caring for them and being very polite. The dragon couldn't fly yet because of the scratch on its wing.

After being bitten hard on a paw, Pumpkin had learned not to try to pounce on either of them. The dragon was quick to defend itself and its rider.

When Katrina's aunt arrived, she was forced to spend less and less time with them.

One afternoon, she sighed as she put on "real people" clothes in her bedroom. At least the t-shirt displayed a dragon on the front. She preferred her princess clothes, but her mother insisted that she wear boring stuff.

Aunt Candace stood in the hall to greet her when she walked out of her room.

"Hello, sweetie," she said in a syrupy voice that sent shivers down Katrina's spine. Curly blond hair dangled around her face. Loose, teal and blue clothing draped over her ample figure. "I have a gift for you if you'd come to my room for a moment."

That was the last thing Katrina wanted to do, but she didn't want their plans for the zoo to be canceled if she got in trouble for being rude. "Okay, Aunt Candy."

She meekly followed her aunt into the guest room.

"Sit down here," her aunt invited.

Katrina obliged and plopped down in the wicker chair. She didn't like this chair. She associated it with any time her aunt visited, but aside from that, it was fairly comfortable.

"You've been growing up so much," her aunt said as she sat on the foot of her bed.

Katrina fidgeted. Where was the present? She wanted it so she could leave. She didn't really care what it was.

"Look at me when I talk to you," Aunt Candace demanded firmly.

Katrina reluctantly raised her gaze to meet her aunt's hazel eyes.

Katrina felt fuzzy when she left her aunt's room with a new model horse in her arms. It was an Appaloosa. Very pretty. But she couldn't even remember it being handed to her. It felt like mere seconds had gone by, but she had an uneasy inkling that much more time than that had passed.

She didn't quite know how she knew it, but then her mother's voice rang out impatiently, "Katrina, it's time to leave!"

Katrina walked into the living room, blinking and trying to focus. Her brain felt as if a blanket had been thrown over it. She clutched the horse in her arms. "I'm ready."

"Where have you been?" her mother demanded. "I've been calling you."

"I…um…Aunt Candy wanted to give me a gift. See?" She held the horse up, but her stomach twisted with queasiness.

"Oh." Her mother's expression softened. "It's lovely. Why don't you put it on a shelf in your room and let's get going?"

"Okay." Almost robotic, Katrina turned to head back to her room.

Most mages moved their hands around as a tool to help them visualize and focus what they were doing. Movement engaged the whole body in the act of spell casting, which in turn helped control the magic.

Bree had never learned to do it that way. She was more of a "sit in one spot, very still, trying to focus every centimeter of her being" type of mage. She huddled, eyes shut as she tried to pull magic together to make a portal. Everything felt like it worked, but when she opened her eyes, no portal glowed before her.

Her personal audience of fairies zoomed around the room, glittering and giggling.

A knock on the door made Bree jump a foot up from the bed. She landed lightly. "Who is it?"

"It's Amiah. Can I come in?"

"Oh, I suppose."

Bree sighed in consternation as she sat back on her hind legs. She fiddled restlessly with her tail as Amiah stepped inside.

Everything in the room was too small for a human except one chair that Bree had requested so that when Amiah came to visit, she had a place to sit that wouldn't shatter beneath her. That wasn't a crack at her weight, for Amiah was quite plump. Even a slender human might break furniture made for goblins.

Aside from the furniture being small, the room itself was quite spacious.

"You know you missed classes today," Amiah said as she sat down.

"I'm doing independent study," Bree responded stubbornly.

"I'm not sure that's a recognized course," Amiah said with a smile. She brushed her hands over a lace-up tunic. Flowery embroidery decorated the hems. It hung long over comfortable leggings that vanished in lace-up boots.

"I need to order mouse-sized clothes," Bree remarked, distracted from the current subject. "You get to dress in the most interesting things. All I have is boring fur."

"You can wear clothes if you want to." Amiah laughed lightly.

"Perhaps a stylish cape." Bree scratched at an ear with a forepaw.

"We could dye your fur," Amiah suggested.

"Oooh!" Bree liked that idea.

The fairies darted around Bree in a small whirlwind. When they withdrew, her fur was pink, purple, blue, and yellow.

"AHHHH!" Bree squealed.

Amiah almost fell out of her chair laughing. "They tie-dyed you!"

Bree shook a tiny fist at the fairies. "Go away! Go clean something!" She was fed up with their nonsense, especially since they had been less than helpful with her chocolate problem.

Apparently, that offended them. They created a room-wide tornado of furious glitter.

Bree shielded her eyes. She heard Amiah exclaim something unintelligible. She couldn't see anything except wild sparkles everywhere as the wind from their momentum nearly knocked her over.

The fairies left, funneling away underneath the door, leaving the room in ruin.

"You guuuuuuys!" Bree wailed. The bed blankets were everywhere. The desk and coinciding chair lay upside down. Papers scattered all over the place.

The walls looked like someone had shot them with a paint gun.

"Wow," Amiah said. "You really upset them."

On the upside, Bree's fur was white again.

Bree drooped and hugged her tail close like a teddy bear. "I didn't mean to. I'm just so frustrated. I really want chocolate! It's all I can think about."

"It's very difficult to make a portal from one world to another," Amiah gently said. "Landon said it was impossible. And he's the head mage here. He should know."

"Except that we got here," Bree pointed out.

"That's true," Amiah agreed. "But those were special circumstances."

Long story short: They both had started out on Earth, but due to magical adventures, they now lived on Deart.

"Chocolate is a special and desperate circumstance."

"Maybe you should focus on what you do have," Amiah advised. "Instead of obsessing over what you can't get."

Bree scowled at her. "Don't you try to be wise with me. I'll turn you into a newt!"

Amiah stood and began to straighten the room. "Okay, but wait 'til I've picked up all the heavy stuff, first."

"Argh!" Bree threw herself over backward on the blankets. She wrinkled her nose, whiskers twitching. "Chocolate chocolate chocolate," she chanted. "I can smell you!"

She bounced to her feet, swaying slightly.

"Have you been sleeping at all?" Amiah asked as she picked up the mug that had been recently emptied of kaffey.

"Who needs sleep when chocolate is at stake?" Bree made grabby motions with her paws, trying to collect threads of magic and pull them to her. "I just need one chocolate bar. Is that too much to ask?"

Lights coalesced around her.

Amiah straightened in alarm. "Bree! What are you doing?"

"I neeeeed chocolate-covered coffee beans!" Bree cried. A kaleidoscope of magic whirled around her. She squeaked when the bed vanished and sent her tumbling through space.

She flailed wildly, arms pinwheeling, tail spinning. "AAAAAH!"

Stars flitted past as she traveled at warp speed.

Shortly after, she tumbled down a small hillside, rolling and bouncing before she landed on soft grass, spread-eagle.

Alyn drank the last few drops of water and set the cup aside. He studied Katrina worriedly. Lately, she had been acting strange. Almost lifeless. Perhaps she was not entirely his concern, but he wondered what was happening. Ever since this "aunt" of hers had arrived, he saw much less of the child.

She loyally brought food and water for him and Shade, even when he could tell that she wasn't supposed to be out here. Apparently, this aunt demanded a lot of time and attention.

Not unlike when he sensed a threat in the wilds, he felt that hair-raising alarm as he looked the girl over. Was she not getting enough sleep? Was she ill? He wished he could ask her, but the language barrier made it tricky.

A flash of light suddenly filled his vision. He shielded his face with a flung arm, flinching away.

Shade shrieked.

Katrina squealed.

Skittering paws indicated the cat fled.

Alyn slowly lowered his arm, trying to blink dazzlement from his eyes.

Bree bounced to her feet, excited. "Is there chocolate? Am I on Earth? Maybe even America?" She used English out of pure hope that she had arrived in the right place.

A human child rubbed at her eyes and then stared at Bree in disbelief. "First a dark fairy and a dragon? Now a talking mouse?"

Bree took a quick moment to look around. "A dragon?! Where? Oh! There!" She peered curiously at the dragon.

"That's…that's a very small dragon. I always imagined them to be a lot bigger."

And then it hit her. "Noooo!" She flopped on her stomach in despair. "If there's a dragon and lidra here then I'm not on Earth!"

"Yes, you are," the little girl said.

Bree jumped to her feet again. "I am?"

"Yeah," the girl said. "I'm not sure where else you'd think you were. Or did you come from the land of fairies?"

Bree noted the plethora of fairy doors decorating the scenery. The way the tree branches hung over half of a small hill made the place a magical alcove. Sunlight sprinkled through, dotting the grass and hill, shifting slightly over a variety of adorable doors.

It also finally clicked that the little girl spoke English. She appeared to be around eight years old or so, wearing a frilly princess dress.

"I did make it to Earth!" Bree jumped up and down, overwhelmed with joy.

Next thing she knew, there was a cat on top of her.

"No, Pumpkin!" the girl cried.

Bree couldn't really see anything. "Mmmph…you…mmmage, cat!" she tried to talk through the paw pinning her face.

The weight abruptly lifted and the girl set the cat aside. "You can't eat this mouse, Pumpkin."

Bree pried herself from the ground. "I'm a mage, you nitwit!" she scolded the cat. "Cats like mages." However, that didn't necessarily negate the automatic pounce reflex when they saw a mouse.

Turning her attention on the dragon and lidra, Bree hopped over to them. "Hello."

The dragon eyed her suspiciously. The man grimaced. He looked like a lidra, but his skin was silver instead of gold. Odd.

"He doesn't understand English," the girl said helpfully.

"Ooh. Well then." Bree switched to Lidran. *"Hello."*

The man's finely shaped eyebrows lifted in surprise. *"Greetings. You…speak Lidran?"* He had an accent different from what Bree had grown up with.

"I am a lidra," Bree explained. *"Or I was. But…I didn't know lidra with silver skin existed."*

"I wasn't aware there was any other color," the man responded.

"Gold," Bree told him brightly. That was the hue she was familiar with.

But on to more important things.

She turned to the girl. "Do you have chocolate? I am desperate for chocolate!"

Chocolate smeared Bree's face as she happily filled her stomach full with the delightful stuff. "Thanks so much, Katrina." Introductions had finally been made after Bree had cast a Sphere of Understanding around the cozy nook. Now they all understood each other and would slowly learn each other's languages.

"Portals were randomly appearing around your home?" Bree asked Alyn partway through his explanation about his arrival on Earth.

"Yes."

"Do you know what caused them?"

He shook his head. "No. We were investigating them when Shade and I accidentally went through one."

Bree's eye twitched. "And this was recently? Ish?"

Alyn studied her, possibly trying to follow her line of thought.

"It's my fault you're here," Bree concluded before he got a chance to answer. "It must be. Only half a handful of people on Deart even know about Earth. I was the only one trying to get here, so it must have been me. I'm so sorry! I was trying to make a portal in my room. I had no idea that portals were popping up in other places. That's so annoying!" She carefully wrapped up the remainder of the chocolate bar. "Why couldn't the portal just appear in my room the first time?"

"Katrina!" came from the house.

Katrina sighed. "I don't really wanna go. I wanna stay with you guys."

Bree waved her off with a paw and then froze when she saw Pumpkin drop into a crouch, watching her intently. She slowly lowered her paw. "Go ahead. It's not like we're going anywhere soon. I have to figure out a way to send us back. Maybe take Pumpkin with you?"

"Sure," Katrina agreed halfheartedly. She picked up the fat cat. He was obviously heavy and difficult for her to carry as she waddled out of what she called the Dewdrop Realm.

Once she was gone, Alyn asked, "Why did we end up here?"

"Oh." Bree eyed the chocolate bar, wondering if she could possibly fit a few more bites in her stomach. "It's probably because Katrina is a resonant."

"And a resonant is?"

"A person who has magic. They can channel it, but they can't really use it. Magic is just kind of around them. Mages can connect to them, though, for an extra power boost. I've done it a few times, but I'm not very good at it. That is, I usually need a resonant who's more experienced than I am in order for it to work. Anyway, for whatever reasons, since she's a resonant, the magic I was using tied the portals to here. Possibly to these doors."

She raced up the side of the hill and tugged at a door. The whole thing came off and tumbled down the hill. "Oops!"

"What are you doing?" Alyn asked incredulously.

"Trying to see if one of these doors became the portal. Help me look!"

Dubious, Alyn checked the doors with her. The dragon watched them both as she carefully stretched her wings, testing the injured one. She sat back, flapping her wings exuberantly.

Alyn smiled. "Shade should be able to fly soon."

"That's good," Bree said cheerfully while peering behind a blue door with bright pink stripes.

That evening, after Katrina had come and gone, Alyn voiced his concerns. Since Bree was a mage, perhaps she sensed something he couldn't.

"Did you see how she acted?" he asked the mouse's tail.

The rest of Bree vanished in a pile of cereal. Os tumbled away as her head emerged. She tried to speak around a mouthful but gave up and rushed to chew it and swallow it down with a big gulp. "What do you mean?"

"Did she seem different?"

"You mean…tired?"

"Yes, that, but more than that."

Bree turned pink eyes toward the house. "She did seem a bit under the weather. Is she coming down with something, I wonder?"

"It's been happening for a while," Alyn explained. "She seems perkier earlier in the day, but when she goes back and then returns here, she's very tired. Almost…" He shrugged, at a loss. "It's difficult to explain, but it worries me."

"Hmmm." Bree eyed the house. She flung a paw toward the sky. "We'll have to investigate!"

The next day, Bree asked Katrina, "Can I ride on your shoulder?"

"Um, people would freak if I had a mouse with me."

"Hmmm." Bree scratched behind an ear with a forepaw. "How about if I hide in your hair?"

"I guess so."

Now that Alyn had pointed it out, Katrina did seem to be getting tireder and tireder. The day had only just begun, so technically, the child was at her peak of energy when they saw her, but it was one very low peak.

"Why?" Katrina asked.

"I just wanted to see more than this little place. I ride a friend's shoulder a lot back home. I do it all of the time."

"Well, okay." Katrina sat down and held a hand out.

Bree scampered up her arm and then jumped up to grab her hair with tiny claws. The cornrows made it fairly easy to climb. Bree wriggled into the thick fluff at the back. She found it to be a lot harder to move around in than she had initially thought.

"This is nothing like hair I'm used to."

Katrina showed only moderate amusement. "Yeah, my hair is different from most people I know."

"I may never get out alive!" Bree hoped to cheer the child with her silliness, but it didn't seem to work. She finally found a position where she was hidden but could see out through a veil of thick curls.

Katrina stood and carefully ducked beneath the entrance to her kingdom before trudging to the house.

As soon as she set foot inside, Bree sensed another mage in the vicinity. Her little heart raced. Hopefully they wouldn't sense her, or if they did, they might mix it up with the magic Katrina already possessed.

Not to be left out, Alyn leapt astride Shade. His spirit thrilled in the familiar leap and swoosh as the dragon took wing. She darted out into open air and flew around the house. They couldn't get inside, so they settled for peeking in windows.

They found one guarded by some kind of mesh, the glass part open.

Katrina sat in a chair within.

The dragon attached herself to the mesh. It didn't seem like they were in danger of being seen as an adult human sat down on the foot of a nicely made bed. The woman was portly, her blond hair a tumble of curls.

"Look at me, dear," the woman said.

Alyn's stomach clenched as Katrina looked up. He possessed no magical senses so he didn't know exactly what was happening, but his other senses screamed that something was extremely wrong.

Katrina's eyes glazed over and the woman's face transformed to an expression of wicked glee.

Bree, on the other paw, knew exactly what was happening! The mage was using Katrina as a conduit to pull more power into herself. But as far as Bree could tell, the woman wasn't well practiced with magic. Probably self-taught since there weren't exactly magic schools on Earth. By pulling magic through Katrina, the mage could gain more energy faster than if she did it on her own.

Not only that, but it would give her a heady sense of euphoria if she drank in a lot at once.

"Why you!" Bree squeaked. She struggled to get free of Katrina's hair. The girl didn't respond at all to the tugging and pulling against her scalp as Bree wrestled free.

"You stop that right now!" Bree yelled at the woman. "I don't care if evil aunts are cliché! You are *evil!*"

The woman stopped, shocked at the sight of the white mouse jumping around on Katrina's head.

For a second, she merely stared, seemingly unsure of what to make of this new development.

But then her eyes narrowed. "I don't know what or who you are." She stood. "But you will not interfere!" She sliced a hand through the air.

A glimmering force smacked into Bree. One of her hind paws caught in the girl's hair, stopping her from flying right off. Bree dangled, turning in circles.

Katrina sat, motionless, eyes staring straight.

The woman stalked forward and reached for Bree with a hand plenty large enough to physically crush the life out of her. And that did, indeed, seem to be the woman's intent. Kill or capture, either was bad news.

Bree struggled to throw some magic together to defend herself, but it was extremely difficult to focus while turning circles upside down. Her impending doom kept twirling in and out of her vision.

A loud shriek filled the room. Bree heard tearing and flapping sounds.

The woman suddenly withdrew with a scream as Shade dove for her face. The dragon left bloody claw marks on her nose and cheek.

Bree bent double and clawed at the hair around her foot, getting it loose. "Eeee!" She fell to the floor, landing on her back, the breath knocked out of her.

"Lung...air...work..." She gasped as she rolled over and picked herself up.

"What are you things?" the woman yelled. She slapped a hand at the air. A half-sphere of magic smacked into Alyn and Shade, knocking them to the floor.

Alyn rolled away from the dragon's back as Shade tried to recover, shaking her head and staggering, stepping on one of her wings.

The woman's face contorted in a furious snarl.

Katrina's body jerked as the mage ruthlessly pulled more magic from her to use against her tiny enemies.

Katrina finally responded, crying out in pain.

Seeing that happen to the child, feeling the magic and knowing the pain it caused, sent Bree into such a fury that her vision filled with red.

"NO!" shook the foundations of the house as a wave of power swept outward from the mouse.

That stopped the aunt from hurting Katrina as she staggered around, grabbing a chair, trying to get her balance and senses back together.

Alyn jumped back on Shade as the dragon leapt into the air. Shade dove for

Katrina and landed on her shoulder. Cooing at her, the dragon rubbed her face against the girl's dark-skinned cheek.

"Katrina!" Alyn called to her. "Wake up! We need to go!"

The bedroom wasn't big enough to contain the magic battle that ensued. Lights flashed as forces collided between Bree and the evil mage.

A crack spread ominously up a wall. It expanded into webs of tinier cracks as it traveled across the ceiling. Dust and debris rained down.

Bree tried everything she could to keep the woman from getting to the child or re-establishing the magical connection between them.

"Get her out of here!" Bree squeaked in desperation as she bounced around, dodging searing bolts of deadly energy.

The aunt had quickly figured out who posed the biggest threat here. Using the word "biggest" loosely.

Shade bit Katrina's earlobe. That finally woke the child from the catatonic state. She shrieked in fear, but Alyn quickly got her attention.

"It's us! We're here to help. Stand up! Can you stand up?" He hurriedly gave Katrina step-by-step instructions to get out of the chair and flee the room.

Bree half-wondered where the parents were. Perhaps they weren't home? No one came running to check on the ruckus. She almost got clobbered by a slash of furious magic when she sighed in relief, seeing Katrina dash from the room.

"Eek!" Bree darted away, running after her friends to make sure they got out all right. More cracks zigzagged down the hallway, taking over the walls, floor, and ceiling as the mage pounded after her.

Bree flung shields of magic behind her, fending off the evil woman on the way. The house shook and the floor abruptly fell sideways. Bree skittered frantically. Her vision honed in on the door which had been left ajar. Things fell around her, crashing and clattering.

The house collapsed with a thunderous roar.

Bree barely cleared the patio as the awning fell in a violent cloud of destruction.

Katrina's parents stood outside of their car, staring in slack-jawed disbelief.

Shade snatched Bree up from the ground before she could even comprehend what happened. She caught a glimpse of Katrina running into her mother's arms.

Katrina looked up at Bree and Alyn where they perched on a tree branch.

"It's this one!" Bree announced, rapping mouse knuckles on a wooden fairy door framed by leaves and roses. It was almost half her size, nailed onto the side of the branch.

Alyn leaned toward it, eyes narrowed. "How did we even fit through that?"

"Magic," Bree answered with a shrug.

He chuckled as he straightened. A slight jerk of his head swept long strands of black hair behind a shoulder.

Katrina slowly packed up her fairy doors, leaving the one Bree identified as the portal. A few tears stung her eyes. "I don't want to leave," she said.

"Well, I kind of accidentally blew up your house," Bree said. "I'm sorry!"

"You did it to save me." Katrina smiled at her. It was as if she'd been in her own fairy tale. Bree had explained everything to her. "I can't thank you enough."

Katrina felt so much better now that her aunt could no longer drain her of magical energy. Funny how that worked. It explained so much. Maybe she would feel grief about her aunt's death later, but right now, she merely felt relief. Her only sadness was that they had to move and she had to leave her new friends behind. Her parents thought a random and tragic sinkhole had been responsible for the disaster.

"Can't I go with you?" she asked.

Bree sighed and shook her head. "No, I'm sorry. Your parents are here and they love you very much. But don't worry! Now that you know about magic and that you can channel it in a way, I'm sure you'll find all kinds of interesting things."

"You will," Alyn agreed.

"Oh!" Bree chirped. "But there is one thing you can do."

"What's that?" Katrina asked expectantly.

"Bring me a box of chocolate bars to take back home with me!"

Katrina laughed. "Okay, I'll do that," she promised.

Bree and Amiah are from my Worlds Akilter *series. If you enjoyed this story, you might have a blast reading about their other adventures involving cats, magic, a soul devouring parrot, killer rutabagas, and many other strange, funny things!*

ajbakke.com

Dragon Ward

Jenelle Leanne Schmidt

Gwyna pressed her back against the rough bark of the tree, fervently wishing she could turn invisible. The cut on her arm stung, throbbing with every pulse of her heart. Her breaths were deafening, and she tried to steady them—to silence them—as the air passed from her lungs through her lips, in and out, in and out. In desperation, she strained her ears, concentrating. Listening for the sounds of pursuit. She was a hunter, unused to being the prey. The terror coursing through her was dishonorable, and shame rose in her throat like bile.

The forest floor shook. Gwyna waited, her arrow notched. She reached for calm, but it eluded her grasp. A roar thundered around her, and she fumbled with her bow as the beast burst into view.

The day had started out so well.

"Careful now," Gwyna's father cautioned as she lowered the final frame into the apiary. He held the smoker up to the hive, keeping the bees quiet. When she finished, they stepped back, pulling off their veiled hats and grinning at each other.

"This has to be the best harvest we've ever had," Gwyna exulted. She surveyed the farm, dotted by orderly hives. The cloudy sky belied the heat of the Warm Term afternoon. It was a relief to peel off the long gloves and heavy outer garments she wore to protect herself from stings.

Her father nodded his agreement and wiped the back of his hand across his forehead. He glanced down at his daughter, a glint in his eyes. "Next thing is to extract the beeswax. You ready to help me with that?"

Gwyna groaned. Her father laughed, putting an arm around her shoulders.

"I'm teasing," he assured her. "Go on. I know you're dying to get out in the woods with your bow. Thank you for your help over the past few weeks. After all that, you deserve at least a few hours to yourself."

Gwyna squealed and threw her arms around his neck. "Thank you, Father! I promise I'll help with the wax tomorrow."

He waved a hand. "Go on, get out of here, before I change my mind." Gwyna started to dash away, but her father's voice halted her, a warning note in his tone. "Remember, stay away from the cliffs."

Gwyna waved an arm at him. "I wasn't planning on going that way," she called back. "Besides, I don't need any more lectures from Nanna Roisin about the dangers of magic."

Her father chuckled, and Gwyna ran into the house to change and retrieve her most precious possession: her bow. Though she worked hard helping tend the bees, archery was Gwyna's true talent. With her bow, she kept food on their table, even through years with less bountiful harvests.

The woods were her favorite place to be, stealthily creeping through the trees in search of a suitable quarry. Here, she was at peace. Here, she was master.

She had not counted on stumbling upon a dragon.

Dragons were rare in Llycaelon—ever since the breaking of the world—but they did exist. The great beasts harbored a bitter hatred of humans; her father said it was because of the wizards, but Gwyna felt that was unfair. It wasn't her fault that her ancestors had broken the world when they tried to eradicate the myth-folk during the war. It wasn't her fault that drops of their blood ran through her veins. But she had learned to keep a wary eye on the sky, never expecting to find one on the ground.

Now, as the dragon roared into view, Gwyna just had time to wonder how the day had turned into such a nightmare before she released her waiting arrow and fled; she did not wait to see if her bolt found its mark. Running, leaping over fallen logs, scrambling over obstacles, she dashed deeper into the forest. The pounding of her footfalls thudded in time with her racing heart. Her feet found a path and she darted down it, leaping over a little brook that sang and burbled its utter lack of concern. A squirrel raced up a tree and chattered angrily at her. From under a bush a pheasant shot into the air, startled by her noisy approach. The forest scattered before her flight.

Knowing that she had no chance against a dragon, her mind whirled off to thoughts of her father. He would never know what had become of her. Her eyes darted frantically, taking in the landmarks as she raced away, her mind churning, reaching, searching for something, anything that might offer her a hope of escape.

The doorway!

The option that suddenly presented itself to her made her miss a step. She stumbled and fell, rolling over and over. Gwyna rose to her feet in a wary crouch, but the sound of pursuit was not as close as she had feared. The dragon must have gotten tangled in the narrow path. Why did it not take to the sky? Surely it would be easier to hunt her from above? As she paused to catch her breath, she considered the idea that had sprung to her mind. She glanced around, examining her surroundings. Yes, she was close; she might make it to the doorway in time. She chewed nervously on her thumbnail, her grandmother's warnings echoing in her mind. Did she dare?

A thunderous roar made her decision. This time, her flight was not one of blind recklessness. Gwyna sped through the forest with grim purpose. Her plan was unthinkable, bordering on insane, but it might save her life. Another roar, this time followed by a wave of heat. The sound of dry branches and leaves catching fire and crackling in the blast of dragon's breath behind her urged her legs to pump faster. Up ahead, the forest thinned out onto an open, grassy hill. Beyond the trees, she glimpsed the stretch of blue sky turning to deep purple. Streaks of gold and pink chased their way through the clouds, telling her that night approached. She assumed the dark would not help her; legends all agreed that dragons could see even better in the blackest of night. But the view of the hill and the sky bolstered her confidence; she now knew exactly where she was. For the space of an eye-blink, she hesitated. Once out of the forest, her cover would be gone; there would be no trees to hide her from the dragon's fury. But there were no other options, and no room for wavering; Gwyna left the forest and dashed up the hill. Beyond the summit, there was nowhere to go. The slope ended abruptly in sheer cliffs high above the ocean. But she did not need to reach the summit. She envisioned the beast behind her sneering with malevolent delight at the thought of its prey presenting itself to be eaten in such a thoughtful manner. But the predator did not know that Gwyna had one trick left on the Karradoc board, one roll of the dice yet to play.

Another crashing sound came, louder than before, as though the entire forest was being ripped up by its roots.

Almost there.

The ground quaked. She glanced back and saw the enormous dragon emerging from the forest. In another moment, she would be a mass of charred ashes or on her way down the creature's throat. Frantically, she wondered if dragons swallowed their prey whole the way some serpents did. She hoped not. Being swallowed alive to die slowly inside a dragon's stomach sounded like the worst sort of fate. If only she could reach the doorway in time. The doorway!

Where was it? Her frantic eyes scanned the hillside before her. Where?

Ah! There! A faint, silver arch shimmered in the waning light of day. Ten more paces and she would reach it. Another would take her through. Gwyna did not allow herself to think; the time for faltering was done. No matter that nobody knew what the doorway was or that nobody had yet been brave enough to enter. What mattered was the chance it offered. A slim chance. If not to survive, then at least to die on her own terms. A wave of heat washed over her and she shuddered in mid-flight, but it was not fire, not yet. Fire would come next. With a strangled scream, she squeezed her eyes shut and dove through the portal.

When she finally opened her eyes, Gwyna was unprepared for the sight that greeted her. She pushed herself to her knees, blinking in confusion. Blackness surrounded her, pricked by thousands of tiny specks of light. Were those…stars?

"What hast thou done?" a voice roared, so near that Gwyna flinched.

She reached for the comfort of her bow but found that she had lost it somewhere. Her father would be furious. It was a good bow—beautifully crafted—and expensive, but worth it for the food it brought to the table. Her fingers scrabbled, searching for it on the smooth ground, but it was not there. Desperation filled her as an angry roar reverberated through the darkness. She had not expected the dragon to follow her inside! She crawled forward, hunting blindly, her heart in her mouth.

Suddenly, the world changed and shifted. The blackness surrounding her slid away, and without warning, she found herself back in her village. The Dragon's Eye rested on the tops of the trees to her right, a fiery red orb sinking toward the horizon. Gwyna blinked as friends and neighbors rushed past, shouting and jostling. What was going on?

"Daughter!" Her father's voice made her spin around, a ready excuse on her lips for not bringing home any game, but it died as she began to remember. They were under attack! She had been heading to the watchtower. Why had she stopped?

Her father appeared next to her, his arms wrapping around her, pulling her close. "May your arrows fly true," he whispered. Then he was gone.

With a full quiver rattling against her back, Gwyna raced to the watchtower where the other archers would be gathering. The hill upon which the tower stood provided the village with a fair amount of defense against any attack from the ground and the best vantage point from which to shoot anything that attacked from the sky, but the lack of cover also brought a certain amount of danger.

When she reached the watchtower, the others were already assembled. She saw the familiar faces of her friends and fellow archers. She had trained with them since her youth, and they greeted her now with tight nods. They were arrayed in a well-ordered line beneath the illusion of safety provided by the tall wooden structure, their bows strung, arrows out, as they waited for their target to appear. Gwyna joined them, lacing up the bracer on her arm. She drew an arrow and held it loosely in her bow, point trailing toward the ground in preparation.

A massive shadow winged overhead. Gwyna heard her friends counting quietly and she joined them, taking deep, calming breaths. One, two, three. The winged beast dove closer, unaware that he had been spotted. Four, five. He grew larger, filling up the sky. Six, seven, eight. His wings beat once, twice. She raised her bow. Nine. A glint of golden eyes pierced through her. He opened his mouth to rain fire down upon her defenseless village. Ten. But they were *not* defenseless.

"Now!"

The air filled with the slight thrum of bowstrings as the archers loosed their arrows into the sky. Gwyna released her own arrow with a deep satisfaction— her aim was true.

Her chest lit on fire as though pierced by a blade. The dragon's scream of pain cut like a whip through her soul. Anguish coursed through her. An answering shriek burst from Gwyna's own throat. She collapsed even as the dragon plummeted from the sky. The voices of her friends were garbled and concerned, asking where she was hurt, but she could not answer. She curled up into a ball around her inexplicably shattered heart, weeping.

"Gwyna! Gwyna!" Somebody shook her by the shoulder. "Gwyna, are you well?"

Slowly, she opened her eyes, surprised to find that she was not covered in blood; the hole in her heart still ached, but there was no visible wound. At the base of the hill lay the enormous creature she had helped bring down. Ignoring the concerned inquiries, Gwyna descended. With faltering steps, she approached the mighty beast. Trembling, she reached out her hand and laid it on the mighty head just above his eye, out of which protruded the shaft of an arrow. Gently, she brushed her fingers over the wild pheasant feathers, taking note of the hint of blue dye on the tips, her own personal fletching pattern. Sorrow overwhelmed her and tears spilled down her face; sobs wracked her body as she sank to her knees. She did not understand why she was crying; she only knew that she felt as though a part of her had been slain with the dragon. Out of the corner of her eye, she caught the hint of a silver glimmer. Despite her tears, she was drawn to look up. Beyond the corpse stood a doorway outlined in radiant light. Without conscious thought, she rose to her feet and drifted toward the door. Her father called out to her, urging her to stay and celebrate. The victorious shouts of her friends beckoned, but she could not join them. A driving, compelling force directed her to walk through the doorway, and she could not refuse. Straightening her shoulders, Gwyna obeyed the command. With sure, purposeful strides, she passed through the door.

She collapsed on the other side in the cool twilight air. Her fingers dug into the grass and dirt of the ground, and she wondered if this were real or just another vision. Her breath came in great, gulping sobs left over from the remembered pain of the strange vision she had received. She was aware that she no longer stood on the hill; she was back in the forest. Tall trees and a ledge of mossy rock rose up on her right. And on her left… Gwyna froze as she realized that she was not alone. A great, dark shape loomed to her left, radiating warmth and emitting the same shaky, shuddering breaths as herself. Instinct took over and she crouched, ready to either flee or stand and fight, whichever course of action offered her the best chance at survival. As her eyes adjusted in the dusky haze spreading over the land, Gwyna's breath caught.

Before her stood the most magnificent beast she had ever seen. It boasted four powerful legs ending in sharp, deadly talons. Its body was covered in scales; she thought they might be red, but she could not be certain in the near-darkness. A long, graceful neck arched up into the sky. Two golden eyes—the eyes from her vision—peered at her with suspicion and mistrust, and yet, there seemed to be a hint of curiosity in them, as well. Over its back were folded massive wings.

"Oh! You beautiful creature!" Gwyna gasped. She stared, unable to utter another word. Never had she dreamed that such majesty could exist in a single being. Her feet were frozen to the spot, but her spirit urged her to move forward, to touch the scales, to climb up and sit between its wings, to experience the freedom of flight.

The moment of awe was broken as the dragon shied away, rearing up on its hind legs away from her.

"What trickery is this?" He roared the words into the air. "What didst thou do to me?" The dragon whipped his head around and stared. "The doorway, where did it go? Did I truly come out the other side or is this another cursed vision?"

"What?" Gwyna gasped.

"Where hast thou brought me? This place…" The creature spun in a circle, knocking Gwyna to the ground with his great tail.

"I didn't bring you anywhere!" Gwyna shouted, scrambling back to her feet. "You were the one chasing me, remember? I've never been through the doorway before, for obvious reasons. I mean, it's magic, and magic is dangerous! My people stay away from that place. I only went in to avoid being burned to a crisp and eaten. You didn't have to follow me!" Heat filled her cheeks as she shouted each word.

The dragon lowered his great head to peer into her face. "Thy words ring true," he said. "Then we have come out the other side?"

Gwyna hesitated. "I…I think so." This felt real, but she could not be quite sure. She was, after all, talking to a dragon, not exactly a common occurrence.

The dragon shuddered. "The things I witnessed in there… The things I did…" He straightened. "I am Keltarrka of the Windlash Kin. Forgive me for chasing thee, I merely sought to protect myself."

"Protect yourself?" Gwyna's eyes widened as she noticed the awkward way Keltarrka was holding his right wing and the thick blood dripping down his side. "Oh!" She gasped. "You are hurt!"

"Careful!" he cautioned as she moved to get a better look at the wound, but it was too late. A drop of the molten liquid fell on Gwyna's shoulder and she cried out as pain seared through her. Her vision narrowed and grew foggy. As she fell into darkness, she thought she heard a new voice speaking, but she could not place it.

When Gwyna regained consciousness, she found herself lying on a cot in a small house not unlike her own. She blinked and sat up, groaning as the skin on her shoulder stretched and burned.

"Ah, you are awake. I was beginning to think you would sleep the day away." A thin, blond man looked at her from where he sat at a small table, mashing something in a wooden bowl.

"Where am I?"

"Not far from where you fainted. You are lucky I happened to be passing by. I did not know which village you came from, or I would have taken you home." He tilted the bowl, revealing a thick paste. Kind, blue eyes twinkled at her in concern. "I am making this to put on your burn, if you will allow me."

Gwyna looked down at her shoulder and winced as the sight of the reddened blister sent a new wave of fire shooting down her arm. "Please!" She gasped.

The man stood and limped over to her. Seating himself on a chair by her bed, he applied the paste to her wound and then carefully wrapped a long, clean cloth around her shoulder.

"I am sorry about your shirt." The man's words barely registered. "I needed to cut off the sleeve to treat your wound. No, don't do that!" he exclaimed as Gwyna shrugged, an instinctive gesture that ended with her gritting her teeth against a new wave of torment that sent bright flashes across her vision.

As the man applied the poultice, the pain diminished. Though it did not immediately disappear, it was no longer all-consuming, and Gwyna found herself wondering about a great many things. The last thing she remembered was looking at the dragon…the dragon! She struggled to throw off the heavy blankets.

"Whoa now," the man said. "The poultice will help, but you are in no condition to…"

"The dragon!" Gwyna cut him off. "Where is he? Is he…?"

A knowing smile ghosted across the man's face. "He is well. Keltarrka is currently outside, sleeping in my garden. I am fairly certain he has crushed my tomatoes…" A woeful expression filled the man's face, and then he waved a hand. "But no matter. Plants have never been my specialty anyway."

Gwyna breathed a sigh and rested back against the flat pillows. "Good. I thought maybe he had flown away."

"You care about what happens to him, do you?"

"No! I mean… Yes. I mean… I don't know. We went through something in that…that…*corridor*. I'm not sure I understand any of it, but until I get answers, I don't really want him flying off and leaving me to puzzle through it on my own."

"I don't think there's any danger of that."

"What do you…."

Her question was interrupted by a forceful ringing in her mind. She clapped her hands to her head.

"Ow!"

The man glanced at her in concern, but she could not focus on him over the sudden throbbing in her temples.

Forgive me. The pain lessened, leaving behind nothing more than a quiet voice, not altogether unpleasant.

"What?" Gwyna asked.

I did not mean to overwhelm you. I can read your thoughts, though I'm not sure why. You're not a dragon, are you? The voice brimmed with curiosity, and she noticed a lack of formality in this mental communication.

"No, I'm not a dragon! What is happening?" Gwyna all but shouted.

The man raised an eyebrow. "Should I be concerned about you?" he asked. "Are you often prone to these sorts of nonsensical outbursts?"

Gwyna waved a hand at him. "Not you, the voice in my head. I mean…" She stopped, her ears heating up as she realized how ridiculous she sounded.

A strange expression crossed the man's face. "I see. Try answering without speaking out loud."

Gwyna gave a frustrated shake of her head. "How do you propose I do that?"

"Just try," the man urged.

Gwyna gave a sigh and leaned back against the thin pillows. Squeezing her eyes tightly shut, she focused her thoughts. *Hello?* She tried a single, tentative word.

Hello. The reply was cautious, nowhere near the eager bounding it had been earlier.

What is this? Gwyna wondered. *Who are you?*

My name is Keltarrka.

You are… Gwyna's eyes sprang open as awareness struck her. She stared at the man. "Are you a dragon?" she asked.

"No." The man chuckled. "I am not. And neither are you, it would seem. But apparently going through the doorway together has awakened a bond between you and Keltarrka that has not been seen before."

"Between me and a dragon?" Gwyna scoffed. "That's impossible."

"It was," the man agreed.

Are you still there? The voice had returned. *Are you well?*

She did not want to answer. She could not be speaking to a dragon with her mind. This was not possible; it was not safe. She would not... She could sense the creature's worry, his anxiety as he waited for her answer. She sighed. *I am well.*

His answering joy was a sunburst in her head, but this time it did not hurt. This was a warm, sweet ray of happiness that cradled her in its embrace. She felt a twinge of astonishment. She had not realized that dragons, those cold-blooded, scaled monsters, could experience such depth of emotion. Her own feelings seemed suddenly pale and shallow in comparison.

The man was still stealing furtive glances from the corner of his eye even as he appeared to be busying himself with more herbs.

"Can I go outside and see him?" she asked.

The man considered it, his head listing to one side as he studied her. At length, he reached for a cane and used it to push himself to a standing position. "Other than the wound on your shoulder, I do not believe anything is terribly wrong with you," he said. "We can go out. It's time to change his poultice, anyway."

Gwyna swung her feet out of the narrow bed and stood. The room swayed dangerously, but she gritted her teeth when she saw the stranger's concern and willed the world to right itself. It did, slowly, and she took a tentative step. The floor became stable beneath her feet, and she felt a surge of triumph. She followed the man outside and found to her surprise that the Dragon's Eye was just beginning to rise, throwing the gardens into misty dawn. Hues of lavender and gray painted the landscape. The air had taken on a chill through the night, and Gwyna wrapped her arms around herself, wincing as the movement sent a fresh throbbing through her shoulder. She gazed around the garden, taking in the neat rows of flowers, the beds of herbs, the trimmed hedges, and wondered how this little homestead could have escaped her notice. How had she missed seeing this cottage, this well-cared-for garden, in all her traversing of the forest surrounding it? She reached out to tug at the man's shirt and ask the question, but the words died on her lips as her eyes found the dragon.

He was enormous. Even in his recumbent pose between day lilies, hyacinths, and tall tomato plants, he towered over her. Her glimpses of him before did not do justice to his true size. He was easily larger than the cottage.

"Ruining my tomatoes. I knew it." The man snorted, jabbing his cane in Keltarrka's direction, but neither anger nor regret tinged his tone. It was more as if he said it because it was the expected thing to say. As he approached, no fear or timidity tainted his movements, and Gwyna envied his ability to appear so at ease. She, on the other hand, was rooted to the spot, planted like one of the garden flowers. Though a part of her yearned to move closer, a spark of fear prevented her from taking another step.

"Good morning, Keltarrka," the man said. "May I take a look at that wing of yours?"

The dragon shifted so that one of his golden wings lowered. The man peeled away the poultice, and Gwyna glimpsed the slash of crimson. Concern bolstered her forward. Her feet tumbled one after the other until she stood right behind the stranger. Keltarrka swung his great head at her movement, and suddenly, Gwyna found herself nose-to-nose with the beast.

Hurt clouded in his eyes, a swirl of silver in their golden depths. *Beast? Is that how you perceive me?*

Gwyna cursed herself for letting the startled thought loose. *Forgive me, I did not mean it. My people do not encounter dragons often, and the stories about you are the kind we tell around the fires to frighten one another. Your people hate mine, and my people fear yours.*

A sadness poured through her. Keltarrka's thoughts rolled through her mind. *It is true. The Mystic Wars still haunt us. My people still remember it; some are still alive who fought in it, though it is unfair to hold you responsible for the actions of your ancestors.*

He raised his head and looked at the man tending his wound. "What is happening?" he asked aloud. "How is it that I can speak mind-to-mind with this youngling? What was that place that showed me her death and pierced my heart as though it were I who had died a thousand deaths?"

"You had a vision?" Gwyna asked. "Inside the doorway? You saw me die?"

Keltarrka lowered his head in assent. "By my claw," he rumbled.

"I experienced the same thing!" Gwyna bounced on her toes, her fright forgotten. "Except I watched you felled by my own arrow. It was like my own heart was being torn in two." She glanced at the blond man. He had paused in his ministrations, his brow furrowed as he considered them both. "Do you know what that place is? My nanna says the door is magic, and that we should stay away from it. She tells a story about the people who first discovered it. One of them threw a rock inside and it disappeared. After that, nobody wanted to investigate any further."

"The door appeared shortly after the Mystic Wars ended," he replied. "I have my suspicions as to its origin and purpose, but I needed time. Time to rest and to heal. Until today, nobody had gathered the courage to step through the doorway—I made sure of that. But my wards were not enough to deter true need. And now..." he trailed off then shook his head, a rueful smile touching the corners of his mouth. "Well, it appears that the two of you have been linked, perhaps forever: two halves of a whole, separated to protect you and reunited to make you stronger. You are the answer to the breaking of the world."

"What?" Gwyna asked, her chest constricting. "What does that mean?"

"I cannot tell you what it means, for I am certain that it means many things," the man replied. He paused and then nodded, as if to himself. "But I think it is safe to say that the doorway is a gift from Cruithaor Elchiyl himself." He paused again. "It will require study. There is wisdom among your peoples, is there not?" He directed the question at both of them.

The girl and the dragon nodded together.

"Good," the man replied. "We will need to gather them. This is a puzzle that must be solved." He grinned. "But first, we must be off." Abruptly, he strode away, back to the cabin. Gwyna stared at Keltarrka and found her confusion reflected back at her in the eyes of the dragon. Before they could speak, however, the man returned, a pack in his hands and a mandolin slung over his back. He handed the pack to Gwyna. "Here, you can carry this. I believe you are both up for a bit of travel."

"Where are we going?" Gwyna asked as she took the pack.

"To your people, of course," the man replied, as though this were the most obvious thing in the world.

"Why?" Gwyna dropped the pack on the ground in horror.

"To tell them what has happened," he said. "They will need to see proof of your bond, and once they do, I think everyone will be more reasonable. It will be easier to convince the Kin."

"We cannot go to my people!" Keltarrka thundered, and a shock of dread coursed through the bond between them. "I wasn't supposed to be this far from the enclave to begin with. If I go home with a weakling human…" he trailed off, and she felt an apology waft toward her. She waved it aside.

"My people will not attack us if they see me, though Nanna is going to be so furious," Gwyna said. "But how can we make them understand? And why must we? Can't we just pretend this never happened?" A quiver of anguish shuddered through her as she said the words out loud, but she could not be certain whether the emotion was her own or if it came from Keltarrka.

"No," the man said patiently. "The bond has been forged. It cannot be unforged. You are connected, and to be separated would not be healthy for either of you. No, we cannot go back. You must go forward. Strengthen this bond, learn its limits. Teach others. You are the first of something new! There will be more like you, and you must be ready to lead them."

Gwyna shivered. She did not like what he was saying, but she could not deny the veracity of his words. They rang with a truth that echoed within her soul.

"Father and Nanna will not be happy about this," she said grimly.

"Not at first, perhaps," the man acknowledged. "But, in time, they will come to see the benefit of having a family member warded to a dragon."

Keltarrka growled and his talons dug into the soft earth. His tail lashed, and as his wings spread, Gwyna feared that he would take to the skies and disappear.

The sudden heartbreak at the thought of never seeing him again left her gasping for air. As she gulped, Keltarrka grew still, his golden eyes turned toward her in wonder. Then he nodded slowly.

"We will try it thy way," he said. Then he tilted his massive head and eyed the man. "Thou hast not told us thy name. With whom are we to be traveling?"

The man gave a jaunty grin and spread his arms wide. "My good dragon, my dear girl, surely you recognize me from the legends! Why, I am the minstrel: Kiernan Kane!"

Keltarrka's whole body rippled with surprise and he half rose. "Kiernan Kane? *The* Kiernan Kane?"

The man gave a flourish, his cane whipping out to one side. "The one and only."

Keltarrka lowered his mighty head in a formal bow. "My Kin have waited a long time to offer thee thanks, Minstrel. We will never forget what thou hast done for us."

A beatific smile lit the man's face. "And I thank *thee*, Keltarrka, for reminding me of my true calling." He tossed his cane away. "I have rested here in convalescence long enough, and the world has rested with me. But I am not a gardener, nor am I a guardian. I am a minstrel, *the* minstrel. And your arrival has convinced me that it is time Llycaelon moved past the war and started healing."

Gwyna stared from the man to the dragon and back, her mind awhirl with questions, but the one that burst from her lips had nothing to do with the confusing words exchanged between Kiernan and Keltarrka. "When your wing is healed, can I..." she began then faltered to an embarrassed halt, unsure if her request would be considered presumptuous or, worse, insulting. And yet, the yearning which began the moment she exited the cottage had only grown as each moment passed until she could no longer keep it to herself.

But in the end, she did not have to ask the question, for Keltarrka understood.

When my wing is strong once more, little Ward, we will fly together, he promised.

Jenelle first fell in love with stories through her father's voice reading aloud to her before bed each night. A voracious reader of fantasy and relentless opener-of-doors in hopes of someday finding a passage to Narnia, it was only natural that she soon began making up fantastical realms of her own. If you enjoyed "Dragon Ward," you can read more about that world and its enigmatic minstrel in Schmidt's Minstrel's Song *four-book series. Jenelle currently lives in the wintry tundra of Wisconsin with her husband and four children.*

http://jenelleschmidt.com

What Lies Ahead

Lauren Lynch

Vassus
Caucasus Foothills, 80 A.D.

Both desire and desperation drove me to seek out the past I should have had—the one the Romans had stolen from me. My dogged mind couldn't accept the likelihood that I might not belong anywhere. A last ember of hope had sparked my journey, and only now was I beginning to question my choice.

For hours, we'd trudged up steep terrain, Hortensia, my sure-footed mule, trundling behind Leonidas and his doddering donkey. I had no idea if I could trust the wizened Greek I'd hired as a guide, but he'd been the only one I could find willing to venture north alone with me. While not much of a physical threat himself, he could still lead me into an ambush, take my remaining coins, and toss my body into the ravine carving a desolate path to the south. Few ventured this way, as the overgrown trail attested. But then I was given to bouts of self-defeating thoughts. It took much less than eccentric old men to sidetrack me from my intended path.

I stretched my aching back and chided myself for my waning spirit of adventure. This was the journey I'd yearned to take for years and before I'd even crested the first peak of the Caucasus Mountains, I'd begun to doubt my purpose.

"Here we are," Leonidas proclaimed, his crotchety donkey staggering to a halt.

What? I ground annoyance between my teeth. Had I wasted my precious few coins on a senile old man? Hortensia lumbered up the last few paces of rocky incline and came to a stop beside Leonidas. Had I not already clenched my jaw in frustration, it might have dropped open.

A stone stairway, half-reclaimed by its surroundings, carved a precarious path to a ridge towering over the coastline. At the cliff's ledge, an ancient-looking doorway stood, its heavy cedar plank door shut against a sheer drop to certain death. The door stood alone with only an ornate stone frame to support it. Had someone built a doorway at the cliff's edge by design? If so, it was diabolical. Or had it once opened into a cliffside structure that long ago tumbled into the Black Sea?

"Who would enter such a doorway?" I completed my musings aloud. Hortensia took a step back. By the rigid stance of her body, I knew she would venture no farther.

"A select few men and women with faith greater than their fears." The awe in his voice somehow made the idea sound more honorable than foolish.

"To what end?" I gave Hortensia a reassuring pat on the neck as her head swung back to eye the trail behind us.

"That is entirely up to you. Why did you hire me?"

I tried to wring out my impatience on Hortensia's reins. "I thought I'd made that clear. I need to find the Siraci Tribe."

The man was unruffled by my scowl. "Then this will take you to them."

"You can't be serious."

"Have I done anything to make you think otherwise?" His gaze was not that of a madman's, and yet...

"Being led to a cliff's edge is not what I'd had in mind. I was looking for someone to navigate me through the mountains and help me track down a very specific tribe."

"I was certain you knew me by reputation. To hire an old man and a half-crippled donkey for a trip of that magnitude..."

He had me there. "What is it you believe this doorway leads to?"

"When you're lost—when you seek a more perceptive path, it takes you where you need to go. Everyone has a birthright, but few fully embrace it before it is too late. If you choose to enter, your life will never be the same."

By coming to an abrupt end, I suspected. "That door has no handle. Even if I wanted to, I don't see how I could enter."

"Think about what you most desire—the purest desire of your heart. The door will only open by the power of your longing."

I pinched the bridge of my nose and tried not to sigh aloud. I'd learned long ago not to indulge in wishful thinking. It only led to torment. Born into slavery, my life had offered little hope. And yet—a vague and childish recollection fluttered through my mind: lean arms enfolding me in tenderness, dark lashes never quite masking the wariness in her eyes, a rare glimpse of the weary smile she offered with the promise that one day all would be made right. On that particular evening, however, it eluded her eyes—the brave smile, meant to bolster me in times of trouble.

"Tomorrow, you will begin your journey," she'd said, tucking her own thin cloak over me as I lay on my pallet.

BANG!

My eyes flew open. Hortensia reared beneath me. I lunged toward her neck, grabbing a fistful of mane. The great cedar doors stood wide. Blinding white light poured from the now open portal.

"Steady, steady—" I whispered, as much to myself as to calm my panicked mule. I straightened and turned to my guide.

Leonidas shook his head. "I was going to tell you to meditate upon it carefully, but…"

"You did not warn me soon enough." Had I not been on Hortensia's back, I might have fallen to my knees.

"I had no idea that the force of your desires would be so great." Leonidas balked.

"When you are ripped from your mother's arms at a tender age, the longings you suppress haunt you daily. It did not take much to summon them."

The old man's brows bunched. "You thought of your mother?"

"It's a lifelong habit," I confessed. "One I cannot seem to control."

Leonidas was quiet for a moment. Beyond him, the fierce white glow of the doorway took on subtle detail as my eyes adjusted, revealing jagged, snow-covered mountain peaks within—the kind of snow that appeared everlasting.

"You told me you intended to find the Siraci. Perhaps you must close this door before you can open another," he added with a frown I could only hope was concern for my future. "Should this opportunity arise again, guard your mind against frivolity."

"You believe a quest to discover my heritage is frivolous." I slid from Hortensia's back and turned to face him.

Leonidas dipped his head. "I didn't mean to imply that at all. I am merely here to point the way and embolden you in your choice."

"After you," I prompted.

"Only the seeker may pass through the portal. This is something you must experience on your own." The lines on Leonidas's brow faded in the light pouring through the doorway. His age-thinned lips wore a young man's smile, hinting at the adventurous youth he'd once been.

Seeker… Greeks had such a flair for the dramatic. I couldn't resist rolling my eyes.

Although it was dusk where we stood, the snippet of landscape revealed through the ancient portal seemed to glint with the brilliance of midday sun.

I slid from my mule, my trail-weary joints betraying me as I stumbled forward a step. Leonidas unfolded his gangly limbs and began to disentangle himself from his donkey.

"What if—" I hesitated, unable to fully form the question chipping away at my resolve.

"Precisely." The old man's face spread into a wide grin. "You understand more than I gave you credit for."

The half-formed question died on my lips as I clambered to the foot of the stairway. My mind headed in a new direction. "How do I control this sort of travel?"

"You don't. Are you willing to take the risk? Faith greater than your fears, my boy. Faith greater than your fears."

The scenery in the doorway shifted, as if from a bird's-eye view, swooping downhill toward patches of green foliage and into a densely treed hillside. I lurched with the sudden change in visual perspective, nearly losing my footing on the moss-slick steps.

I filled my lungs with fresh mountain air. "This is what I came for. I don't have enough of a life that risking it could result in much of a loss."

Leonidas slid from his donkey with a deep groan. "Why your mother, may I ask?"

"I was born into slavery and separated from her at a young age. When she spoke of her past, she did tell me of our Sarmatian heritage. She spoke of her life as a Siraci warrior. Perhaps it was just a story to bolster the courage of a small boy about to be snatched from her arms, but I was desperate for meaning and purpose. I drifted off to sleep most nights amid her stories of bravery and honor." I clenched my jaw as if it could contain the surge of resentment that inundated memories of my hapless childhood.

"Your mother is freed?"

"I haven't seen her in over two decades. I don't know if she is dead or alive, slave or free—but if she had a choice, I'm certain she would return to her people. She spoke of her homeland with a glint in her eye."

"And you wish to make some sort of connection."

"I suppose, I—"

"You suppose?" the old man sputtered. "*You suppose?* To open this portal with such force took a great deal of passion."

I shook my head. "There is anger and bitterness in me to be sure—but few people would describe me as passionate."

"Perhaps you inherited your mother's *glint?*" Leonidas rubbed his chin as he studied me. "And what has your life's work been?"

I gave a snort of contempt. My life's work? A life of slavery courtesy of the Roman empire? Self-loathing, perhaps? "I spent most of my life in arenas."

Leonidas's gaze leveled on mine. "You must have possessed great skill to survive."

"I was not a gladiator. My work—if you could call it that—was to remove bodies from the arena…dressed as Pluto no less."

"Ah."

Yes. There was little to say in response to my life's work. My escape from it—and the part a mountain had played in it—was the more interesting question, but that story would have to wait.

"I will think on this while you are gone. You should proceed. The portal won't stay open indefinitely."

This is what I'm here for. No turning back now. I took a few hesitant steps up the mossy stairway then sprinted forward, leaping across the threshold to the shadowy forest on the other side. I skidded to a stop on the forest floor detritus beyond and turned back. There was no sign of the portal.

Pockets of dense smoke hovered among the fir and aspen trees, burning my eyes as I stifled the urge to cough. Firelight danced in the woods ahead of me. *What had I jumped into?* Despite the haze of smoke, it appeared a mere campfire with a group huddled around it.

I'd known my mother's people were nomads at heart. What had I expected?

I crept closer, my heart pounding. With each cautious footstep, I anticipated the group turning as one as I snapped a twig, but they sat embroiled in a heated debate.

"They think us fickle barbarians, quicker to beg kings from Rome than we are to keep them," a deep voice grumbled.

"Well, Eunones certainly proved them right. The Aorsi tribe now fights with Rome," another hissed.

"Rome bought them years ago—the moment the Aorsi set up trade with them, peddling Babylonian wares to profit from the Roman hunger for the exotic."

"All they've really traded is a once-proud Sarmatian heritage for a few silver denarii—turning against their own to fight alongside their Roman masters."

"The traitorous swine have no respect for themselves, much less their kinsman tribes."

"May their fortune slip through their fingers. May they never return from the house of the dark one."

"And our dead drive away their sleep."

"May they be split and dragged apart by avenging horses."

"And their spirits struggle long to leave their tortured bodies."

I sank to my knees in the bushes. These were warriors—angry ones at that. *No turning back now.* What had I been thinking? I exhaled slowly, hunkering down into what I hoped appeared as shadows to them. Fear had just settled over me like a paralyzing blanket when I was seized in a suffocating chokehold. The tip of a blade pressed against my throat before I could release a yelp of surprise. I raised empty arms in surrender as I was yanked back to my feet. A large hand grabbed me by the back of my tunic and shoved me toward the firelight.

"It is one of the Roman dogs, come to spy on us."

I turned to face my accuser. "No—I—"

"Silence!" His dark eyes reflected the flames.

I gulped back my half-formed denial as the sharp blade pierced the skin at my throat. A warm trickle of blood slid down my neck. Of course, I would appear Roman. It was all I knew. Now that I could study my captors up close, I could see how filthy they all were—a mishmash of old battle scars, fresh injuries, and soot-stained skin.

Hands fumbled over my body from behind, searching for weapons and finding none. In my impulsive haste, I'd left all behind in my pack on Hortensia. One of my captors—a husky fellow with stringy hair—pointed a spear at my chest and shook his head. "What is this?"

What kind of lame Roman spy was I? I could only shrug like an idiot. It dawned on me then that they'd spoken my mother's native tongue until they'd addressed me in Greek. I'd long understood more of her dialect than I could speak.

I must not have appeared as much of a threat because they shoved me against a sapling birch, binding my hands behind it and returning to more pressing matters.

A hulking man with a bleeding head wound lumbered to his feet. "Perhaps we were fools to side with Mithridates. Our rebellion has proven fruitless."

The man beside him shook his head. "No river can stop them. Our ditches and fortifications barely slowed them down. We always believed Uspe's defenses lay in her high ground, but our earthen ramparts are nothing to the Roman siege engine. Our spears and arrows couldn't even reach their front lines."

Voices came in a torrent from around the fire.

"What are we to do?"

"They've already sent troops ahead. Surely they mean to surround us."

"I'm sure they already have."

"By morning, our settlement will lie in ashes. They nearly finished us off before nightfall with their torch-lobbing siege towers."

The fire crackled as the group faded to silence, apparently waiting for their leader to speak. A large man with a circlet on his head stood—their king. "I'm afraid we have no choice but to surrender. Perhaps the offer of hostages—"

"Who would you offer?"

Their king heaved a sigh. "Ten thousand slaves might appease them."

Slaves. The mere idea of the exchange—one life for another—lodged in my throat. So many lives, such callous disregard by the very people I had thought to be my own.

"Who will you send with such an entreaty?"

"I will go, Father." That voice. A woman stood, lean arms crossed over her chest. *Mother?* No—impossible. This woman was far too young. Not to mention she was the king's daughter.

"Absolutely not—" the king growled, thrusting away the idea with his hand.

Undaunted by his anger, the warrior woman continued. "Perhaps they would find a woman less threatening and be more open to negotiation."

"They do not respect their women as we do. They view them as little more than chattel, perhaps because they are reduced to performing as such. I will not put you at risk when there is little chance they'll listen."

"I believe they will recognize me as a warrior. At the very least, I should catch them off guard."

The king paced in silence for a moment before speaking. "Very well. We are already defeated. Take our prisoner here with you. You can offer him with the promise of more. Perhaps they will see the return of one of their own as an act of good faith. Do not under any circumstances reveal yourself as my daughter. It would result in nothing good."

She dipped her head. "Of course."

As if fortified by the formulation of a plan, the king issued orders to the men, sending one to find the healers, several more to gather survivors, and yet another to search for the Roman camp. "I will survey what remains of Uspe and meet you here before dawn."

He pulled his daughter aside as any in the group still able to walk dissolved into the woods.

"Question our prisoner. I will return as soon as possible," the king commanded, his gruff words at odds with the kiss he pressed against her forehead.

She turned to me then—the woman who couldn't be my mother—and the resemblance was unmistakable: her high cheekbones, that strong jaw. The same faded scar near her hairline I'd traced with my finger as a child was here a fresh and ragged cut. She circled me as if calculating my weaknesses.

"I'm not Roman," I said, gulping back alarm at the familiar eyes assessing me as if I were a stranger. If I could accept that a cliffside portal could transport me to the object of my desires, I supposed I'd also need to embrace the possibility that it had ushered me into my mother's past.

She stopped. Gave me the look—one eyebrow arched. The one that meant she didn't believe me. I'd seen it enough times as a young boy.

"Moon fingers," I said. It was a phrase she'd coined to describe an odd defect we shared. Both of our fifth fingers were as curved as a crescent moon.

A flicker of horror chased away the disdain in her eyes, quickly replaced by confusion. "Just how long have you been spying on me?"

"I'm not a spy. Don't go to the Roman camp. Let them send someone else," I pleaded like the child I had been the last time I saw her. Even as I said it, I was painfully aware that I might not exist if she didn't.

My mother cast me a withering glance. Her eyes contained a fire I'd never seen in them as a boy. "That is not who I am. All my life I have trained for this, and I am good at what I do."

"But you will be taken prisoner."

"What would make you say such a thing? Do you imagine yourself some kind of prophet?" She clutched her bow with the same determination in which I'd seen her clutch a spindle in my early childhood. Beautiful. Not yet broken. So magnificent tears stung my eyes.

"No." I sighed. "You wouldn't believe me if I told you."

"You underestimate me again. I am a great believer in things to come. There is a prophecy—that I one day travel to a faraway land, that I give birth to the one who guides our people to enlightenment."

"But—" The words I'd intended froze on my lips. That couldn't be right. Unless she had another child. Which I supposed was possible…

"Why are you here?" She shook me as if it might snap me out of my stupor.

"I have spent a lifetime in Roman captivity. Trust me, it is no place you want to be."

"We will offer them many slaves and have already suffered a grave loss of life—enough for them to consider this a victory. I am merely a messenger."

"You're my mother," I blurted, raising a hand for her inspection.

Her eyes widened, the fire reflecting in them as she pressed her hand to my own, a mirror image of oddity.

"Moon fingers," I repeated.

Her jaw tightened with resolve—another mannerism I recognized in her. Her will, once set in motion, would not relent. "Then the prophecy is true and you are where you belong."

"What prophecy?"

"I don't have time to explain. You can't imagine how happy it makes me to know that I am successful in this. Are you trained in archery?" She shouldered a quiver of arrows.

"No." My face burned with the confession.

She tilted her head. "Spears?"

"A little." Only what I'd observed in the arena. Knowing their slave population outnumbered them, Romans kept their slaves and weapons separate.

My mother's mouth opened and closed. A crease appeared between her brows. "How did I fail in this? No don't tell me. I don't want to know. You must not engage our enemy yet. You are not ready—and you are too important."

"I must be such a disappointment to you." My stomach clenched with my own inadequacy. Why would a woman of royal birth risk her life for a future that involved me as an outcome?

My mother's eyes narrowed—without the deep lines that would one day point like arrowheads to the outer corners of her unfathomable brown eyes. "No—never. You are my greatest achievement. My crowning glory—or so I've been told."

She laughed. It was amazing. I'd never heard her laugh before. I would have ventured through a dozen cliffside doorways to experience that alone.

"If you really are my son, then obey me in this."

I gave a hesitant nod, my mind already rebelling. I wanted nothing more than to escape with her, to grasp onto as much time as I could by her side, burning each precious moment into my memory.

I relived the parades to the arena in my mind as we strode toward the Roman camp. While this trek lacked all the fanfare, it held every bit as much danger.

"This is hopeless," I muttered under my breath, reverting to the comforting familiarity of negativity.

"No—quite the opposite. It is the march to my destiny. It is my path to you." My mother's eyes nearly sparked with her fervor. "There is no doubt in my mind why you appeared here at such a time. You arrived to fortify my confidence in this task I am given, the beginning of my great journey to the faraway land. You are proof of my success. This is all playing out exactly as it should."

The irony stung me. The beginning of her journey? Had she known this all along? When I was a child? Is that why she'd filled me with the stories of her homeland? Filled my mind with hope beyond reason? Is that why she'd so carefully prepared me for my own journey back to her? Her future held more trials and bitterness than she could imagine—bitterness toward Rome, and yet—

"This is where we part ways," she said, interrupting my thoughts.

"What do you mean?"

"Go back. Go back to your own time. I will be fine. I will survive this—as you must well know from your childhood memories of me." She took a deep breath and her voice softened. My youthful mother took my hand in hers, bringing my knuckles to her lips and closing her eyes. "You are not meant to linger here. I am on my way to you already. Now go. Obey your mother."

She released my hand and turned. I watched her ramrod-straight back, the proud back-thrust shoulders as she disappeared into the haze of smoke hovering over the smoldering city. I hoped with every fiber of my being that this would not be the last time I saw her—knowing that she had my early childhood yet ahead of her—and fighting the urge to run after her.

"She's a warrior to her core, isn't she?"

I flinched, realizing how oblivious I'd been to my surroundings as I began to mourn the loss of my mother a second time. An elderly woman hunched in a nearby wagon, appearing little more than a heap of smoke-stained rags at first glance. I could only hope the shock of her proximity had erased the childish frustration from my face.

"We must let her go. Her time has come." She tilted her head and placed a gnarled finger on her lower lip before shaking it at me. "I know you. You're the one. You're on your way to us now, aren't you?"

What was the deranged old crone babbling about? I was standing right in front of her.

She shook a finger at me again as if reading my thoughts, and I gulped back my insolence. I was relieved when she turned her shrewd eyes from me to rummage through a large basket beside her.

"Here," she said, pressing a leather satchel into my hands. "Go now—and take this with you. You will need it once you return."

"Who are you?" I asked, too disheartened to keep any pretense of politeness.

The shriveled woman gave a casual flick of her wrist. "An advisor to your mother and grandfather—and now to you as well. Go."

"Did you advise her to sacrifice herself to the enemy?" I winced at the bitterness lacing my words.

"We must all let go of our past before we can fully embrace our future." The smoke shifted and her gaze drifted to an exchange between my mother and the Roman soldiers in the meadow below us.

A centurion grasped her elbow, yanking her toward their camp. She turned once, her gaze sweeping the hillside where I stood, before disappearing into the maze of Roman tents.

"They can't do that." I clenched my fists—aware of the pointlessness of the gesture.

"This is war. What did you expect?"

"Where is her father?"

A misshapen hand rose from the tattered robe, one bony finger pointing farther down the ravine to where the king rode at the head of a sullen mob. "Zorsines surrenders slaves against my guidance. It will do no good. He plans to use them to beg for pardon, but the Romans will not burden themselves with transporting so many slaves. They would sooner slaughter them and be done with it."

The king rode ahead, meeting the Roman cohort in the same place his daughter had only moments before. "Do they know who he is?"

"I would say so," the crone rasped, her voice as dry as the fires still crackling among the rubble within Uspe's ruined walls.

Zorsines limped forward, pausing just short of the front line where three soldiers stood draped in bear hides, each carrying a standard. A soldier marched forward and dragged the despondent king from his horse, yanking the circlet from his bowed head.

"They've brought the effigy of Claudius," the old hag hissed.

A bear hide-clad soldier stepped forward, raising his wooden staff high. Atop it, a golden disc gleamed through the residual haze, evidently bearing the image of their emperor.

King Zorsines sank to his knees before it, lowering his forehead to the ground.

"Wise move. They'll prefer a victory without further bloodshed—except for the lives of the unwanted slaves, of course." The thin bands of smoke shifted and the woman doubled over in a fit of coughing.

I stumbled forward, clawing blindly through underbrush hidden in low-hanging drifts of smoke. Tears stung my eyes. Thorny vines snagged my tunic, but I ripped myself free. A campfire flickered in the distance, and I ran toward it. If I stumbled across another group of surviving warriors, perhaps they'd be willing to fight to free my mother.

As I drew closer, I realized that the fire blazed on the other side of a doorway—*the* doorway.

I skidded to a stop, my heart pounding in my ears. Where I belonged, I couldn't be certain. Leonidas hunched over the fire, poking at it with a stick. Looking up, he waved me toward him.

Words echoed in my ears, at odds with the desires I'd been foolish enough to dwell on. *Let her go. Her time has come… It is not yet your time.* My legs buckled as I stumbled across the threshold, tumbling down the first few steps on the other side.

"Leonidas, help—" I screamed. Hinges creaked behind me. Before I could turn, the door groaned shut. *Mother.* What had I done? *Mother!* I crumpled where I'd landed on the moss-covered steps.

Leonidas struggled to his feet and tottered to my side. A fire-warmed hand gripped my shoulder.

"Was that real?" I turned on him, grasping his threadbare tunic in my fists. "Or some sort of cruel sorcery? None of this should have happened. I should have had a life beside my mother—there among her people."

He shook his head at my outburst. "Such thoughts are childish fantasy, my friend. Without her years in slavery, you would not exist."

Bile rose in my throat. "Is there no other circumstance where we could exist together?"

"What is done cannot be undone, but there is always the possibility of a second chance."

A second chance. I couldn't ask for much more than that.

I attempted to brush away ashes still clinging to my hair and clothes. "She was taken prisoner and there was nothing I could do to stop it. I couldn't stop anything."

"You weren't there to change the outcome—only your understanding of it. What did you learn?"

"I've never felt so powerless."

"Good. That's a start. What else?"

"Good? There was nothing good about it. If I couldn't change anything, then why was I there?"

"I didn't say you couldn't change anything."

"Then I failed horribly. I changed nothing. Everything was set in motion already. It was out of my control."

"Precisely. But it's not too late to change the one thing that matters the most."

"What is that?"

"Your heart."

I shook my head at the absurdity of it all. "What do you mean?"

The look he gave me was one of compassion. "You will understand if you keep searching, but you cannot search half-heartedly. Begin by softening your heart. Forgive. Move forward."

It's not that easy, I wanted to whine, but I held my tongue.

He pointed to the leather parcel under my arm with his staff. "What did you bring back with you?"

"I don't know. Some babbling old crone shoved it at me." I tugged at the drawstrings, revealing a bundle of fine-spun fabric. I unraveled layer after layer, growing impatient.

Our sharp intake of breath was simultaneous as I pulled back the final gauzy layer of cloth. A golden diadem lay in my hands, studded with pearls, amber, and garnet. Centered at the top was a tree of life crafted of gold with a deer figure on either side.

An odd sense of guilt plagued me. I had made off with an item of great value from my mother's people. "What does it mean? Why would she give this to me?"

Leonidas's bushy brows disappeared into his hood. "It would appear that what lies ahead is much greater than the past you're so desperate to hold on to."

I rewrapped the crown, mulling its potential role in my future. Whatever its significance, one thing was certain. I had to move forward. I would leave the past behind me and make my way toward whatever future these mountains held in their craggy heights.

"Continue on your journey. I believe you will discover a birthright beyond your wildest dreams."

For the first time in my life, I allowed my bitter hold on the past to slip. "You're right. I need to look forward, to press on. I will continue to search these mountains until I find my people. Care to join me?"

While I had made the offer half in jest, the old man tilted his head as he took in the majestic scenery beyond. "I suppose I have nothing to return to myself. I am but a mist that will soon vanish, but perhaps enough of the youthful adventurer in me remains to conquer these vast mountains."

A smile twitched at my lips, catching me unaware as I climbed onto Hortensia's back.

So many wasted years. Any illusions of the past I'd clung to faded like stars dissolving in the light of dawn. It was easier than I might have imagined to let go of my childish notions—to reach for the endless possibilities awaiting me.

Lauren Lynch writes historical fantasy novels and short stories designed to captivate readers of all ages. Join Vassus on other adventures in books two and three of The TimeDrifter Series. Learn more at www.laurenlynch.com.